WHAT READERS ARE SAYING ABOUT KAREN KINGSBURY'S BOOKS

"I've never been so moved by a novel in all my life."

—Val B.

"Karen Kingsbury is changing the world—one reader at a time."

—Lauren W.

"I literally cannot get enough of Karen Kingsbury's fiction. Her stories grab hold of my heart and don't let go until the very last page. Write faster, Karen!"

—Sharon A.

"Whenever I pick up a new KK book, two things are consistent: tissues and finishing the whole book in one day."

—Nel L.

"The best author in the country."

—Mary H.

"Karen's books remind me that God is real. I need that."

—Carrie F.

"Every time I read one of Karen's books I think, 'It's the best one yet.' Then the next one comes out and I think, 'No, this is the best one.'"

—April B. M.

"Novels are mini-vacations, and Karen's are my favorite destination."

—Rachel S.

Other Life-Changing Fiction™ by Karen Kingsbury

Stand-Alone Titles

Fifteen Minutes
The Chance
The Bridge
Oceans Apart
Between Sundays
When Joy Came to Stay
On Every Side
Divine
Like Dandelion Dust
Where Yesterday Lives
Shades of Blue
Unlocked
Coming Home—The Baxter Family

Angels Walking Series

Angels Walking
Chasing Sunsets
Brush of Wings

The Baxters–Redemption Series

Redemption
Remember
Return
Rejoice
Reunion

The Baxters–Firstborn Series

Fame
Forgiven
Found
Family
Forever

The Baxters–Sunrise Series

Sunrise
Summer
Someday
Sunset

The Baxters–Above the Line Series

Above the Line: Take One
Above the Line: Take Two
Above the Line: Take Three
Above the Line: Take Four

The Baxters–Bailey Flanigan Series

Leaving
Learning
Longing
Loving

Baxter Family Collection

A Baxter Family Christmas
Love Story
In This Moment
To the Moon and Back

9/11 Series

One Tuesday Morning
Beyond Tuesday Morning
Remember Tuesday Morning

Lost Love Series

Even Now
Ever After

Red Glove Series

Gideon's Gift

Maggie's Miracle

Sarah's Song

Hannah's Hope

e-Short Stories

The Beginning

I Can Only Imagine

Elizabeth Baxter's 10 Secrets to a Happy Marriage

Once Upon a Campus

Forever Faithful Series

Waiting for Morning

Moment of Weakness

Halfway to Forever

Women of Faith Fiction Series

A Time to Dance

A Time to Embrace

Cody Gunner Series

A Thousand Tomorrows

Just Beyond the Clouds

This Side of Heaven

Life-Changing Bible Story Collections

Family of Jesus

Friends of Jesus

Children's Titles

Let Me Hold You Longer

Let's Go on a Mommy Date

We Believe in Christmas

Let's Have a Daddy Day

The Princess and the Three Knights

The Brave Young Knight

Far Flutterby

Go Ahead and Dream with Quarterback Alex Smith

Whatever You Grow Up to Be

Always Daddy's Princess

Miracle Collections

A Treasury of Christmas Miracles

A Treasury of Miracles for Women

A Treasury of Miracles for Teens

A Treasury of Miracles for Friends

A Treasury of Adoption Miracles

Miracles—a Devotional

Gift Books

Forever Young: Ten Gifts of Faith for the Graduate

Forever My Little Boy

Forever My Little Girl

Stay Close Little Girl

Be Safe Little Boy

www.KarenKingsbury.com

KAREN
KINGSBURY

The
BAXTER
FAMILY

TO THE MOON AND BACK

a novel

Howard Books
New York London Toronto Sydney New Delhi

An Imprint of Simon & Schuster, Inc.
1230 Avenue of the Americas
New York, NY 10020

This book is a work of fiction. Any references to historical events, real people, or real places are used fictitiously. Other names, characters, places, and events are products of the author's imagination, and any resemblance to actual events or places or persons, living or dead, is entirely coincidental.

Published in association with the literary agency of Alive Literary Agency, 7680 Goddard Street, Suite 200, Colorado Springs, Colorado, 80920, http://aliveliterary.com.

First Howard Books hardcover edition May 2018

HOWARD and colophon are trademarks of Simon & Schuster, Inc.

Interior design by Davina Mock-Maniscalco

Manufactured in the United States of America

10 9 8 7 6 5 4 3 2 1

Library of Congress Control Number: 2017040246

ISBN 978-1-4516-8765-1
ISBN 978-1-4516-8767-5 (ebook)

To Donald:

Well . . . we are ending our second year as empty nesters. I never liked that term. And I can tell you now with all my heart that there's been nothing empty about the last few years. They've been full of beautiful walks and meaningful talks, nights when we randomly jump into the car and spend an evening with Kelsey and Kyle, little Hudson, and now our newest grandbaby. We play tennis and Ping-Pong and hang out with our wonderful friends. And yes, we miss having our family all together every day. But when they come home the celebrating never ends. What I mean is, I've loved raising our kids with you, and now I love this season, too. God has brought us through so many pages in our story. The Baxter family came to life while we were raising our kids. When they told stories around the family dinner table, we were doing the same. And when their kids auditioned for Christian theater, our kids were singing the same songs. Our family is—and always will be—inexorably linked with the Baxter family. So thank you for creating a world where our love and life and family and faith were so beautiful I could do nothing but write about it. So that some far-off day when we're old and the voices of our many grandchildren fill the house, we can pull out books like this one and remember. Every single beautiful moment. I love you.

To Kyle:

You will always be the young man we prayed for, the one we believed God for when it came to our precious only daughter. You love Kelsey so well, and you are such a great daddy to Hudson and your newest little one. I literally thank God every day for you and for the friendship all of us share. Thank you for bringing us constant joy. We pray and believe that all the world will one day be changed for the better because of your music, your love and your life.

To Kelsey:

What an amazing season this has been, watching as you went from being the best mommy ever for Hudson, and now as you've welcomed your second precious baby. Little Hudson is so happy, and I know that Baby Nolan is, too. Your home is full of love and joy, peace and patience and God's Holy Spirit. Because you and Kyle have intentionally welcomed the Lord into your home. What a beautiful time for all of us! Hudson is strong and kind and joyful, with a depth that tells all of us that some way, somehow, God is going to use him. I can't wait to see all the ways God pours His gifts into your newest little angel, also. I believe God will continue to use your precious family as a very bright light . . . and I know that one day all the world will look to you and Kyle as an example of how to love well. Love you with all my heart, honey.

To Tyler:

I remember that long-ago day when you were a ten-year-old and you said, "Mom, someday I'm going to write music and make movies. But I think I'm also going to write books in my spare time. Like you do!" And now, my talented son, that's exactly what you're doing. How amazing is it that we have the privilege of writing together? Already we've had one screenplay—*Maggie's Miracle*—show up on the Hallmark Channel, and now a series of books about the Baxter children. I always knew God had gifted you with great talent. But I never would've imagined the ways God would work it all together. You're still songwriting, still writing original screenplays and dreaming of making movies. But now you're writing books in your spare time, too. I love it! God has great things ahead, and as always I am most thankful for this front-row seat. Oh, and for the occasional evening when you stop by for dinner and finish the night playing the piano. You are a very great blessing, Ty. Love you always.

To Sean:

Later this year you will finish your time at Liberty University, earning a degree and growing in your faith and strength as a man. You have listened to God, Sean. You have taken the difficult moments of your earlier years and turned them into strengths, and for that your dad and I are so proud of you! From the first day we held you, we knew your spirit was bright. You love God and people with a passion and joy that defied your first five years.

Yet we agreed with you that it was time to take your faith to another level. I am convinced God has amazing plans ahead for you, Son. I love you forever.

To Josh:

You are out on your own, finding your way. What a blessing to know that wherever you go, you take us with you . . . and Jesus with you. Always remember that having a relationship with Him is the most important gift you will ever give your family. You belong to Him, Josh. You always have. As you lead your family in the years to come, as you walk out your faith together, walk humbly. And just know how much we love you. We are here for you, always.

To EJ:

What a tremendous time this is for you, EJ. You are doing so well at Liberty University, so excited about the career in filmmaking you have chosen. Isn't it something how God knew—even all those years ago when you first entered our family—that you would need to be with people who loved God and loved each other . . . but also people who loved the power of storytelling. I'm so excited about the future, and the ways God will use your gifts to intersect with the gifts of so many others in our family. Maybe we should start our own studio—making movies that will change the world for God. Whatever the future holds, remember that your most powerful hour of the day is the one you give to Jesus. Stay in His word. Pray always. I love you.

To Austin:

I'm so grateful I can see you when I travel to Liberty University to teach. You are tall and strong and a godly presence on that campus. But not only that. You are a loyal friend with a very deep heart. During breaks we will continue to have many happy times together. But I still miss you in the everydayness, Austin. You have been such a light in our home, our miracle boy. Our overcomer. You are my youngest, and no question the hardest to let go. At times the quiet here is so . . . quiet. Even with your dad's jokes and two little grandchildren in our lives. So . . . while you're at Liberty, on nights when you lie awake in your dorm, just know that we have cherished every moment of raising you. And we are still here. We always will be. Love you forever, Aus.

And to God Almighty,

the Author of Life, who has—for now—blessed me with these.

Jessie
RJ
KARI ∞ TIM
(deceased)
∞
RYAN
Annie
Maddie
Hayley
BROOKE ∞ PETER
Sophie
Egan
DAYNE ∞ KATY
Blaise
THE BAXTER
FAMILY

Cole
Devin
Sarah Marie (deceased)
ASHLEY ∞ LANDON
Janessa
Amy
Heidi Jo (deceased)
ERIN ∞ SAM
(deceased) (deceased)
Clarissa (deceased)
Chloe (deceased)
Tommy
LUKE ∞ REAGAN
Malin
Johnny
JOHN BAXTER ∞ ELIZABETH
(deceased)
∞
ELAINE

This book is part of the Baxter family collection, but it can be read as a stand-alone novel. Find out more about the Baxter family at the back of this book. Whether you've loved the Baxters for a decade, or you're finding them for the first time—*To the Moon and Back* is for you.

TO THE MOON AND BACK

1

The roots of the tree had taken residence in Amy Hogan's heart, where they wouldn't let go. She could see it in her mind, feel the rough bark against her fingertips. The way its branches spread out like the hands of God. Amy had never seen the tree, but she would soon.

The Survivor Tree.

A hundred-year-old American elm growing out of what used to be a parking lot in front of the Alfred P. Murrah Federal Building in the heart of Oklahoma City. Now its boughs shaded the highest part of the memorial site. The place where an evil man parked a moving truck loaded with fertilizer and blew the federal building to bits.

Amy was only twelve. She wasn't alive when the Oklahoma City bombing happened way back in 1995.

She had no idea what it was like to be part of the terrible morning when the truck bomb ripped through the building that April 19. She didn't know the specific aftermath of twisted metal and broken bricks and battered men, women and children that made up the imagery of that horrific day when 168 people died.

But she could imagine the screaming and anguish; she could almost feel the glass in her skin, the blood on her body. She could picture the looks on the faces of the survivors.

Because Amy was a survivor, too.

And that's why the tree meant so much to her, why she could hardly wait for spring break to begin. When her family would take a road trip to a dozen different destinations. But one of them would be the Oklahoma City National Memorial.

It all started with a photo Amy had found.

She lived with her Aunt Ashley and Uncle Landon, and their kids. Her cousins, Cole, Devin and Janessa. In every possible way this family had taken her in as one of their own. Sometimes she even thought of her Aunt Ashley as her mom. Because her aunt loved her that much.

One of the ways Aunt Ashley proved it was how she had set up Amy's room. In the corner was a chair that faced the window. So Amy could sit and talk to God about her family in heaven—any time she wanted. Next to the chair, against the wall, was a bookcase full of everything that reminded Amy of her childhood.

A teddy bear her daddy gave her when they went to the fair the year before the car accident. A small treasure chest full of notes her mom had written while Amy was growing up. Notes just for her. Because taking time to put her feelings on paper was important to her mother. That's what Aunt Ashley said.

Amy took a break from packing for the trip. She sat on the bench at the end of her bed and stared at the bookcase. There were also a dozen framed photographs scattered on the different shelves. Photos of Amy and her mom, Amy and her dad. One of both her parents and her all snuggled up on the couch on an ordinary day.

Back when they thought they had forever.

And then there was Amy's favorite photo. The one of her whole family. Her parents and three sisters and her. They had been getting pictures taken for their Christmas card and the photographer had already snapped a million shots. Amy stared at the image across the room and let it fill the broken places in her heart one more time.

She could still hear her mother telling their story. How her mommy and daddy had been praying for a child when a social worker told them about Amy. Of course, Amy was just a little baby back then. But her birth mother had been a drug addict, and at the last minute the woman decided to keep Amy. That's when God brought Heidi Jo along. The littlest olive-skinned sister in the group. But as soon as her parents adopted Heidi Jo, they got a call from the social worker. The woman was on drugs again and she had been arrested. Which meant not only Amy but also her two older sisters were available for adoption.

Her parents were thrilled and pretty much overnight they went from having no children to raising four little girls. Clarissa, Chloe, Amy and Heidi Jo. The first three all tan with pale blond hair. They were the closest four sisters anyone ever knew.

Until the accident.

Amy stood and walked to the bookcase. A layer of dust dimmed the black frame. Amy hated dust. She picked up the photo and lightly brushed the edges clean, then she looked again at the people she missed so much. Her mom and dad were on either side of Amy and her sisters. The girls had their arms around each other and they were laughing. Laughing so hard that this picture had turned out to be the best that day.

For a few seconds Amy closed her eyes. The sound of her family still filled her heart. Still made her smile on days when she wasn't sure she'd survive the missing and hurting. The terrible losing. She blinked and her eyes focused on Clarissa. It was Clarissa, her oldest sister, who had said something funny that day. Something about her mouth feeling frozen or how she was glad she wasn't a model because of all the smiling.

The details weren't as clear as they used to be.

Whatever Clarissa had said, the day instantly became one of their favorites ever. Amy touched the glass over her sister's face. It was good to have these memories. That was something Aunt Ashley talked about a lot. Memories were God's way of saying something had actually happened. And it mattered a great deal.

Amy returned the frame to its spot in the bookcase. Then she stooped down. The bottom shelf was filled with eight photo albums. All the ones Amy's parents had ever put together. When everything from Amy's old home in Texas was gone through and sorted, after the furniture and the house had been sold, her Aunt Ashley had collected a few boxes of things for Amy.

She would always be grateful to her aunt for saving them. Every item and picture mattered. They were all she had left of her old life. Before the car accident that took everyone else in her family home to heaven. Everyone but her.

Yes, she understood what it meant to be a survivor.

Amy pulled the fourth book from the bottom shelf and took it to her chair by the window. She flipped to the back page and looked for the photo that had started her interest in the Oklahoma City bombing.

Before they'd adopted Amy and her sisters, her parents had taken a trip to Oklahoma. Amy's daddy had cousins in Oklahoma, and one of them had hosted a family reunion.

The album told the story. There were pictures of Amy's parents with people Amy didn't know or couldn't remember ever meeting. Most of them had reached out when the accident happened. A few of them had written letters since then. Her daddy's parents were dead, but his great-aunt had started a scholarship account for Amy. So she would always know how much they cared about her. They came to visit every summer for a few days.

Amy scanned the images. There were photos of sunsets and scenery, her mom and dad happy and in love. But the picture that caught hold of Amy's heart was one of her mama. While they were on their trip, her parents had gone to the Oklahoma City National Memorial. In the photo her mother was standing at the base of the Survivor Tree, her hands on its thick trunk, eyes lifted up to its beautiful branches.

Amy read her mother's words, written next to the photo: "*Me at the survivor tree. With God, there is always a way to survive. I love this living reminder.*"

Amy ran her fingers over the image and then lightly over her mother's words. Her mama was tender. That's what Aunt Ashley said. She had a heart deeper than the ocean. No wonder she and Amy's daddy went to the memorial site while they were in Oklahoma.

Amy hadn't heard of national memorials until last fall, when her history class was studying them. But the idea filled her heart. Places of recognition and honor for very great losses suffered by Americans.

A few weeks after that lesson in class, Amy was looking through her photo albums when she saw the picture of her mother at the Survivor Tree. She Googled what had happened that day.

That's when she found the history of the Oklahoma City bombing. And the tree.

Amy looked out the window at the storm clouds drifting closer. The tree had been there before anyone thought about putting a federal building on the site. When it came time to pave a parking lot, someone must've decided the tree was too pretty to cut down.

So they built around it.

And that's how the tree stayed for lots and lots of years. Decades, really. Right up until the bomb went off. The bomb was so big it had something called shock waves. It meant that cars parked nearby exploded and the tree caught fire. Pieces of glass and metal from the blast shot out and struck the old elm's base. Most of its branches were cut off by flying debris. When the dust settled, all that was left was a smoldering, blackened, barren trunk.

In the weeks that followed, the people cleaning up after the bomb intended to cut the old tree down. The elm was dead, they figured. Of course it was dead. But they left it standing because of the glass and metal lodged in its bark. The way the pieces were positioned told investigators what they needed to know about the location of the bomb.

So since the tree trunk was evidence, it stayed.

Then something beautiful happened. On the one-year anniversary, survivors of the bombing and family members of the victims, as well as firefighters and police officers, all gathered at the old parking lot to remember.

That's when a police officer noticed something amazing about the tree. Sprigs of green were coming from the bark. The tree was alive! Horticulture experts were called in to tend to the tree and help nurse it back to health. The glass and metal were removed from the trunk and the tree was fed good nutrition. One year led to another and its branches began to grow again.

Today it was one of the biggest, most beautiful trees in Oklahoma City. Each spring workers at the memorial swept up seeds from the boughs. The seeds were grown into saplings, and every year those little baby trees were given out to people who wanted them.

People who had survived something.

People like Amy.

It was just as her mama had said all those years ago. The Oklahoma City tree was proof that with God, there was always a way to survive.

So Amy had gotten an idea, and a few months ago she shared it with her aunt. Maybe they could go to the memorial site for spring break, and maybe Amy could get one of the saplings.

She could plant it out back near her Grandma Elizabeth's flower garden, and it would grow and give shade and comfort and a reminder of the family she'd lost. Then Amy would have her own Survivor Tree.

For spring break, they had been planning to visit Branson, Missouri, and Silver Dollar City and spend time on a houseboat on Table Rock Lake. But her Aunt Ashley and Uncle Landon talked about it and decided, yes, they would go a little further and visit the Oklahoma City National Memorial, too.

They were going with Amy's Aunt Kari and Uncle Ryan and their family. Two cars, caravan-style. Aunt Ashley said that on the day they'd visit the memorial it would just be the two aunts and the older kids. The younger kids would go with the uncles to Frontier City for rides and stuff.

The memorial would be too sad for them.

But it wouldn't be too sad for Amy. She wanted to be there, wanted to see the empty chairs and tall gates that had been built in honor of the victims. She could hardly wait to stand next to the tree and feel its trunk against her hands.

The way her mama had felt it.

Because the tree's roots really had taken hold of her. And somehow, she knew that God was letting her go there, not only to see the tree. But to learn something from Him.

Something about surviving.

2

The guys made the decision to leave at six in the morning that Saturday. Ashley Baxter Blake wasn't thrilled with the idea, but by the time they were on the road the sense of adventure had gripped them all. Even her.

The older kids had agreed to turn off their cell phones until after dinner each day. So they used walkie-talkies to keep up with their cousins in the other car. The old-fashioned way, as the kids had said earlier.

"We're stopping for gas at the next exit, right, Dad?" Cole shifted forward and looked at Landon.

"Yes, sir! Next exit!" Landon grinned.

Ashley could only admire him. Landon had always loved road trips with the family. These were his favorite vacations. He'd told Ashley that a thousand times.

Cole sat in the seat directly behind Ashley. He grabbed the walkie-talkie from the cup holder and held it to his mouth. "Stopping for gas at the next exit." Cole loved the handheld device. "Roger?"

A static sound came from the speaker. Then RJ's voice. "Roger! Over."

"Over and out." Cole leaned in to the space between

the two front seats. He looked at Ashley. "This thing is amazing. I can't believe you talked like this in the olden days."

Ashley looked at Landon. *"Olden days?"* She mouthed the question.

"Hey now!" Landon shook his head. "We're not that old, Cole."

"I know." Cole patted both of their shoulders. "Just teasing."

They'd already been on the road for two hours. Ashley watched Landon pull off at the next exit. Her husband was more handsome than ever. He wore a white T-shirt and dark jeans, his arms and face tanned from his daily jog, his dark hair short to his head. The muscles in his shoulders were as defined as they were back when the two of them got married.

Ashley flipped the visor down and used the mirror to check on the kids. Devin was in the seat next to Cole, and Amy and Janessa were in the back row. Last night when they were loading up the car, Ashley had pulled Amy aside and taken her to a quiet bench in the backyard. Ashley was glad for the moment. She had been meaning to ask her niece if she felt nervous about the trip.

After all, it was on a road trip from Texas to Bloomington that Amy's family was rear-ended by a semi truck. For weeks now Amy had seemed excited about the adventure ahead—especially seeing the Oklahoma memorial site. But Ashley thought she should hear from her niece on the subject. Just in case.

"Are you worried?" They had settled in on the bench and Ashley had taken hold of Amy's hand. "About the drive?"

Amy hesitated for a minute. "Sometimes." Her voice was quiet. "When I really think about it." She looked across the field toward the stream that ran behind the old Baxter house. Then she turned to Ashley. "The Bible says to live is Christ. To die is gain." Her smile didn't quite fill her face. "I believe that."

"Me, too." The Scripture had helped Ashley learn to live in such a way that she didn't feel heartbroken for Amy every time she saw her. All of them had learned to live normal lives again. Almost. Ashley felt tears well in her eyes. "Just look how many people we have in heaven. Right?"

"Yes." Amy's expression softened. She lifted her eyes to the starry sky. "When I think about that, I have nothing to worry about."

Her wisdom was breathtaking.

Ashley watched Amy now, curled up with her pillow in the third row. She and Janessa had been sleeping for the past hour. Before that they were playing I Spy and giggling over things they'd spotted along the drive.

Ashley flipped the visor up and exhaled. She shifted so she could see Landon better. "Amy's come so far."

"She has." Landon smiled. He kept his voice low. "Thanks to God . . . and you."

"And you." Ashley reached for his hand. They had all helped with Amy's healing. "You're wonderful to her."

Landon squeezed her hand as he turned in to the gas station. Ashley's sister Kari and her husband, Ryan Taylor, and their three children had followed them the whole morning. Ryan towed a pair of Jet Skis behind his truck, and he pulled the entire rig up to the pump across the way. It was supposed to be unseasonably warm this week. But they had brought wetsuits just in case.

Fifteen minutes later they were on the road again. During the next stretch, Cole chose the music and everyone sang along. There was Colton Dixon's "Through All of It" and Danny Gokey's latest hit, along with songs from Francesca Battistelli, Newsboys, Natalie Grant, MercyMe, and Matthew West.

At one point they were all singing at the top of their lungs. "Hello, my name is . . . Child of the One True King. I've been saved, I've been changed, I have been set free!"

Ashley grinned at Landon. Most of them weren't the greatest singers. Amy probably had the best voice in the family. But the sound was joyful all the same and it made the final leg of the trip fly by.

They reached Branson just after three o'clock and checked into their hotel. Then both families climbed back into the cars and drove the short distance to the beach. They laid out their blankets not far from the boat launch.

Half an hour later the Jet Skis were flying across the lake. Landon and Ryan took the first round while the kids cheered them on from the shore. Ashley and Kari settled into chairs near the blankets.

"What a great day." Kari looked at her and took a deep breath. "Easier than when the kids were little."

"Right?" Ashley laughed. "Diaper changes at gas stations. I don't miss that."

Kari stared at the kids still jumping around on the sand. "So true. But still . . . I sometimes long for those days." She blinked a few times, like she was just seeing their kids for the first time in awhile. "When did they get so old?"

Usually Ashley tried not to think about that fact. This was Cole's junior year, and already he was talking about colleges. Liberty University was at the top of his list. He had heard about it from Connor Flanigan, the son of their good friends. Every time she thought about Cole moving away, Ashley's eyes filled with tears.

"Live in the moment, appreciate every day." Ashley watched Cole pick up Janessa and run toward the water as she shrieked with delight. A smile filled Ashley's words. "God gives us only so many days with our families. As long as we know that, we can live without regret."

"Agreed." Kari stared toward the water. "Even when it seems they're growing up right before our eyes."

Ashley appreciated the time with Kari. Sure they saw each other at family dinners and holidays, at Clear Creek Community Church each Sunday and on the occasional day at the nail salon. But there was something very special about having a week together.

Kari stretched her legs. "I wish the others could've come. I really thought Brooke might."

"It should be a law—all spring breaks must be on the same week." Ashley uttered a light laugh. "I guess that's not very likely."

Kari shaded her eyes and nodded toward the kids. "They love playing together."

"If they don't kill themselves!" Ashley laughed. Devin and RJ were running up and down the shore, trying to push each other into the water. Just at that moment they both wound up in the lake, splashing and dunking each other. Ashley sighed. "At least it's all in fun."

Kari laughed. "Boys." They were quiet for a moment. "What's the story with the new movie for Dayne?"

The setting sun was warm against Ashley's shoulders. Perfect after the chilly start to spring. She filled her lungs with the fresh lakeside air. "Dayne said he'll produce it, and he and Katy will star in it."

"Really?" Kari looked surprised. "They haven't done that in years."

"They miss it." Ashley smiled at her sister. "They think this one will be big. Not just at the box office. Dayne said the message is just what our country needs. It's called *Shades of Blue*. About healing after abortion."

"Wow." Kari faced the water again. "Powerful. I'm glad they're working together."

Ashley was happy for Dayne and Katy, too. "I only hope they don't stay in L.A. too long. Their kids love Indiana."

"True. They're crazy about their cousins." Kari grinned.

Ashley stood and stretched. "Come on. Let's join the kids."

"I was just thinking that." Kari smiled.

The sand felt warm on Ashley's toes. Everything about Table Rock Lake reminded her of Lake Monroe back home and the dozens of beautiful times their family had shared there. She glanced at Kari. "One of these days we'll get all five of us and our families together for a family vacation. Somewhere at the beach. Florida, maybe." She paused. "Even if we need to plan it a year in advance."

"I agree." Kari smiled. They were almost to the shoreline. "Can you imagine? So fun!"

Cole was the first to run to them, a football in his hands. "I'm next on the Jet Skis. Jessie, too." He tossed the ball to Ashley. "You and Aunt Kari should play catch."

Kari laughed. "Last time I caught a football I jammed my finger." She shook her head. "It's Frisbee for me."

Devin must've heard the conversation. He was Cole's Mini-Me, an almost exact, younger, blond replica of his older brother. His eyes lit up. "I'll play with you, Mom!"

Ashley wasn't very good at throwing a ball, but for Devin she would try. They found a spot a few yards from the others and Ashley gave it her best effort.

"Mom!" Devin snagged the ball from the air. "Look how good you are! You've been practicing!"

Everyone laughed, and Jessie and Annie high-fived. "Yay for Aunt Ashley!" Jessie jumped around, her hands in the air. "You should play for the Colts!" She skipped closer and fist-bumped Ashley. "I'll be the cheerleader!"

This was what Ashley loved about vacations together. No clocks. No reason to leave the beach. Just fun and family and laughter. And on this occasion, even a little football.

Ryan and Landon pulled up on the Jet Skis and turned the machines over to Cole and Jessie. Landon came up the beach and watched Ashley. The sun glistened on his bare arms as he brushed the water from his shorts.

Ashley could feel his admiration without looking at him. She caught the ball, repositioned her fingers on the laces and threw it back to Devin.

"See, Dad?" Devin grinned. "Mom's crazy good at this!"

Landon closed the gap between them and kissed her cheek. He winked at Devin. "I taught her everything I know."

Amy was building a sand castle with RJ. She yelled out her approval, too. "You taught her good, Uncle Landon! Just watch her!"

Ashley held on to the moment. The sun almost to the horizon, the sky still warm and clear and blue. Diamonds of light dancing on the lake and her family gathered around her. Everyone whole and healthy and happy.

Even Amy.

An hour later they were done for the day. The sky was nearly dark as they loaded the Jet Skis onto Kari and Ryan's trailer.

When they were back in their SUV and the kids were buckled in behind them, Landon smiled at her. "You really were impressive with that football."

She could feel the sparkle in her eyes, the way she felt it so often around Landon. "I did know a little before I met you." She stifled a laugh. "Truth be told."

He chuckled and fixed his eyes on the road ahead. "Whatever happened to the idea of your dad and Elaine joining us?"

"They talked about it." Ashley would've loved that. There were only so many chances for her dad and his wife to join them for a spring break like this. She turned to see Landon better. "Dad had a conference at the hospital." She thought about how healthy her father was, how committed to the field of medicine, to helping people. "He might be retired, but that doesn't stop him. The younger doctors need someone to teach them, you know."

Landon smiled and gave a slight shake of his head. "I want to be like him when I grow up."

"Mmm." Ashley rested her head against the seat. "Me, too."

Back at the hotel, they got ready and met in the lobby for dinner. After they ate, everyone gathered in the hotel's private theater, adjacent to the restaurant. That night both families filled the place and Amy sat next to Ashley as they watched Disney's *Tangled*.

Ashley took a mental snapshot of the evening.

If today were a painting, the most obvious setting would be the scene from earlier, her family playing at the beach. But Ashley felt more drawn to paint the one here, inside the theater. Not the movie screen or the seats or the entire group of them. But just Amy and her, and the fact that even at twelve years old, Amy still felt comfortable to hold Ashley's hand.

That simple gesture was proof that Ashley had become more mom than aunt to the girl. Even if Ashley would never replace the mother her sister Erin had been. Still, Amy's hand in her own assured Ashley that however much healing was still ahead, they were on the right path.

And God, in all His mercy, was with them.

• • •

THEY SPENT THE first four days of the trip in Branson, playing on the beach and letting the kids take turns on the Jet Skis. A couple times, Ashley and Kari even took the little ones, Janessa and Annie, for a slow ride along the shore. Then in the late afternoons they'd head into town.

Each day was a different adventure. They played mini golf and rode go-karts and toured the Ripley's Believe It or Not! museum. All the kids loved the room with the slanted floors and the mirrors that made Cole look two feet taller than Landon.

"You wish." Devin laughed.

Landon raised his brow. "It's not too far-fetched." He put his arm around Cole's shoulders. "Cole's about to pass me up. Any day now."

By the end of the four days, Ashley had already taken hundreds of pictures—some with her camera, some with her heart—memories to hold close years from now.

When the kids were grown and gone.

As for the pictures on her camera, once they were back home she would make an album of their fun times this week. Each of the kids would get a copy. Photo books were among Ashley's favorite ways to create proof of the years gone by.

Wednesday afternoon they packed up their vehicles and headed to Oklahoma City. Tomorrow was the anniversary of the bombing. The day Amy wanted to be at the memorial. The day they gave out saplings from the Survivor Tree. After they checked into their hotel rooms and once the kids were tucked in and asleep, Landon hit the lights.

In the darkness, Landon reached for her hand and rolled onto his side. He spoke close to her face. "I love you, Ashley. Everything about you."

"Thanks." She slid closer and kissed him on his lips,

quiet so they wouldn't wake the kids, sleeping in the bed beside them. "I love you, too."

Landon paused, and even in the stillness Ashley could tell something was weighing on him.

"What are you thinking?" She kept her voice quiet.

"About Amy's sapling." He put his hand on Ashley's cheek. "I've been praying she gets one. There's no guarantee."

"I know." She thought for a minute. Then she whispered, "We'll get there right when it opens. That should help."

Landon kissed her again and another time. Then he settled in on his side of the bed. "You'll have to tell me all about it."

"I will. Good night, love."

"Good night."

Ashley rolled onto her back and stared toward the window. Their new hotel was in the heart of Oklahoma City, not far from the memorial. Her eyes were adjusting to the dark, and now she could see lights from adjacent hotels and buildings.

God, please . . . let Amy get a sapling. I have no idea how we'll care for it on vacation, but we'll figure it out. It's just . . . it matters so much to her.

Ashley lay there, silent. Waiting. Sometimes when she prayed she heard from God. A Scripture or something He had been laying on her heart. But not tonight. Tonight there was just the soft breathing of the kids sleeping and the nearness of Landon. She closed her eyes. God would come through on this. Ashley was sure.

Because if anyone deserved their own Survivor Tree, it was Amy.

3

Thomas "Brady" Bradshaw had been counting down the days for a month. The way he always did when springtime rolled around. For the past few weeks, his work as a firefighter for Oklahoma City had taken second seat to his memories and heartache, his confusion and anger. And all of it led to this one day. This one morning.

The anniversary of the Oklahoma City bombing.

Brady had the day off. He pulled his motorcycle into a spot near the back of the memorial parking lot and killed the engine. For a long time he just sat there, helmet and sunglasses still in place.

He was twenty-eight now. Twenty-three years removed from the little boy he had been when the bomb went off. The sky overhead was clear today. Some years it rained. A few years had seen storms and even a tornado warning or two. Brady could see today's events as clearly as if they'd already happened.

It was the same every anniversary.

People would stream through the front gates, quiet and somber. Some of them tourists, curious people passing through, remembering for the first time in years the terrible terrorist attack that had happened here. In America's heartland. They would walk the grounds and take pictures. Look at the exhibits in the museum and stop by the gift shop. A mug and a postcard later and they'd be on their way. Off to explore the nearest park or Frontier City.

Brady released his grip on the handlebars and stared at the memorial. The people here today wouldn't all be tourists. Some would be connected to the bombing. They might've lost a friend or a family member. Or they may have survived the attack from inside the building. For those people—like Brady—the anniversary of the bombing was reverent. A day they would never forget.

But only a small number were really anything like him. For Brady, the Oklahoma City bombing was personal.

He shoved up the sleeves on his navy sweatshirt and stared at his forearms. When people looked at him they didn't see the scars. They saw the guy who had done a season on the *Survivor* show. A guy modeling agencies once fought over.

Brady never wanted any part of it.

He didn't do *Survivor* to become famous. Battling fires in Oklahoma City was his passion, not standing in front of a camera. He only did *Survivor* because he was one. And if anyone could prove it, he could. Never mind that he lost in the second round. The show couldn't hold a candle to real survival.

The way it felt twenty-three years ago, when he was buried in the rubble of the Alfred P. Murrah Federal Building.

A quick look at his arms and he could see them. Jagged scars that crisscrossed his forearms. Sure, they had faded, but they were still there. He ran his hands over the marks and looked up again. Yes, today would be the same as every anniversary that had come before it.

He would go through the gate with the others and make his way to the outdoor area. In utter silence he would find the chair with his mother's name and he would leave her a single long-stemmed rose. Then he would place his hand on the trunk of the Survivor Tree and he would try to separate his memories from the long-ago news accounts of the day. The ones still up on YouTube.

Brady took a deep breath and removed his helmet. He set it in the compartment at the back of his bike and pulled the paper bag with the rose from the same spot. Then he headed for the front gate.

Of course, there was one more reason he came every year. At least for the last eleven years. The reason was simple. The chance that he might see her. Brady clenched his jaw and stood a little straighter.

Her name was Jenna.

He didn't know her last name. She was a girl he'd met only once, here at the memorial site on the twelfth anniversary of the bombing. Back when they were both only seventeen. Back then she'd been a wisp of a girl with forever long legs and the face of actress Emma Stone. At least that's how he remembered her.

And Brady remembered her every day.

Jenna. The only girl in the world who would ever fully understand him.

Brady paid his admission and thought the same thing he did every year: Survivors should get in free. He shoved his free hand into the pocket of his black jeans and made his way out back to the field of chairs.

Like every anniversary there were more people here than usual. The noise wasn't soft and reflective, but more an intentional somberness. As if people knew they should be quiet. Respectful. But it was forced. Because they didn't have a million memories clawing and fighting their way to the surface.

The way Brady did.

His sunglasses were still on, where they would stay. No one ever saw Brady Bradshaw cry. He would make sure about that. Also because he didn't want to be noticed. The *Survivor* show had highlighted his history, his connection to the Oklahoma City bombing. Since then occasionally he'd responded to a call and someone would identify him. Dark hair. Tall. Built like a professional quarterback. At least that's how they described him on television.

Whatever. People recognized him. That was fine. Brady liked the people of Oklahoma. They were the family he didn't have. He enjoyed talking to them. Signing the occasional autograph, taking the handful of selfies in a month's time.

Not today.

Her chair was in the third row, somewhere near the middle. Brady moved past the people taking pictures and whispering. Beyond the handful of visitors carrying saplings from the Survivor Tree. No one seemed to notice him as he made his way. He was as familiar with this walk as if he lived here. And in some ways maybe he did.

Always would.

Three chairs down, and then—

There it was. Her chair. The one with her name etched into it. Proof once again that she had died here on that terrible day. Brady felt the first sting of tears. The routine was the same every year. He set the rose in the vase. Every chair had a vase attached to the side of it.

But not every chair had a rose.

With both hands Brady gripped the edges of the seat. He closed his eyes. There it was. The familiar feeling that came over him, the same one that hit him every anniversary. An aching, desperate, deep sense of protection. As if Brady Bradshaw, strong, tall, broad shoulders, could certainly do something to keep his mother safe.

The way she had done for him that horrible day.

"Mom. I'm here." He choked on the words. Then he ran his fingers over the plate with her name.

Sandra Bradshaw.

Two tears trickled down his cheeks, but Brady ignored them. Almost didn't notice. This was his time to remember. He wasn't in a hurry.

A few photographs of Brady's mother had been collected from their apartment after her death. Brady kept them in a small flip-book in a drawer near his bed.

That was it. Six pictures. The only evidence that his mother had ever existed. Brady thought about the photographs. One was his mom in her first year of college. The year she got pregnant with him. She had blond hair past her shoulders and a graceful, athletic build. She had gone to school on a tennis scholarship.

But that had ended when she found out she was having a baby. Brady had no idea who his father was or why he had abandoned his pretty mom. From what Brady could piece together, his mother hadn't been close with her parents. She had moved in with a few girls and gotten a job waiting tables.

The second picture was of her with two friends, all of them in their restaurant uniforms. In both photos, his mom's eyes were bright and happy. Young and full of life. The rest of the images grew less carefree. Deeper. But whatever the details of her story, Brady could see his mother had loved being a mom. She had loved her boy. Brady was everything to her.

The next four pictures were of the two of them. Her and him. One when he was hours old, lying in her arms, still in the hospital. Another when he was maybe two. He wore overalls and sat on his mother's hip, him grinning up at her. The next must've been taken at Christmastime when he was maybe four, and the last one was from his fifth birthday. In that photo, his mom stood beside him, her arm around his shoulders while he blew out the candles on what was the last birthday cake she'd ever make.

Yes, Sandra Bradshaw had loved being his mom.

The only other keepsake Brady had was an old weathered children's book. The one his mom had read to him every night at bedtime.

To the Moon and Back.

Brady gripped her chair and let the memories come. There were so few, he had to concentrate. Even then he wasn't sure if they were real or something he imagined. One moment he recalled was of his mom at nighttime. Maybe a few weeks before the bombing.

In the memory, Brady was wearing green race car pajamas. He could see himself, running into his room and hopping on his bed, his mom behind him. It was the clearest real-life picture Brady had. The one he held in his heart. His mother's blond hair windblown. Beautiful. Happy. Her eyes bright with laughter.

No hint of the tragedy to come.

"Brady boy, it's time for your story." Her singsong voice had called to him then. It called to him still.

And she was sitting on the bed beside him and opening their favorite book and reading every line, every page. "I love you to the moon and back, Brady. I always will."

He had giggled and laughed and yawned through the story. And she was turning off the light and lowering her voice. "Let's pray to Jesus."

"Yes, Mommy." In his memory it was always *Yes, Mommy.*

And she was praying for God to put His angels around Brady and their little apartment and for God to show him the good plans He had. "You're going to do great things when you grow up, Brady. Very great things."

Her smile had lit up his heart and then she was leaning close and kissing his cheek and tucking him in. Her hands soft against his arms. "I love you, Mommy."

"I love you, too, Brady."

Brady blinked and two more tears slid past his sunglasses and onto her memorial chair. There were only a handful of other memories. Mainly ones from the building that day. He and his mom had done errands together. Brady hadn't felt good. He'd had a cough, so he'd stayed home from preschool.

They had gone to the bank to pay bills. At least he thought that was why. And then they went to the Murrah Building to see about getting help. That's what his mom had told him. Brady had long since understood that the help must've been financial aid. Housing assistance or food stamps. Something to ease the burden of being a single mom and living with very little income.

Whatever the reason, they were in the building that

morning. Brady felt his heart rate speed up. The way it always did at this point in the flashback. They were in line and Brady was playing with the stanchion.

The gray weathered filthy stanchion.

And his mom was saying, "Don't touch that, Brady boy. You'll get germs." And she was looking right into his eyes and he was staring into hers. Her sweet blue eyes. She smelled like minty toothpaste and flowers. The way she always smelled. She smiled at him. The warmest, most wonderful smile. Her blond hair spilling over her shoulders, framing her face. And she had touched his cheek. "We're almost done here."

Those were her last words before the bomb exploded.

We're almost done here.

Brady's next memory was cold and frightening and painful.

Even still.

The next thing he knew, he was lying in a hospital bed with tubes attached to his arms. His mom's friend was there. He couldn't remember her name, but she had dark hair and she was crying. Crying hard. She had her hands over her face.

Brady tried to talk and she must've heard him because she jumped up and came to the side of his bed. "Brady . . . can you hear me?"

The room was spinning a little. Brady could still feel the dizziness every April 19 when he allowed himself to go back. He looked at the woman, stared at her and tried to feel steady and strong and brave. "Wh . . . where's my mommy?"

And the woman cried harder. Tears streamed down her cheeks. Or maybe those were the tears sliding down Brady's face now. The memory was old and grainy and fainter every year.

That's when the woman put her hand on his little arm. She smelled like pizza. Nothing like his mother. "Brady . . . I'm so sorry, honey."

Whatever was she sorry for? Brady couldn't understand. And why was she crying? Those were the thoughts in his little five-year-old mind. But before he could spend any real time wondering, the woman told him.

His mother was dead.

She rambled on, doing her best to explain what she thought he wanted to know. How a bad guy had parked a big truck near the building and blew it up, and how there had been flying glass and metal and concrete. Which was why his arms had bandages all around them. Brady was almost certain he could remember the woman saying all that.

But the part he was absolutely sure about was what she said next. She told him the reason he didn't have any cuts on his face or his head was because the very last thing his mother did before she died was cover him.

She protected her little boy. Guarded him at the expense of her own life.

When the bomb hit that Wednesday morning, it

ripped the front off the building, leaving a gaping hole and exposing every floor. Brady and his mom hadn't fallen to the ground along with the mountain of people and debris that collapsed that day. Instead, they were buried under rubble on the fifth floor. Later Brady learned from the paperwork in his mother's things that a chunk of steel had hit his mom in the head while she lay over Brady.

That was how she died.

The rest of the details were a mix of Brady's memories and news accounts he'd studied. For years after the bombing he had been obsessed with details about survivors and the monster who did the deed.

At least until five years ago. At that point he'd had enough of the true accounts. He still visited the memorial each year, but otherwise he lived his life. Brady let the memory fade into the cool wind around him. With no family to take him in, his mother's friend had kept him at her house. But only until the state found his first foster home.

After that, his childhood was more like a court dossier as he was passed from one foster home and social worker to the next, shifting between three elementary schools, one middle school and two high schools until he graduated.

His sophomore year, on the anniversary of the bombing, Brady connected with a couple who had lost their baby in the attack. The little boy was one of nineteen children killed in the daycare center on the second floor of the building. From their first meeting, the woman and her husband had embraced Brady. They would've done anything for him. But Brady struggled with one thing.

The husband and wife were Christians.

Brady didn't hold that against them, exactly. Faith was a personal thing. He just didn't want to be around it. If God was for him, then why did the bombing happen? What about the good plans God was supposed to have for him? And how come evil was so much a part of this world? None of it made sense. So while he still stayed in touch with the couple, he mostly kept to himself.

When he turned eighteen he started volunteer work with the Oklahoma City Fire Department. Two years later they hired him. Ever since then he'd been doing something for strangers that no one had been able to do for his mother.

Helping people survive tragedies.

Brady used the fabric of his sweatshirt to dust the top of his mother's memorial chair. The *S* in *Sandra* looked grimy. A little spit on his sleeve and he used it to work the dirt free. He stood straight again and studied her name. Yes. That was better.

He ran his hand over the letters one more time. "Next year, Mom. I'll be here."

The tears welled up again. He blinked them back, his sunglasses firmly in place. Then he turned and walked away. He knew where to go next. He moved across the open space to the reflection pond.

He took a seat on an empty bench and stared at the

two bronze walls on the other side of the water. They stood four stories high. Engraved at the top of one was a simple time stamp: *9:01*. The other was engraved with a different one: *9:03*.

The first one represented the minute before the bomb went off. That morning at 9:01, when life was still whole and innocent and beautiful. Not just for Brady and his mother, but for everyone in the building.

Right up until the explosion.

Brady closed his eyes. The dirty gray stanchion. The smell of the musty government office. The people in line ahead of them. *We're almost done here. Almost done.*

He squinted and shifted his gaze to the second one. *9:03*. The minute after the bomb went off. People in Oklahoma City liked to say that time stamp represented the first minute of whatever would come next. The beginning of life after the bomb. The start of recovery. The numbers were meant to give victims and their families and all who loved the city a belief in one important idea:

Healing was possible.

Brady worked the muscles in his jaw. Never mind any of that. For him it would always be 9:02. The minute the bomb went off. There was no fancy wall memorializing that moment. An ache filled his chest and pushed down on his soul. *Breathe, Brady. Take it in.* He lifted his gaze to the sky. The explosion ripped through his life every morning, keeping him from something that came easily for most people:

Love. All kinds of love.

Letting someone in would mean the possibility of losing that person. Brady hadn't figured out how to do that, so he hadn't found healing. And he was almost certain he never would. Every now and then his buddies at the firehouse tried to set him up with one of their sisters or friends. Brady would last one or two dates. Once in a while he would spend a couple weeks or a month interested in a girl. But always things fell apart. Brady was never surprised. Not only did he have trouble loving, but the reverse was true, also.

He wasn't easy to love.

Girls didn't understand him. One date put it succinctly: "You're gorgeous on the outside, Brady. But you're a haunted house on the inside. I don't want to get caught in the cobwebs."

Brady thought of it another way. His heart was like the Murrah Building. Still in pieces from the aftermath of the bombing. The way it had been since he was that five-year-old little boy, waking up in the hospital.

Since high school, Brady lived alone, no roommates. He liked it that way. Besides, he was hardly ever home. When he wasn't working, he volunteered with several city service groups. The work gave him purpose. If God wasn't going to help the people of Oklahoma City, then Brady would step in. It was what he lived for. Helping other people. That and one other thing.

The hope that someday, somehow he might find Jenna.

Brady stood and walked around the pond to the

hundred-foot section of chain-link fence. Here was where he would spend most of his time this morning. Looking at the letters and pictures and hand-drawn cards people would leave today.

Eleven years ago, Brady had met Jenna here at this very spot. But that was another story. Something he wouldn't think about until later. Depending on how he felt. Right now he only wanted to find a spot in the fence for the letter and wait. In case she showed up the way she had that day.

Brady took the letter from his pocket. It was a copy. Every year he wrote her a letter and always he kept the original. That way if he ever found her, she could have the whole collection. One for every year.

Proof that Brady had never forgotten her.

He took a deep breath and read this year's letter once more. He'd written it last night. Usually that was when the words came to him—the day before the anniversary. From his other pocket he pulled a piece of blue ribbon. He rolled the letter like a scroll and tucked it into the chain link. Just above a large red paper heart with the words *We miss you, Papa* scribbled in crayon across the front. Next to a faded copy of an older photo. A husband and wife on their wedding day. Four words were handwritten across the top: *I miss you still.*

Sorrow rushed at him like a tsunami. Brady tried to steel himself against it, but then he moved closer to the fence. Closer to the heartache. He grabbed the chain link and squeezed his eyes shut. Why? Why would someone fill a truck with fertilizer and blow it up in front of the federal building?

How could anyone hate that much?

Brady felt his tears become sobs. Deep. Quiet. Relentless. He fought them with everything in his being. It was time to move on, time to get past this. If only he could. Because for all the people he had ever rescued, the one person he couldn't save faced him in the mirror every morning.

For a long moment Brady didn't let go of the chainlink. Couldn't let go. So much pain. So much hurt and loss. Generations changed forever. Brady clenched his teeth and finally . . . finally he found control again. He sniffed and willed his tears to stop. He wanted only one thing. The same thing he always wanted.

9:01.

We're almost done here . . . almost . . .

Brady stepped back from the fence. A woman was watching him. She was beautiful. Older than he was, but still very pretty. *Probably remembers me from* Survivor, he thought. But she wasn't Jenna, and Brady didn't feel like talking.

He started to walk away. There was still the tree and the museum to visit. He needed to look through it all, every detail. Every memento and remembrance, like he did every year. Before he left he would take a piece of chalk and write something on the children's patio. Visitors were encouraged to do that. It was another part of Brady's routine.

And the whole time he would keep his eye on the fence. Checking it. Looking back at the spot where his letter remained. Just in case he might see her. Maybe walking the fence the way she'd done all those anniversaries ago. Just in case this was the year.

The year Jenna actually showed up.

4

The bad news came when Ashley and Kari and three of their older kids had been standing in line for thirty minutes. No more saplings. Apparently, there were more people wanting a piece of the Survivor Tree this year. There were still dozens of people ahead of them when a man with a megaphone stood on a picnic table at the front of the line and made the announcement.

"Sorry, folks! We're all out!" He wore a park ranger shirt and a sympathetic expression. "Try again next year. We do this every anniversary."

Amy didn't seem to grasp the information at first. She looked up at Ashley. "Wait. Is he serious?" Alarm filled her eyes and her cheeks looked suddenly pale. "Does he mean . . . I can't get a sapling? Even though we got in line so early?"

Ashley felt terrible. "Yes." She put her hands on her niece's shoulders. "They might find more. We can ask someone inside." Ashley glanced at Kari. Maybe her sister would have something more to offer. But Kari managed only a sad shake of her head.

Defeat seemed to come over Amy all at once. "I can't believe it."

Ashley looked into her niece's eyes. "I'm sorry, honey." Next to Amy, Cole and Jessie stood, silent. All of them helpless.

For a few seconds Amy said nothing. Then she nodded, her eyes dry. "That's fine. I just . . . I really hoped . . ." She hesitated and looked off. "It's okay. Can we see the tree now?"

"Of course." Ashley's mind raced. How could she still get a sapling today? Her niece wouldn't cry or make a scene or even complain. The poor girl had lost her whole family, after all. At twelve, she was used to disappointment. But there had to be a way.

Ashley ached for her precious niece. The baby tree was a big part of the reason they were here. And now . . .

Ashley felt like she was responsible. Like she'd let Amy down. She hung back with Kari while Amy, Jessie and Cole walked ahead. Cole must've said something kind, because Ashley saw Amy give him a slight smile.

"I really blew that." Ashley linked arms with her sister for a few seconds. "We should've gotten here at six. Clearly."

"You didn't know." Kari patted Ashley's hand. "It'll be okay. She can get a sapling another year."

But they both knew what the little tree would've meant to Amy. They were quiet as they followed the kids. Ashley crossed her arms and looked around. The feeling of the memorial was one of complete serenity. Ashley had expected something more hopeless.

Instead somehow the place felt inviting. As if many people who had walked these grounds had made peace with the past. A quick glance around told her that most of the people here today were likely tourists. Patriotic types. Oklahoma natives. Visitors from out of the state and even out of the country.

Ashley wondered if the families of victims and survivors visited anymore. There would be fewer now, twenty-three years later. People might have moved or passed away.

Following Amy's lead, their group walked into the museum. She didn't stop to look at any of the exhibits. That would most likely come later, Ashley figured. Instead Amy was moving more quickly now, her cousins working to keep up. Like she had a single-minded mission, and nothing could distract her until she'd carried it out.

Amy walked through the back doors of the building and there on the landing she stopped, her attention locked on one thing. Ashley and Kari were close enough behind her that they could see it, too.

The Survivor Tree.

It stood much larger and grander than Ashley had imagined. The five of them continued outside and up a few flights of stairs. And there they were. In the shadow of the big old tree.

Ashley and Amy had searched online for photos of other American elms. None of them looked so grand.

This one had a trunk thick and proud, if somewhat slanted. The branches spread out like a canopy.

A hundred people could've sought cover under its shade.

With quiet steps, Ashley moved next to Amy. After a while, Amy looked at her and smiled. Not with her mouth, but with her eyes. "It's beautiful."

"Yes." Ashley gazed at the tree. There was definitely something special about the tree. "No wonder your mama loved it."

The others came closer. "It's the prettiest I've ever seen." Jessie leaned against Kari. "Right, Mom? Don't you think so?"

"I do." Kari nodded, her eyes on the old elm.

Cole stood on the other side of Ashley. "It's almost a hundred years old. I can't believe it's still here."

Amy didn't stop staring at the tree. "I saw pictures of it after the bombing. It looks like a totally different tree now."

"I know. I Googled it." Cole nodded. "It was basically just a burned-up tree trunk, all black and shredded from the bomb and the cars that caught fire around it."

Amy's eyes grew noticeably soft, her attention still on the elm. Her voice grew quiet. "But God let it survive."

Disappointment came over Ashley again. She lifted her eyes to the blue overhead. *We should've gotten that sapling for her. Please, Father, help us get one. No one deserves one more than Amy.* They had already researched how the little tree would look when it was grown and Amy had even found a place to plant it. Ashley let the thought go.

There were two other groups of people nearer to the tree. When they were gone, Amy walked to the trunk. At one point she stopped and looked straight up through the branches. "I can't believe it's so tall."

The others didn't say anything. This was Amy's time and Ashley wasn't going to miss the moment. She pulled her phone from her jacket and as soon as Amy put her hand on the trunk, Ashley captured it.

For a long while, Amy closed her eyes. When she opened them she turned to Ashley and then Kari and her cousins. "I asked God to let my mama and daddy see me here. So they'd know the truth about me."

They all watched her, like they were waiting for more explanation. Amy looked at the tree and then back at the rest. "You know. That I'm a survivor. Just like the elm."

Cole joined Amy at the tree, and put his hand on the bark. "God really can get us through anything." He turned to Ashley. "I think that's why He let it survive."

"I think so, too." Ashley walked to the trunk and touched it. Pressed her hand against the rough bark. Suddenly she knew what she was going to do. She was going to paint the tree. She could see it in her heart already. A bright blue sky, two or three puffy white clouds. And there in the middle, in all its glorious splendor, the Survivor Tree. At the base, a blond girl. Amy. Sitting against the trunk, her hands raised toward heaven.

Yes, she would paint it for her niece. Ashley smiled. She would start as soon as they got home.

Kari and Jessie joined them, too. "Amy . . ." Kari took a step closer, her words gentle. "Your mom always loved trees."

"She did?" Amy leaned against the trunk.

Ashley loved the privacy of the moment. There were no other tourists on the patio near them. They could take their time. She slipped her arm around Cole and listened as Kari explained.

"Yes. They were some of her favorite things." Kari linked arms with Jessie, her attention on Amy. "She once told me she felt closest to God when she looked at a tree. She liked to say we could learn a lot from them."

Tears filled Ashley's eyes. Dear Erin. The revelation was sweet and poignant. Something Ashley had never known about her youngest sister. She looked at Kari. "I love this. How long ago did she tell you?"

"We were at church camp one summer. Taking a walk." Kari gazed into the distance, clearly remembering. "Ash, you and Brooke were back at camp for some reason."

"Probably cleaning our cabin." Ashley uttered a light laugh. "I was always in trouble. Too much talking. Not paying attention."

Kari grinned. "Probably." She turned to Amy again. "Anyway, your mom said that trees raised their arms to praise God, no matter the season. Even in the dead of winter, when no sign of life existed. When its leaves might never come again, the tree's branches were still lifted high toward heaven."

"Really?" Amy's eyes brightened. "I love that. I never knew."

All of them seemed caught up in the story. Ashley looked to the beautiful elm, grasping the imagery as deeply as Erin once had.

"She said something else." Kari's voice was soft, gentle in the breeze around them. She had a way of bringing a memory to life. This was one of those times.

"The reason a tree can survive the storms of any season is because its branches bend in the wind. Otherwise it would blow over and die." Kari gave Amy a slight smile. "Your mother said she wanted to be that way, too. Whenever God's Spirit might talk to her or lead her in a certain direction, whatever He whispered for her to do or not to do . . . she wanted to be sensitive."

"That's beautiful." Amy kept her eyes on Kari.

"She said the Holy Spirit was like the wind." Kari patted Jessie's arm and separated herself so she could go to Amy. In the most tender way, Kari took hold of both Amy's hands. "I want you to know something." She looked into the girl's eyes. "Your mom *was* like the trees she loved so much. She moved easily to the sound of God's voice in her heart."

A few tears slid down Ashley's cheeks as she listened. She wiped them and put her free hand on Amy's shoulder. "It's true. Your mom's faith was everything to her."

"Wow." Cole took a deep breath. "That's powerful. The tree in the wind analogy."

Amy hugged Kari and then Ashley. "Thank you." She kissed each of her aunts' cheeks. Kari put her hand alongside Amy's face. "I'll remember that about your mom as long as I live. Every time I look at a tree."

Ashley's heart ached. The story was indeed one of the most precious she had heard about Erin. She had been at the camp that summer, too. And somehow she had missed that moment. The way she had missed so much about Erin while she was alive. The two of them had often been at odds. Erin, close to their mother. Ashley, more rebellious, independent.

She blinked back another few tears. At least she had stories like this. And she had Amy. One day in heaven she would have forever to get to know her little sister in ways she never did here on earth.

Several tourists were headed their way. God had given them private space here at the Survivor Tree. Now it was time to move on. Ashley took another few photos, including one of Amy and Kari. A reminder of the story that had come to life today.

"Can we see the fence next?" Amy was at Ashley's side again. "Do you know about the fence?"

"I don't." Ashley put her arm around Amy's shoulders as their group started to walk toward the steps.

"None of us do." Cole looked at Jessie and then Kari. "Tell us about it."

Amy had done her research on the memorial site and while they walked, she told them what she knew. The site had opened in 2000, on the fifth anniversary of the bombing. It sat on three acres in the heart of Oklahoma City and included the museum and the open space behind it.

"See those?" She pointed to a nearby field with rows of chairs made of bronze and what looked like blown glass. Amy stopped. "There's one for each of the people who died that day."

"How come some of the chairs are smaller?" Jessie shaded her eyes.

Amy was quiet for a moment. "Those represent the children. Nineteen little kids were killed. Most of them were in the daycare on the second floor."

Again Ashley's heart felt the weight of the tragedy. The realness of it. Good thing the guys had taken the younger ones to Frontier City today. The sadness here would be more than they could understand.

They were passing a large rectangular pond. Amy motioned toward it. "That's the reflecting pool. Come on." She stepped away from Ashley and headed toward a low stone wall. "Look into the water."

Everyone followed her lead. The only thing Ashley could see was her own reflection—almost as clearly as if she were looking into a mirror.

"I see myself." Cole looked from the water to his cousin.

"Exactly." Amy smiled, but her eyes held a deeper sorrow. "It's meant to show you the face of someone harmed by the bombing. Someone changed by it." Amy looked at the others. "Because when terrorism hits, we are all affected. Always."

Ashley could hardly believe her niece's depth and insight. She had definitely studied the memorial. The reason for the pond was spot-on. Of course every American had been harmed by what had happened that sad day. Ashley had been in high school. The feeling then was the same now: only God could heal America. For this bombing and for 9-11 and so many other ways the people of the United States had turned against Him.

Amy sat down on the stone bench and the rest of them did the same. "See those tall thick walls?"

They were impossible to miss. Covered in bronze and at least a hundred feet high, each of them glistened in the morning sun. Amy explained that the walls were called gates, and that the times engraved at the tops of them represented the minute before the bomb went off and the minute after.

"The bronze is so that people would see more sunshine than memorial. The promise of life outside of the disaster site."

"Wow." Cole patted her shoulder. "You did your homework."

Amy looked more relaxed. She smiled. "My history teacher said I could do an extra-credit report on it."

"So what about the fence?" Jessie turned and looked over her shoulder at the long stretch of chain link at the far end of the grounds. "It has things all over it."

"Right." Amy stood and looked that way. "Come on. I'll show you."

As they walked, Ashley kept her eyes on Amy. *I couldn't be more proud of her.* Amy's composed way of sharing the details about the memorial. The way she carried herself, head high. Smile ready. Even surrounded by reminders of her own loss.

Amy wasn't a victim. No matter what had happened to her because of the car accident. Even though the rest of her family was in heaven, Amy was whole. Of course she had moments of feeling sad and missing her parents and sisters. But she was determined to live life.

Coming here to see the Survivor Tree was further proof.

Her cousins walked on either side of Amy as she talked about the fence. "The original bombing site was fenced so people wouldn't disturb it. But crowds still came to see the area, to remember. Some of them because they'd lost a person they loved here." Amy pointed to the fence, now just ahead of them. "People began to leave things tucked in the chain link. Letters and cards, photos and teddy bears. Whatever reminded them of the husbands and wives, daughters and sons they had lost."

"This part of the fence." Cole pointed down the length of it. "Is that what they kept when they opened the memorial?"

Amy nodded. "Exactly." She motioned to a pink teddy bear. "Every day people leave things here. And every day the memorial site workers collect everything and put it in storage."

"All of it?" Kari sounded as amazed as Ashley felt.

Amy thought for a few seconds. "I guess. I'm not sure."

They reached the fence and for a few minutes Ashley looked at the items. A faded baseball cap with the words *Hey buddy . . . still think about you every day* written across the bill. A birthday card tied to the fence so the inside could easily be seen. Ashley stooped low to read it.

"Every birthday. Every Christmas. Every time I see a sunset. I still miss you, Son. Love forever, Dad."

Ashley felt her tears again. She wanted to spend an hour here. Reading the notes and messages. Imagining the heartache behind them. But they didn't have that much time, which was just as well. The sense of grief and loss was bound to be overwhelming.

Kari walked up, dabbing at the corner of her own eyes. "It's beyond sad. I mean . . . the emotions here. Just heartbreaking."

"So much pain." Ashley looked at the birthday card again, then at her sister. The three kids were a few yards away, still studying other items on the fence. "Are they ready to move on?"

"Actually, Jessie and Amy and I are headed to the restroom. Cole, too." Kari took a step toward the kids.

"Okay." Ashley hesitated. "You go ahead. I'll stay

here." She glanced at the fence and then back at her sister. "Come find me when you're done."

"Okay." Kari smiled. "This has been so special."

"For me, too." Ashley searched her sister's eyes. "I feel closer to Erin because of the story you told."

For a quick second Kari reached out and squeezed Ashley's hand, then she turned and met up with the kids who were a few yards away, and the group headed toward the museum.

Ashley faced the fence once more. As she did, she noticed she wasn't alone. A few feet away stood a guy who looked like he could be Landon's brother. Tall, dark hair. Strong and fit. Maybe in his late twenties. He wore sunglasses and held what looked like a rolled-up letter. Ashley took a few steps back and watched him.

The guy was clearly caught up in his own world. He took a blue ribbon from the pocket of his jeans and tied it around the rolled-up paper. Then he slipped it into the fence. Ashley narrowed her eyes. Who was the letter for? And how was the man connected to the bombing?

Something about him looked familiar, but Ashley didn't think she'd ever really seen him before. Maybe just that he resembled Landon. The guy turned and caught her staring. She managed a weak smile and a quick nod before she focused her attention again on the fence. In her peripheral vision she saw the man shove his hands deep into his navy blue sweatshirt pockets and walk the other direction. He definitely didn't want to talk to a stranger.

Ashley watched him go. *What's his story, God? He looks so hurt.* The man seemed isolated and distant. Like whatever his connection to the bombing site it was deeply personal. Maybe even devastating. She stared at the white paper and the blue ribbon. Why was the man here today? Ashley wished she could've asked him. But more than that she wanted to know something else.

What was in the note?

5

Somehow, Amy felt closer to her family here at the memorial site. As they met up with Aunt Ashley and headed toward the field of empty chairs, she breathed in the quiet air. Maybe it was the other people who had come here today. Some of them were probably tourists.

But she had a feeling lots of them were survivors like her.

Long ago when she was little, her mother had read her a story about an ugly duckling. The little duckling was different from his siblings. Everywhere they went, he felt set apart. He imagined the other ducks whispering about him, feeling sorry for him.

Then one day the ugly duckling came upon a family of swans. And suddenly he realized he wasn't different or ugly after all! He was a swan.

That's how Amy felt today. Her aunt and uncle loved her as much as they loved their own kids. Amy knew that. Her cousins treated her like she was a sibling. No one was mean to her and she'd never seen them whispering about her.

But they felt sorry for her. Of course they did. Her

entire family was dead. Amy understood that, and she was thankful for her home and the way she had been accepted and loved by her aunt and uncle. Still, no matter how much they cared for her, no matter how much they still hurt over their own losses, none of them could ever really understand how it felt to have your whole family die.

Here, though, it was different. At the memorial—especially on the anniversary of the bombing—there had to be at least some people walking around who knew what it was like to be so young and to lose a parent in a sudden moment. Amy was sure of it. They were here because they were still healing. Here because they wanted to remember the person they'd lost.

Amy and the rest of them reached the chairs, and quietly they walked the rows. That was Amy's idea. Because each person should be remembered in some special way, she told the others. They didn't stop and read every name, but they paid their respects.

That's what Aunt Ashley called it.

Amy could picture her parents walking these very rows, noticing each of these exact chairs. Of course they had. Her mom had loved visiting here, she definitely would have taken time to see the chairs.

They were almost done. Today's time would end in the museum, where they would read about the events of that April 19.

Amy wished she could meet everyone here who was just like her. The family of swans. The survivors. People still stuck somewhere between 9:01 and 9:03 that Wednesday morning. But since that couldn't happen, she let herself believe that everyone she could see, everyone they passed by knew her pain. She smiled at a few of them and nodded at others.

Her aunts and uncles and cousins were her family and she loved them with all her heart.

But these were her people.

• • •

THE GUY KEPT returning to the fence. Checking on the letter. Looking one way and then the other, like he was waiting for someone. Ashley noticed him the whole time they visited the chairs and afterward as they left for the museum.

Amy was doing well. She hadn't brought up the sapling again, and she seemed at peace having spent time here. But through it all, Ashley kept an eye on the fence. Whoever the guy was waiting for, the person apparently hadn't shown up.

As they neared the museum, Ashley watched the man leave the fence again. He seemed on a mission now. He actually passed by them, apparently unaware of Ashley's surveillance. Only Kari noticed. "Who was that?"

"Who?" Ashley blinked and turned to her sister.

"The guy." Kari laughed quietly. "Ash . . . you've been staring at him for ten minutes. He was standing by the fence, right?"

"He was." Ashley drew a quick breath. "I don't know. There's just . . . something about him."

"Yeah." Kari raised her brow. The two of them were walking a few feet behind the kids. "Every girl here today noticed something about him."

"It isn't that." Ashley felt embarrassed. "Come on. You know me better." Ashley watched as the guy entered the building. "He looks like Landon. Maybe that's it."

"Yeah." Kari nodded. She seemed content with that explanation. "He kind of does. I can see that."

"Plus, did you see the pain on his face? The guy's hurting for sure." Ashley pointed back at the fence. "He left something. A note. Tucked into the fence." She turned to her sister again. "I saw him leave it. When you were in the restroom."

"Got it." Kari's tone grew more serious. "You think he lost someone here?"

Ashley paused. "Absolutely. I wanted to say something. Offer to pray for him." She shrugged. "He just looked so . . . like he needed help."

They reached the museum and walked up the steps to the double glass doors. "You didn't say anything, right?"

"Definitely not." Ashley scanned the building as soon as they stepped inside. She didn't see the guy anywhere. "He looked like he wanted to be left alone."

"Mmm." Kari appeared to understand. "Probably a lot of people like him here today."

"Probably."

They moved from one exhibit to another. Amy had done much of the research about the bombing, but the rest of them had not. Kari and Ashley were old enough to remember it, of course. But details of that day were hazy. So they read every display.

Ashley was trying to pay attention. She was. This truly interested her. It was a part of history, after all. But she couldn't stop thinking about the letter back in the fence. If the person never came, if he or she never found it, then what would happen to it? What if no one ever read it? The staff would collect it and throw it in storage and the message would be lost forever.

Which would be another kind of tragedy.

The letter could be written to someone who had died here. In which case it was never actually meant to be read. But then why had the guy kept searching, looking one way and then the other? He must've been waiting for someone. A living person.

Finally she tapped Kari on the shoulder and whispered, "I'll be right back."

"What?" Kari walked with her a distance from the kids. She seemed slightly alarmed. "Don't tell me you're looking for that guy again?"

"No!" Ashley gave a hurried shake of her head. "Of course not. He's gone, anyway. I saw him leave."

"Ashley." Kari studied her. "You're freaking me out a little here. He's a stranger."

"I know. But what if he needs help?" Ashley kept her voice low. "I'll be right back."

"Where are you going?"

"To the fence." She was already moving toward the exit. "I won't be more than a few minutes."

"What am I supposed to tell the kids?" Kari looked exasperated. She folded her arms in front of her. "This is crazy, Ash."

"Tell them I'll be right back." She blew Kari a kiss, turned and opened the door. Before she stepped outside she looked back. Amy and Cole and Jessie were completely caught up in a lengthy survivor account posted on the far wall. They'd never know she was gone.

Out in the sunshine again, Ashley flew down the steps. She jogged toward the fence as fast as she could without drawing attention. The mood was still somber, reflective. Calm. She couldn't break into an all-out sprint. But she didn't want to leave without at least looking at the letter.

The urgency that filled her heart reminded her of other times in her life when she couldn't walk away from someone else's heartache. Like years ago when she worked at Sunset Hills Adult Care Home. She spent her off-hours studying the elderly residents. Learning their stories so she could find reasons for their behavior. One Alzheimer's patient at the home screamed when she used the bathroom. Every single time. Ashley's research showed that six decades earlier the woman had been a beauty queen. No wonder the mirror terrified her. Ashley's investigation paid off. She put a sheet over the mirror and the woman never screamed again.

Now her feet moved a little faster. Maybe it was her creative nature, or the fact that she was drawn to hurting people. Either way she couldn't stop herself.

After having watched the guy return to the exact spot along the fence, Ashley knew right where to go. The rolled-up scroll with the blue ribbon was next to a big red heart. Ashley stopped right in front of it and stared, breathless. There were two words written across the front in blue ink. The writing was too faint to see from far away. But from here Ashley could make out the message clearly.

For Jenna

That was all. Just "For Jenna." As if whoever Jenna was, if she came here today she would know the note was for her and she would take it from the fence without hesitation. Ashley blinked a few times. Or maybe not. Maybe Jenna was the guy's family member. Someone he had lost in the bombing. The note might just be his form of therapy. Maybe he did this every year. Wrote a letter to the person he'd lost so that somehow this Jenna would know from heaven how much the mysterious, hurting guy still missed her.

Ashley tapped her foot.

What if the guy came back? He might be watching her now, wondering why she'd been stalking him, waiting to prevent Ashley from touching the note. She looked to the right for a long while and then to the left. The man wasn't anywhere near the fence.

She must be losing her mind.

Of course the man wasn't here. Ashley had seen him leave. She spun around and searched the grounds. No, he definitely wasn't here. But what about Jenna? If she was alive, then there was still a chance she'd come by today. A chance she could be walking by this very spot even now, looking for her letter.

Be discreet, Ashley, she told herself. *Don't look like a crazy person.* She studied the people on either side of her. There were no single women of any age. No one moving along the fence searching for a letter. At least it didn't look that way.

No one seemed to notice Ashley.

She really should leave. The letter was for Jenna. That's all she needed to know. It was the reason she'd come back to the fence. Just so she'd know. Ashley stared at the scroll again. Wrong. *Be honest with yourself, Ash. You came back to read it.*

Fine. Ashley took a deep breath. Her heartbeat picked up speed. If she was going to do this she needed to get it over with. Fast. Before someone accused her of stealing notes from the memorial fence.

Which would almost certainly be a crime of some sort.

With shaking fingers she removed the letter from the fence and untied the ribbon that held the scroll in place. Then she unrolled it and there, inside, was a full-on letter. Ashley held her breath. She had gone too far to stop herself. She let her eyes race to the top of the page and she began to read.

Dear Jenna,

Like I do every year, I wrote you a letter. In case you come to the memorial today. In case you want to find me as much as I want to find you. Every year I-

"Excuse me." A woman tapped her on the shoulder.

Ashley gasped. She dropped the letter and the ribbon and then immediately bent to pick them up. "I'm sorry, I didn't . . ." This was it. They were going to arrest her right here and then Kari and the kids would come out in time to see her handcuffed and hauled away and—

"Oh, my." The woman took a step back. "Sorry. I . . . didn't mean to startle you." She looked around. "I was hoping you might know where the restrooms are."

Only then did Ashley realize that the person talking to her wasn't alone. There were others in her group and all of them seemed to be waiting for Ashley's reply.

"Oh. Right." Ashley grabbed a breath. "They're . . . back at the building. Where the museum is."

The woman nodded. "Sorry again." She pointed to the note. "I didn't mean to disturb you."

"It's fine." Ashley forced a light laugh. "I just . . . I didn't see you walk up." She was rambling now. Already the group was turning away, toward the museum. Ashley waved and then looked back at the paper. Her breathing was fast and jagged. She had no idea if it was a crime to take a letter off the fence and read it. But she needed to get back to Kari and the others.

No way could she stand here and read the whole thing. She skimmed over it and then an idea hit her. Holding the paper in one hand, she pulled out her phone and tapped her camera app. Carefully she opened the note enough so she could see all the words.

Then she took a picture.

If reading other people's letters was a crime, surely taking photos of them must be, too. Ashley didn't know. But she had to get out of here. She rolled up the paper, tied it with the blue ribbon and slipped it into the fence again.

She positioned it so the words were clear once more.

For Jenna.

Then she took another picture.

Without hesitating she returned to the museum as fast as she could. Kari and the kids were only a few exhibits down from where they'd been when she left. Cole spotted her as she walked up.

"Mom, where were you?" He didn't look worried. But clearly he wanted an answer.

"Hi." Ashley smiled. Her heart was still racing, shooting adrenaline through her veins. "I . . . uh, I wanted to see something at the fence. I didn't get a good look before."

Cole hesitated, but only for a couple seconds. "Okay." He took her hand and led her toward the wall where Kari and Jessie and Amy were still reading. "You have to see this. You won't believe how God saved this one guy."

Not until Ashley reached the exhibit and Cole had resumed his place between Amy and Jessie did Kari finally notice she was back. Her sister turned and looked at her. Then she mouthed, "Did you steal it?"

"Of course not." Ashley straightened her jacket and focused her attention on the display. "Cole . . . you mean this one?" She could feel Kari watching her.

"Yes." Cole and his cousins were already on to the next display. "You've gotta read the whole thing."

Ashley fought the guilt rising inside her. She would tell Kari later about what had happened, how she'd thought she was going to be arrested and how she'd taken a picture of the letter. She and Kari could read it together. Ashley tried to focus on the exhibit, but she couldn't. Her heart was still pounding.

Maybe God wanted her to see the man today. Or maybe not. Sure, the timing could've been a coincidence. But what if the Lord had lined up the two of them so that Ashley would be intrigued? So she'd come back and take a picture of the letter and maybe even help the guy somehow?

It was possible, right?

Whatever the reason Ashley couldn't forget him. Not because he was attractive. But because of the hurt on his face. There was something familiar about him. Beyond the fact that he looked like Landon.

Stop, Ashley. This was ridiculous. She would put the whole thing out of her mind. He was a stranger. What could she possibly do to help? She moved on to join the others. *Put it out of your head*, she told herself. *Enough*.

On the way out of the museum, Amy led them to a patio with chalk drawings. A man who worked there stood nearby, supervising. Beside him, on a small table, was a bucket of chalk. Amy looked from Kari to Ashley. "So many kids were killed that day, they decided to make this chalk yard, with squares for drawing and writing. That way children and parents . . . whoever wants, can leave something behind."

The patio was a good distraction. Ashley watched as Amy sorted through the chalk. This was why they were here. For Amy. And if this was the last thing she wanted to do before they left the memorial, then they would all take part.

Ashley studied the childish illustrations and simple words written across the concrete. There were still many open squares. Each of the kids took chalk from the bucket. Then she and Kari followed suit. As they walked together, Kari whispered, "Ashley. What did you do?" She shot her a doubtful look. "You have to tell me."

"Later." Ashley sounded urgent. Friendly, but urgent. She didn't want the kids hearing them. She returned the whisper. "Everything's fine."

They spent another ten minutes on the chalk yard. Amy drew the Survivor Tree. Beside it she wrote, *Dear God, help me be like this tree. Amen.*

Ashley studied Amy's artwork. "It's beautiful." She put her hand on her niece's shoulder and worked to control her emotions. What had she been thinking? Concerned with a stranger? This day was about Amy, not helping some guy she didn't know.

"I really liked the story about my mom. How she loved trees." A softness filled Amy's eyes. More peace than pain. "Today was perfect." She smiled. "Thanks for bringing me."

Ashley worked to keep her emotions in check. "I'm glad we came."

"Are you gonna draw something?" Amy laughed. "You almost have to. Professional artist and all."

Ashley breathed deep and steadied herself. "Yes. That's exactly what I'm going to do." She stared at a blank square. How would it feel to be Amy today? Or the dark-haired young man? Or all the others who had suffered such loss?

And what about Jenna? Whoever she was.

Ashley bent down and began to write. *Beauty from*

ashes. Please, God. The words came easily. When her letters looked swirly and artsy, she surrounded them with a wreath of springtime flowers.

"Not fair." Cole was standing over her. "Mom, you're so good."

Ashley stood up and dusted off her hands. "Not at basketball."

Cole laughed. "True."

"God gives us different gifts." Kari joined them. She smiled at Ashley's drawing. "He just happened to saturate your mother with the gift of creating art. Even from chalk."

Jessie walked up and added her voice to the others'. Kari pointed at Amy's drawing. "I think we have another artist in the family." She kissed the top of Amy's head.

"Really?" Amy's eyes shone.

"You have a gift. I've been telling you." Ashley put her arm around Amy. "How about we get some basic supplies next week when we're home."

"Okay." Amy grinned. "Thanks."

When they were finished, they washed their hands and headed for the car. As Ashley drove to the hotel, Kari shot her another look. She hadn't forgotten about the letter.

Ashley definitely didn't want to talk about it now. She kept her phone in her pocket on the short drive. As soon as she had a minute alone, she would read the letter. And of course she'd share it with Kari and later with

Landon. They could all brainstorm how to help the guy. Which actually might not be possible. Ashley had gotten only one detail in the brief time she'd had the note open. Something she couldn't stop thinking about. It was the guy's name. The guy who clearly had a broken heart.

Brady Bradshaw.

6

Brady gripped the handlebars and leaned his motorcycle into the curve ahead of him. He took the ramp onto the freeway faster than he should've, the wind rushing at him like it was alive, washing over him. He lowered his head to cut the draft and picked up speed.

Jenna hadn't come.

Eleven years in a row and still she hadn't been back. At least not that he'd ever seen. And she'd never found his letters. Otherwise she would've at least contacted him. Because you don't just have the best day of your life with someone and not reach out if you get the chance.

That's what Brady figured.

Back in the beginning, on the second and third years after the two of them met, Brady assured himself that his feelings for her would grow less over time. If he never saw her again, eventually he would forget they'd ever met. He might even stop going to the memorial.

But it was more than a decade later and Brady hadn't forgotten her. Not at all. Her image in his mind had grown stronger, clearer. His determination to find her had never been more consuming. He exited the freeway and slowed for a stoplight. What was it about her?

Brady knew the answer. He had convinced himself that she was the only girl on the planet who could understand him. Or was it something deeper? Maybe having feelings for a figment of his imagination was easier than falling for someone right in front of him. One of the girls he'd met over the years.

The light turned green. Brady clenched his jaw as he sped through the intersection. Whatever it was, the girl had hold of his heart. That much had never changed. He lowered his head again, the wind pushing at him. If only it were tomorrow already. Then he would've survived another anniversary.

He wove in and out of traffic until he saw Jefferson Street. A quick right and he picked up speed again. Images from earlier filled his mind. The people along the fence, the way none of them were Jenna. And who was the pretty brunette who kept staring at him? For a few minutes back at the memorial he'd even wondered if she maybe knew Jenna. Maybe the girl Brady dreamed about had sent this woman to see if he'd be there.

The idea was crazy. Whoever the brunette was, Brady didn't know her. It had to be she recognized him from *Survivor,* or maybe from some news show about the bombing. He leaned hard into a left turn. Speed like this wasn't his usual style. Only once a year, when he wanted to outrun the brokenness inside him. Most days he drove his pickup truck. He'd been at the scene of too many motorcycle accidents. He knew better than to drive like this.

But the anniversary had its own rules.

A right turn at the next light and another right. Two lefts and there it was. The house where he had first learned he might actually survive all this. The home of Cheryl and Rodney Fisher. The couple he'd met at the memorial when he was still in high school.

Brady cut the engine, parked his bike and locked up his helmet. He removed his sunglasses and set them in the small compartment next to his helmet. He wouldn't be here long. Just enough to let the couple know he remembered them.

He still appreciated them.

Cheryl opened the door before he reached the front walkway. She stepped onto the porch and smiled. Not the typical smile of a person expecting company. Not the smile Cheryl would've had before April 19, 1995. But the smile of someone wounded. The closer Brady got the more he could see she'd been crying.

And of course.

This day was a nightmare for them, same as it was for him. The day all of them wanted to rewrite. That they might be anywhere but the Alfred P. Murrah Federal Building that fateful Wednesday. The Fishers had lost their two-year-old son, Jimmy, in the bombing. He wasn't actually in the daycare center. His nineteen-year-old aunt—Cheryl's sister—had just entered the building, intent on signing Jimmy in at the facility.

They were ten yards away from the front desk when the bomb hit.

Cheryl's sister had died, too.

Brady reached the top of the stairs and immediately Cheryl's arms were around him. He was never sure, but Brady had a feeling that in some ways he took the place of Jimmy. Never mind that Jimmy was black and Brady was white. Brady felt like Jimmy was his sibling. The boy would've been a few years younger than Brady. Like a little brother. Or maybe a best friend. Jimmy had been the Fishers' only child. They never had another baby after the bombing. Their doctor said sometimes high levels of stress could make a woman infertile.

Collateral damage after the bombing.

"Brady." Cheryl pulled back from the hug and found his eyes. "Thanks for stopping by." She kept her arm around his waist as they headed into the house. "Rodney's waiting for you." Brady followed her inside and there was Rodney, sitting at the kitchen table, newspaper spread out before him. One of the last of a generation who still read one.

Brady took a step forward. "Mr. Fisher."

"Brady." He closed the paper and stood, stretching out his arms. "Come here."

This was their way. The Fishers saw Brady as family. One of their own. They had moved past handshakes and formalities years ago. Rodney hugged Brady the way parents hug their kids when they return from war. The older man drew back and studied him. "You look good. Still doing that workout?"

"CrossFit? Yes, sir." He chuckled. "Gotta be ready for the next big fire."

Cheryl patted his hand. "You'll be ready." Her tone told him she was proud of him. "No one's more ready than you, Brady." She motioned to the living room. "Let's sit down. I put out coffee and snacks."

Of course she did. Sweet Cheryl Fisher was one of the kindest people Brady had ever met. On the table between the two sofas Cheryl had set a pot of coffee and a plate of chocolate chip cookies. Brady didn't typically do either. But he would fake it today. He could at least do that for Cheryl and Rodney.

Brady sat next to Rodney while Cheryl poured the coffee. "Still no cream?"

"No cream. Thank you, though. You're too nice." He looked from Cheryl to her husband and back again. "You don't need to do this."

"Brady, don't you know?" Cheryl handed him the coffee. Fresh tears filled her eyes. "We look forward all year to this visit with you."

Guilt thudded Brady in his chest. He lived seven miles away, but he made this trip just once every twelve months. On the anniversary. He glanced at the nearest bookcase. Had to be six Bibles on the various shelves, and on the wall was a framed print. It read: *With God all things are possible.*

Brady narrowed his gaze. Try telling that to his mother. Or to Jenna.

There you go again. Thinking mean and cynical. Trapped in hate and unforgiveness. Brady forced the slightest smile and turned back to the couple. He knew about God, of course. He just didn't believe in Him. That's why he didn't come more often. Brady set the coffee down. "You gonna tell me about Jimmy?"

They did this every year. A smile lit up Cheryl's eyes as she took her seat at the table. The first real smile since he'd gotten here. She looked at her husband. "Rodney, should we tell him?"

"Let's do." Rodney put his arm around her. He nodded at his wife. "You start."

"Jimmy, Jimmy." Cheryl shook her head and sighed. "Sweet little baby boy. Biggest brown eyes you ever saw." She looked long toward the front window. Like she was seeing all the way back to 1995. "Oh, how that boy loved life. Right straight out of the womb."

"True." Rodney poked his finger into the air as if to highlight the fact. "Other babies cry when they're born. Not Jimmy."

"No, not Jimmy." Cheryl glanced at her husband, and then at Brady. "Doctors thought something was wrong with him. How come he wasn't wailing like a baby's supposed to do?"

She stood and found a photo album on the nearby coffee table in the next room. When she was back at the table, she opened it. The same photo album they looked through every anniversary. "Here he is." She pointed to the photo of a newborn Jimmy. His eyes shining with possibility. "Look at that. Grinning right straight from heaven into our arms."

"That boy was always happy." Rodney leaned close, studying the picture.

Cheryl turned the page and raised the book every so often to show Brady. "On his first birthday he put his whole fist in the cake." She looked at Rodney. "Remember that? He learned how to say 'Uh-oh' that day!"

"Couldn't forget it." Rodney shook his head and turned to Brady. "Except he didn't eat it like other babies. He held it out to me and his mama. 'Dada?' That little voice of his. 'Dada?' "

Cheryl closed her eyes for a moment and opened them again. "I can still hear him, still see the way he looked at me that day. Just like it was happening all over again." Cheryl turned the next page.

Brady knew the stories. He knew the pictures. He'd been sixteen when he met the Fishers on the anniversary of the bombing. The couple had bought him lunch that day and listened to his story. Before they parted ways, Cheryl had given Brady a phone number and an address. "Join us for dinner next Sunday. Four sharp." And Brady did. That was the first time he'd heard the story of Jimmy.

In the early years after that dinner, Cheryl and Rodney had been there for Brady when he wasn't sure he had the will to live. When he felt alone and when he couldn't find Jenna. But then the Christian thing kept coming up. Cheryl would invite him to church or Rodney would want to open the Bible. Eventually Brady visited less often and in the last few years just on the anniversary. The least he could do was sit here and listen to them talk about Jimmy. Who else would care about their loss this many years removed from the bombing? Who else would care about his?

Cheryl continued through the photo album. She talked about the exact day Jimmy started walking and the day he threw a ball for the first time.

"He was gonna be the next Michael Jordan." Rodney chuckled at his wife. "Isn't that so?"

"Sure could shoot a basketball." Cheryl touched a photo of Jimmy in a red Michael Jordan T-shirt, number 23, holding a small orange ball and smiling like it was the best day of his life. Cheryl grew quiet. "Played with that mini hoop all day, every day."

Brady knew each detail of the story that followed. Jimmy was running by the time he turned two. Racing through the house, laughing and talking. He loved Bible stories and playing with blocks and Winnie-the-Pooh. He thought he was Christopher Robin. So much so that on his second birthday, Cheryl and Rodney threw him a party with a theme Jimmy had loved: the Hundred Acre Wood.

Two weeks later Jimmy was dead. Christopher Robin never got a chance to grow up.

The story slowed down as it neared the end. Tears

spilled from Cheryl's eyes. Rodney's, too. Quiet tears. Stoic. Tears of regret and loss and what might've been. Especially that. Cheryl took a napkin from the table and dabbed her eyes. "We watched *Winnie-the-Pooh* one more time. Before . . ." Her voice trailed off.

Rodney covered her hand with his.

Cheryl closed the photo album. "That was him. Little Jimmy."

"He's with Jesus now. We know that." Rodney looked straight at Brady. "We'll see him again. Our Jimmy. Closer every day."

Tears clouded Brady's vision. He blinked them back. Struggled for composure. This was always the awkward part. How could he just get up, climb on his bike and ride away? Listen to them tell Jimmy's story and then leave? Rather than be a friend to this kind couple all year long? Brady had no answers for himself.

He clasped his hands and stared at the floor. Until he could hear Cheryl's crying slow some. "Jimmy and I . . ." Brady lifted his eyes to Cheryl's, then to Rodney's. "We would've been friends. Somehow . . . we would've found each other."

The couple nodded. This was what they held on to. The possibility that Jimmy might've been Brady's friend. And in that case, somehow seeing Brady was almost like seeing Jimmy. Grown up and happy and whole. That was the gift Brady gave them whenever he came around.

Even if only once every April.

He stood. "I have to go."

"Brady." Rodney stayed seated. "Let us pray for you. At least that."

This hadn't happened last year or the year before. He'd told the Fishers long ago that he wasn't a praying man. Didn't want to talk about God or open the Scriptures. They respected his wishes, but today . . . well, today, there was an urgency in Rodney's voice.

Brady stifled a sigh. "Yes, sir." He sat back in his chair and clasped his hands again.

"You and God still on the outs?" Rodney narrowed his eyes, like he was trying to see through Brady's soul.

"Yes, sir. I guess you could say that." Brady looked at the man. "But thank you for praying. I know it matters to you and Mrs. Fisher."

They were both quiet. Cheryl spoke first. "It does matter, Brady. It matters to God."

Brady couldn't take much more of this. Not on the anniversary. He bowed his head. The signal was clear, the discussion finished. Across from him Rodney led the prayer. Something about healing a little more every year and asking God to watch over Jimmy and Cheryl's sister and, of course, Brady's mama.

Then at the end the man prayed something he hadn't before.

"Whatever it takes, God. Please. Get Brady's attention. So that when You do, he'll know it was You. Because only God could have done it. Whatever that might be." When Rodney finished, they shared their usual goodbyes and Brady made his annual promises to come around more often. Before he left, Cheryl stood in front of him and took hold of his hands. Hers were gentle, but firm.

The way his mother might've held him.

"Brady." She searched his face. "Nothing good ever came from being on the outs with God." Her eyes were damp again, imploring him to see her. Hear her. "Let this be the year. Please."

He stared at the ground and gritted his teeth. A slight nod and he looked at her again. "Yes, ma'am." He kissed her cheek. "Thanks for the coffee."

"We love you." Rodney hugged him next.

Brady couldn't say a word. His throat was too tight, his heart too broken. He turned and walked to the front door. A look back at each of them, a quick wave and Brady was gone.

On the ride back to the freeway, he couldn't stop reliving Rodney's prayer. He wanted to forget the words but he couldn't shake them. Rodney had asked for a sign from God, and that He would look out for Jimmy and Cheryl's sister and Brady's mama. In heaven. Which left Brady with just one question.

Why hadn't God done that before? While they were still on earth.

• • •

ASHLEY HADN'T LOOKED at the letter. The kids wanted lunch, so the five of them ate at the hotel restaurant. Landon had texted her: They were still a few hours from leaving Frontier City.

Not until they were headed back to the room after eating did Cole come up with a plan. "A cousin plan," he called it. The three cousins would meet in Cole's room and watch a movie. They were worn out from the day.

"Something happy." Amy made the suggestion.

"I love it." Ashley nodded. "You're right, Amy. A little laughter would be perfect right about now."

Fifteen minutes later the kids were settled, and Ashley met up with Kari in her room. As soon as Ashley shut the door, her sister was on her feet. "Okay, what happened? Tell me everything."

"It's no big deal. I took a picture." Ashley pulled out her phone and called up the photo. "I haven't read it." She dropped on the bed opposite Kari. "It's a little blurry."

Kari sat cross-legged, facing her. "I still can't believe you took the guy's letter off the fence." She hesitated. "Or that you took a photo of it."

"Maybe I can help him." Ashley felt completely justified. The stranger could've picked any section of the fence to leave his letter. But he chose that spot. Right next to Ashley. She squinted at the photo and made it larger with her finger and thumb. "There it is. I can read it now."

"You don't feel guilty?" Kari's mouth hung slightly open. Like she was incredulous.

"Not at all." Ashley looked at her sister for a second or two. Kari was the cautious one. Following orders. Coloring inside the lines. Ashley was the risk taker. It was what had gotten her in trouble when she went to Paris after school. But this wasn't like that. Ashley drew a quick breath. "I didn't *take* the letter."

"Okay . . . read it." Kari still sounded concerned. She hesitated. "I'm dying over here."

Ashley found the beginning and started.

"Okay . . . here it is: 'Dear Jenna, Like I do every year, I wrote you a letter. In case you come to the memorial today. In case you want to find me as much as I want to find you. Every year I do this, I leave you a note in case. Anyway, here I am again, eleventh year in a row.' " Ashley paused, taking it in. " 'Eleven times I've come to this fence and looked for you. Eleven times I've written you a letter and left it here. Hoping you'd find it.' "

Kari gasped under her breath. "Eleven times!" She motioned to Ashley. "Keep reading."

"I'm trying." Ashley raised her brow slightly and smiled.

"Sorry. Go on. Really."

Ashley found her place. " 'Every year things wind up the same way. You don't come to the memorial. You don't walk the fence. You don't find my letter.' " Ashley adjusted the photo again. The picture was still blurry. " 'Don't you remember, Jenna? What it was like having that one day together?

" 'We met here and I thought . . . I don't know, I

thought it would be easy to find you. I had your name and number in my pocket when I left that day. It was sitting on my dresser for three days. I know it. But then . . . something happened. Someone moved it or took it or threw it away. I'll never know, but it was gone.' "

"Gone?" Kari covered her mouth. "That's terrible."

"So sad." Ashley picked up where she left off. " 'And now—even after all this time—I still think about you. I guess at first I hoped you would call me, since I didn't call you. The truth is, I don't think about anyone but you. I'm a firefighter in Oklahoma City. It gives me purpose. But I'm alone. I'm always alone.' "

Ashley stopped for a minute and lowered her phone. "He's a firefighter." She said the words more to herself than to Kari. Was that why he had seemed so familiar? The way he stood and moved and walked? She glanced at her sister. "No wonder he looked like Landon."

Kari sat forward. "Ash. Be careful." She waited, watching Ashley. "You don't know him."

Her sister was right. But still.

Ashley lifted her phone again. "I'm almost done." She tapped the photo and made the image even bigger. She took a deep breath. " 'That day, the day we had together eleven years ago, we were only seventeen.

" 'But I knew I'd never meet anyone who shared my story the way you did. I lost my mom and you lost both your parents in the building that horrible Wednesday. There's never been anyone who could understand that.

Not until you, Jenna.'" Ashley closed her eyes for a brief moment. The guy's letter was killing her. She blinked away the tears welling in her eyes.

When she could see clearly, Ashley continued. "'Please find this letter. Look for me. Call me. My number's at the bottom.'"

"Wow." Kari was clearly captivated. "All these years."

"I know." Ashley looked at the letter again and kept reading. "'I'll be waiting for you. And if I don't hear from you, if you don't find this, then I'll be back at the memorial again next year. On the anniversary. And the year after that, and the next one.

"'And one of these days, Jenna . . . one of these days you'll be here. I'll find you. I have to believe that. Remember what you said? Our hearts are the same. And so they are. Always. Brady Bradshaw.'"

Ashley put down her phone and looked at Kari. She felt like she'd been kicked in the stomach. "The guy won't make it another few years."

"I know." Kari wiped at a single tear. "So sad."

The image of Brady at the fence consumed Ashley. Her mind raced. "I have to help him. I can find Jenna. I know I can."

"Ashley." Gentle disapproval colored Kari's tone. "It isn't your place. You're a married woman."

"Yes!" Ashley felt her own frustration rise up. "And I'm more in love with Landon every day." She forced herself to calm down. *Patience, Ashley. Patience*. She exhaled. "This has nothing to do with the guy. How he looks, or whatever you're thinking."

"I'm sorry." Kari's eyes grew soft. "That was out of line."

"It's okay. I get it." Ashley felt the fight leave her. She took her time, sorting through her thoughts. "It's just . . . what if God put him next to me for a reason? What if there's more to the story and I'm supposed to . . ." She looked around the room trying to find the words. Finally she lifted her hands and let them fall to her lap again. Her eyes locked with her sister's. "I don't know, maybe it's up to me to help them find each other."

Kari nodded. "Okay." Her expression was more sympathetic. "I hear you." She hesitated, her voice soft. "But, Ash . . . you don't even know her last name. Just Jenna."

Kari had a point. Ashley tapped her fingers on her knee and studied the bedspread for a few heartbeats. "I could find Brady on Facebook. Somewhere. Maybe even reach out to him." She turned to Kari. "Just to tell him I want to help."

"Or maybe Landon could contact him." Kari wasn't pushing. Ashley could tell. Her sister just wanted to guide Ashley in the right direction.

"Good idea." Ashley smiled. Kari was right. Landon was a firefighter. Maybe he could talk to the guy. Surely, Landon would be in favor of the idea.

There was a sound at the door. A key sliding through the lock. Kari jumped up. "They're back!"

Ashley stood, too. The timing was perfect. She could hardly wait to tell Landon about their day. About the Survivor Tree and the memorial and the chalk patio. And the heartbroken firefighter she'd met at the fence. And her idea.

That somehow the two of them could help him.

7

The heartache that lived in the deepest places of Jenna Davis was a private one.

She didn't tell many people about her past. Her co-workers knew her story, but only the basic details. Her loss that dark April day wasn't something she talked about, the feelings hers alone. And without a close friend in her life, Jenna had no one to share her pain with. No one who remembered what happened to her twenty-three years ago at the Alfred P. Murrah Federal Building.

If she were still in Oklahoma, maybe.

But Jenna lived in Columbus, Ohio, and the tragedy of that far-off April 19 was the last thing on anyone's mind. Even today. Sure the late night news might make mention of the bombing. If more pressing stories didn't fill up the hour. But it wasn't likely.

Jenna smoothed the wrinkles from her black wool pencil skirt and checked her look in the mirror of the staff restroom. Martin Luther King Junior Elementary School had one of the nicest newly renovated facilities in the city. Jenna was blessed to work here. She had the best second-grade class in all of Ohio and her colleagues were some of the finest teachers in the state.

She added another layer of lipstick and fixed her hair. Her eyes looked greener in this light. Same eyes as her mother. That's what her grandma used to tell her. Jenna studied herself. Last night at the science fair one of the parents had told her the same thing Jenna had heard a hundred times.

"You look like Emma Stone." The woman had smiled at her. "Anyone ever told you that?"

"Yes, ma'am." Jenna had thanked the woman and moved on.

She loved the compliment, but not for the obvious reasons. She loved it because that's what Brady had told her. Back then Emma Stone had done her debut film—some teenage comedy. At that point no one really knew the actress.

They had both seen the commercial for the movie, and neither of them liked it.

Something else they had in common.

Jenna took a deep breath. *Where are you today, Brady? Whatever happened to you?* She hesitated, waiting. But there would be no answer. Not from the bathroom mirror and not from God. She had asked enough times to know that. She slipped her lipstick back into her purse, walked to her second-grade classroom, and shut the door behind her. The kids were still at lunch, still running around the playground, laughing and carefree.

Unaware of the anniversary, or the sadness in their teacher's heart.

Music. That's what she needed. She used her phone to start her favorite playlist, something she liked to do before the kids returned to their desks. There were speakers on either side of the room. The set started with Kyle Kupecky's song "Come Home."

As the music played, Jenna couldn't help but sing along.

My life's a different story, than I thought it would be . . . I've collected a few memories, never thought I would see. I've traveled far . . . far away from home.

Jenna leaned against her chair and closed her eyes. She could've written the song herself. She drew a breath and blinked. Ten minutes and the students would be back in their seats. A pile of papers with the afternoon's reading assignment sat on her desk. One for each of the boys and girls.

She took the stack and distributed it while the music played on.

But You tell me You love me . . . and You say to me it's never too late. Wherever you are, no matter how far . . . you can still come home.

They were God's words to her. Jenna knew that. She had lived them, after all. Somewhere along the journey of years since her last visit to the Oklahoma City memorial she had indeed found her way home.

Back to God.

The classroom door opened and a stream of twenty-three children ran inside and took their seats. Other teachers had a rule against running. Not Jenna. Life was too short. Olivia, the smallest child in the class, rushed up to her. "Miss Jenna, Edward hit me with the ball at recess!"

The girl had a red welt on her cheek. Jenna shifted her gaze to Edward. The child's head was practically bald—the result of an outbreak of lice last week. Before that Edward's hair had gone down to his shoulders. Didn't seem to matter, long or short. Edward's eyes sparkled with the possibility of mischief, though he gave her his best impression of an angel.

Something else the boy was good at.

"Edward." Jenna raised her brow. "Come here, please."

The other students were still getting situated, looking at the papers on their desks. Edward did as he was asked. When he reached Jenna, his eyes grew large. Innocence personified. "Yes, Miss Jenna?"

She looked at Olivia's red cheek and back to Edward. "Did you hit Olivia with the ball during recess?"

"Not really." Edward blinked a few times. "I was playing dodgeball." He smiled at Olivia. "Hits happen in dodgeball."

"No!" Olivia's eyes welled up. She rubbed the mark on her face. "We weren't playing dodgeball, Miss Jenna. We were playing kickball. And kickball means you don't throw the ball at someone's face just because they got a good kick."

"You're right." Jenna looked at Edward again. "It's only dodgeball if everyone agrees. Do you understand?"

Edward lowered his chin nearly to his chest. He crossed his arms with a huff. "I was tired of kickball."

"Edward." Her tone was more serious now. "Tell Olivia you're sorry."

"Yeah, tell me." Olivia was small, but feisty. She wasn't having any of this from Edward.

He looked like he was in actual pain. An apology was clearly the last thing Edward wanted to do.

"Fine." He looked at Olivia, his eyes more squinty than before. "Sorry you didn't want to play dodgeball."

"No." Jenna needed to get the afternoon started. She stood and looked down at Edward. "That's not an apology. Say it now. Unless you'd like to spend the afternoon in the principal's office."

"Okay." The boy's expression softened. His tone followed. "Sorry for hitting you, Olivia."

The girl touched her red face again. "I forgive you. I guess."

"Listen." Jenna looked from Edward to Olivia and back. "What's the number one rule in our class?"

Both kids looked at Jenna. Olivia spoke first. "Always love each other . . ."

Edward nodded and finished the statement. "Because second grade doesn't have that many days."

"That's it." Jenna gave the two what she hoped was an encouraging look. "Now go sit down."

Olivia hesitated. She smiled up at Jenna. "You're pretty."

"Thank you, Olivia." Jenna loved teaching kids this age. They said whatever they were thinking. No shame. "You're pretty, too."

The girl should've gone to her desk, but she was fixated on Jenna's necklace. "Why do you wear a key around your neck?"

Jenna fiddled with it. The key was dark bronze on a chain the same color. She'd had it for three years today. A gift she'd bought herself for the anniversary. The year her husband left without looking back. Jenna stooped down. *Focus on the child,* she told herself. "It's called a Giving Key."

"The key's giving something?" Olivia reached up and touched Jenna's necklace. "Seems like a regular key."

"It is." Jenna smiled. "Kind of."

The rest of the class was settling in. They had two minutes until the bell. Olivia lifted her blue eyes to Jenna. "Why's it called 'giving'?"

"Because one day I'm supposed to find the right person to give it to. With a Giving Key necklace, you look for a reason to give it away."

Olivia nodded, but she still appeared confused. "Why'd you get it?"

"Because." Jenna felt the beginning of tears, but she refused them. "It reminds me of my mommy and daddy."

"Oh." The answer seemed to do the trick. Olivia grinned. "Bye!" She skipped back to her chair.

Jenna held the key and ran her thumb along the surface. She wore it as often as she could. Some of the teachers and several of the kids had noticed over the last few years. For Jenna it was a reminder. She'd had it custom-made, with just one thing engraved on the front and back.

She drew a deep breath and stuffed her emotions to the basement of her heart. Thoughts about the anniversary could come later. A smile lifted the corners of her lips. "Who remembers what book we're reading?"

Hands shot up around the room, but several children yelled out the answer before she could choose one of them. *"Noah's Ark! Noah's Ark!"*

Just hearing them say the name of the Old Testament Bible story brought a rush of joy. None of the other teachers had thought she could do it. Get the principal to approve *Noah's Ark* for the reading project this month. But Jenna had done her homework.

The story of Noah and the Ark was listed as approved literature in the Ohio State Board of Education guidelines. Jenna assumed it was an oversight, but nevertheless, the title remained among other classics. Jenna was thrilled for the chance to tell kids the story, to introduce them to the truth. Because even children didn't have all the time in the world.

As Jenna knew all too well.

So when she sought permission to share the story with her class there wasn't really any discussion. Reluctantly, her principal agreed. A few of the parents had expressed shock that they were studying *Noah's Ark* in a public school. Most of them were thrilled but a few seemed on the fence about the idea. One or two were even upset. Jenna had just smiled and shrugged. "It's classic literature according to the state."

Jenna had used her own money to purchase every student a copy of the children's version of the story. Each afternoon they would read a section of the book out loud, and answer the questions on the handout.

They had already talked about the people being wicked, and how God had asked Noah to build an ark even before it started to rain. Today they were reading about the animals coming two by two.

From the beginning the kids' questions were hysterical.

"Miss Jenna, why didn't Noah just leave the spiders and ants behind?"

"Do you think the bear was the scariest animal on the ark?"

"Was there an indoor play yard for the animals to run around?"

Jenna did her best to answer. Spiders and ants must've been part of God's plan. The bear was probably tied with the lion for most scary. And an indoor track would've been a good idea. "I'll bet they had one," she told the child who asked. "They needed some way to get their exercise."

Today's discussion was good. Especially the last question of the day. One little girl raised her hand. "Miss Jenna, do you think the story of Noah and the Ark is real?"

"Absolutely." Jenna smiled and sat on the edge of her desk. "I believe God created the world, and I believe He sent the flood. Because people had turned against Him."

"And only God could do something like that, right?" The child grinned.

"Exactly." Jenna checked the clock on the wall. "Okay, boys and girls. That's it for today!"

Jenna could hardly wait to talk about the rainbow tomorrow. She walked her students outside to the front of the school and waited as every child boarded a bus or was picked up by a parent.

Andy Collins was last to leave. His grandparents had custody of him and most days his grandpa was late. Jenna didn't mind waiting. Andy struggled more than all the kids in her class. His parents were convicted drug dealers, so the hurt from that spilled into his time at school.

"How was your day, Andy?" Jenna often had this conversation with the boy while they waited for his grandfather.

Andy shrugged and looked away. "Not good."

Jenna studied him. "I'm sorry." She put her hand on his shoulder. "What happened?"

For half a minute Andy didn't say anything. Finally the boy looked at her again. "It was those same ones. The boys who always pick on me."

"Oh, no." Jenna knew the kids. They were mean to

lots of the younger students. Andy was quiet and shy, often standing off by himself during lunch and recess, which didn't help.

Andy looked at her. "They pushed me down and kicked me. A lot of times."

"What?" Anger shot adrenaline through Jenna's body. "That's terrible." She worked to keep her cool. "I'm sorry, Andy. That never should've happened. I'll talk to the principal. We'll figure this out."

Andy pressed the heel of his shoe against a crack in the sidewalk. He looked at her, hope in his eyes for the first time that afternoon. "Really?"

A quiet sigh drifted up from her aching heart. "You know why they pick on you, right?" Jenna took both his hands in hers, still at eye level with him.

"Because they're mean." Andy looked so little. He was still so young, like all her students. They needed much love and care.

"Yes." Jenna waited for Andy to find her eyes again. "But the reason is because they're unhappy. Very unhappy."

Andy tilted his head, like he hadn't actually considered that. He managed the slightest smile. "It's okay, Miss Jenna." Andy let go of her hands and stood a little taller. "I have you. That's all I need."

"Okay, then." She smiled. *God, don't let him see my broken heart.* Andy didn't need sympathy. He needed people to believe in him. She kept her tone upbeat. "Tomorrow we'll read my favorite book."

Andy's eyes lit up just a bit. *"To the Moon and Back?"*

"Yes!" She straightened and pushed his bangs out of his eyes. "Because that's how much I love you."

"And that's how much I love you, too." He found his laugh again just as his grandpa pulled up.

Jenna stood and watched him go. A deep satisfaction came over her. This was why she was a teacher. The kids who otherwise might fall through the cracks were the exact boys and girls God put in her path. And one day, if He was willing, she would have her own children. Until then, Jenna had Andy and another twenty-two kids to call her own.

At least until summer.

Andy's words stayed with her as she reported the incident to her principal and later as she drove home to her town house and ate dinner from her Crock-Pot. The principal had promised to deal with the students responsible. Even so, Jenna would do a better job looking out for Andy. His words played in her heart again. *And that's how much I love you, too.*

Sweet boy.

Music made Jenna's beef stew and butternut squash dinner less lonely. Tonight it was Colton Dixon's latest album. She could've eaten with someone else. A group of her teacher friends, maybe. Three of them were single like she was. Sometimes they shared meals together, planning for the school week and swapping stories about their students. But tonight Jenna wanted to be alone. Finally, after dinner, it was time to do what she'd wanted to do all day. What she'd planned to do.

Find a quiet place and remember.

• • •

THE SECOND FLOOR of her home had a back deck. Not very big. Just a couple chairs and a small table. But from there Jenna had a view better than any place in Columbus.

Trees grew behind her condo. Over them, the sky stretched on to eternity, and tonight the stars were brighter than usual. "That's so like You, God," she whispered. "Giving me a sky like this. Just when I need it."

She sat in one of the chairs and looked at the moon. It was only a sliver, the reason the stars were so clear. She stayed still for a moment, taking in the view. Her mother had loved the stars, so the backdrop was perfect for remembering. Which was something she did often. But it was different on the anniversary.

More intentional.

Jenna wasn't in the Alfred P. Murrah Building when the bomb went off. She was at her grandmother's house. The way she always was on Wednesday mornings.

Both her parents worked in the building, on separate floors. Jenna wasn't sure if it was her imagination or an actual memory, but she could picture her mom talking to her grandma about watching Jenna before and after school.

"If she can be with you, that'll always be better." Her mom had stood beside Jenna just inside the front door of her grandmother's house. "She loves you so much, Mama."

In the memory, Jenna was five. Not in kindergarten yet. So little. The images took shape. Her mom was dropping her off before heading to work, and Jenna could see herself, reddish-blond pigtails, pink bows at the end of each, grinning at her grandmother. "I love Grammy's house."

So the decision had always been an easy one, apparently. Jenna would stay with her grandmother while her parents were at work. At the end of the day, her mom would pick her up and the two of them would run errands or stop by the library. They'd go home and read or finger-paint or color. And then Jenna would help her mother make dinner.

The whole time—through every wonderful activity—her mom would talk to her about Jesus. "The reason we're here, Jenna, is because God loves us so much."

"That's why He sent Jesus, right, Mommy?"

"Right, baby girl."

Jenna had another favorite memory. It wasn't clear like it used to be, but the important details were there, safe in the most sacred room of her soul. It was almost bedtime and her mom was reading to her. And she could see her mommy's green eyes, see the smile on her face and hear her voice. "I love you to the moon and back, precious daughter." Her mother's face was forever etched in Jenna's mind. Then and now, Jenna thought the same thing: Her mom was the prettiest woman in the world.

Later, Jenna's grandma would tell her that she looked like her mama. Jenna believed it. The picture in her heart was a lot like the one she saw in the mirror each morning.

Another memory came into view. They were making meatloaf, and Jenna was using her clean hands to work in the bread crumbs. Her mom said something about having meat fingers and suddenly both of them were laughing. Just Jenna and her mom, working in the kitchen side by side, laughing about their meat fingers.

Jenna had a new nightgown that night. A gift from her grandmother. And Jenna's mom was helping take off the tags and slipping it over Jenna's head, kissing her forehead. "Sweetheart, look at you! You're more beautiful than any princess who ever lived!"

And in that moment, Jenna could do nothing but believe her. "Princess Jenna, Mommy." She twirled around in the kitchen. "That's me."

Just then, her daddy came into the room. He was tall and blond and handsome. Her mom used to say he looked like Captain America. Sometimes Jenna liked to pretend that was her daddy's real job. Captain America. But by day he worked as a supervisor in the social services department of the government. There were times the accounting kept him late at work. Nights like this one, preserved forever in Jenna's heart.

Her dad dropped his briefcase and his mouth fell open. "Princess Jenna!" He bowed. "I had no idea I was stepping into the presence of royalty!" Her dad had an imagination bigger than the state of Oklahoma. "Your Highness, I request the honor of giving you a piggyback ride!"

Giggles overcame Jenna and she twirled over to her daddy's arms. He swept her up and onto his shoulders. Then he galloped her around the living room and kitchen until she was laughing too hard to breathe. He was her royal stallion, and she was princess of all the land.

She could never know if that was the night before the bombing or not. But it was close. Sometime during their last week. Jenna knew because they had gone to the zoo that weekend. Her grandma always told her the story. How her dad had Saturday work to do, but he said it could wait. The weather was nice and he wanted to take Jenna to the zoo.

Jenna's grandma had gone, too. She took pictures. The ones Jenna kept in a book by her bed. Proof that she'd had the most wonderful parents and that they had spent their last weekend on earth with her. Watching lions and tigers and laughing at the long-necked giraffes.

Like always, at 8:30 the morning of April 19, Jenna's mom dropped her off at her grandmother's house, just a few blocks away. And like every morning, Jenna's mom got down on her level and kissed her cheek. Then she put her hands on both sides of Jenna's face and they rubbed noses.

"How much do I love you?" Her mom's eyes had sparkled that day. At least that's the way Jenna recalled them.

"To the moon and back." Jenna remembered smiling. Remembered thinking that her mommy must be queen of the whole building where she worked.

Half an hour later Jenna was still at her grandma's when something happened. A call came in and when her grandma answered it, she suddenly let out the loudest cry. Like someone had kicked her leg. That's what Jenna thought at the time. She could still see her grandma's face, the look of raw terror.

Jenna got up from the couch and backed as far away as she could, until her feet bumped into the wall. Her grandmother rushed to the TV and turned it on. And the news filled the screen, fire and smoke and people crying out.

Then in an instant, her grandma seemed to remember Jenna. She gasped and turned off the television. "Jenna!" And suddenly Jenna was in her grandma's arms. "I'm sorry, Jenna . . . I'm sorry. We need to pray, baby."

We need to pray.

They were the words Jenna remembered most from that morning. Her next memories were a blur. All except the funeral. Two caskets. And more tears than any princess should ever have to cry.

That day Princess Jenna died.

In her place was a little girl whose mommy would never hold her again, whose daddy would never give her a piggyback ride. She was just Jenna after that.

The memories faded. A cool breeze seemed to heighten the bright stars, making the night feel special. Which it was. The anniversary always felt different. Like God was meeting her in this place. The memories weren't too sad or painful. They were beautiful. All she had of the parents she loved so much.

Jenna narrowed her eyes and tried again to see back to that time. Her parents had been on different floors, but they had gone home to heaven together that morning. And Jenna had moved in with her grandmother, where she stayed until she left for college. Jenna's grandpa had been dead for a decade by then. And in Jenna's sophomore year, her grandma passed, too.

No matter how distant Jenna grew from God after her parents died, she never told her grandmother. Through middle school and high school Jenna went with her grandma to church and together they read the Bible every Sunday afternoon.

Jenna knew the answer to every Christian question. But the whole time she didn't want anything to do with God. He could've spared her parents, but He didn't. Didn't He know? Jenna needed her parents far more than He did. Her parents were praying people, people who believed in Him. So why hadn't He answered them?

For Jenna, the answer was obvious: God didn't love her.

That's what she told herself, anyway. It wasn't until college that Jenna attended church with a friend. The message that day was about why bad things happen to good people. Jenna would always remember the pastor's words. "God isn't the reason bad things happen. He's the rescue."

God was the rescue.

It was something Jenna hadn't considered. After that, something changed in her heart. She began to see things differently. Her heart softened and she realized the pastor was right. God wasn't the cause of her loss. He was the solution. Because of Him, Jenna would see her parents again one day.

She moved to Columbus after graduation, where the teaching job at Martin Luther King Junior Elementary was her first. By then she was even closer to God, so when her church hosted a financial planning meeting, Jenna attended. That's when she met Dan Davis. International businessman. Financial entrepreneur. They had their first date that Friday. Six months later they were married.

In the beginning they attended church together, and Dan seemed to believe in God the way she did. She made an assumption that would haunt her later. She figured since she'd met Dan at church, he must be a Christian. He must want to live his life according to the Bible. Looking back, she could see that every conversation they ever had about faith was started by her.

They celebrated their first anniversary with news that she was pregnant. She was ten weeks along when she miscarried. In the months after that loss, Jenna would spend hours reading her Bible, memorizing Scripture. She would cry out to God and He would remind her of His promises.

Come to me, all you who are weary and burdened, and I will give you rest. . . . Do not be anxious about anything, but in every situation, by prayer and petition, with thanksgiving, present your requests to God. And the peace of God, which transcends all understanding, will guard your hearts and your minds in Christ Jesus.

And so many others.

Dan said something to her during that time that should've alerted her to what was coming. He walked into their bedroom and found her in the rocking chair reading the Bible. He stopped and lowered his brow. "Really, Jenna? The Bible? Again?" He laughed, but the sound was mean. "You need more books."

She looked at him, trying to figure out if he was kidding. "Dan . . . I couldn't get through this if I didn't read the Bible."

"Sure, but you've read it." He laughed again. "Three times, right?"

Concern came over her even before she knew what was coming. "It's not like that . . . With the Bible, it's different. It's like God's talking to me." She paused. Dan should've understood that. "It's alive and real."

He looked at her for a long few seconds, and then he shrugged. "Suit yourself."

That was it. *Suit yourself.* He didn't ask what she was struggling with. He didn't tell her he was sorry about the miscarriage, and he didn't ask why the Bible spoke to her so deeply. Just *Suit yourself.*

Sometimes she would try to talk to Dan about her miscarriage and even about losing her parents. Especially when the losses built and grew in her heart until she could barely breathe. Dan would usually change the subject. Death and loss made him uncomfortable. When Jenna felt like crying, Dan always found other places to be.

Eventually those places involved other women.

A week before their second anniversary, Dan announced that he was moving to London. A better job, he told her. But the next week he expanded on that. He didn't want to be married anymore. Didn't want the possibility of more babies. Didn't want to be a father. Jenna nearly suffocated from the shock, but she couldn't fall apart completely.

She had her job and her students. She had the strength of God.

Dan left three days later and Jenna never heard from him again. Once he was gone, she drove to Lake Michigan for a weekend. To clear her head and her heart. And there, on a beach chair overlooking the water, Jenna made a promise to God. Never again would she marry a man who didn't share her faith.

The promise was as much for her as it was for God. She would rather be single than raise a family with a man who couldn't understand why she read her Bible. She wanted a man who would read the Bible *with* her.

Period.

But a year passed and then two more, and she remained single. Guys would cross her path, but none of them shared her faith. When she'd find out that they had no interest in going to church, she would move on.

Because she absolutely would not consider breaking her promise to God.

And so she had figured a way to make a life for herself alone. With a small inheritance from her grandmother and her teaching salary she got along just fine. She was even ready to visit the memorial again—something she hadn't done since the year she met Brady.

This summer she would make the drive to Oklahoma City. That was the plan.

She had a reason. Each victim of the bombing had a glass box for mementos in a designated room at the memorial museum. A worker at the memorial had told Jenna that her parents' boxes currently had only their black-and-white photos from the news accounts that day. Nothing more. Jenna wanted to do something about that. So she had gathered copies of several of her parents' photos and letters. Items she could laminate and take to the memorial.

Besides, Jenna had avoided the memorial long enough. This coming summer it would be time. Proof that Jenna was moving forward. Getting on with her life. Ready to distance herself from all things Oklahoma City

Bombing. That's how she felt. Or at least it was how she usually felt. Every day except today, when all she wanted to do was find the one person on earth who truly understood her.

Brady.

Only then could she see if he had made peace with God, the way she had. A month ago when she finalized her plans to drive to Oklahoma City, she began to pray for Brady, asking God to let their paths cross. Even for one more day. So she could see if he was okay. If he believed again.

It was the reason she had bought the Giving Key. The reason she had it engraved with the numbers that represented her life. Her journey of faith. She wasn't stuck at the moment of the bombing. She had moved on. Tragedy and loss didn't define her. Her personalized key was a constant reminder of her healing.

Her life after the tragedy.

It was a key she would give Brady, if she ever saw him again. Whether he was still running away from God or not. The key could at least remind Brady that God wanted his return. Because Brady was the only other person in her world who would understand the numbers on the key, and the healing they represented. Jenna ran her thumb over the etching. It was the only thing she could've engraved on the key.

9:03.

8

Ashley mustn't have explained the situation right, because Landon wanted nothing to do with contacting Brady Bradshaw. Even if the stranger was a firefighter.

When Landon and Ryan had come back to the hotel, they'd dropped the younger kids off with the older cousins. Then both men had listened to Ashley talk about what had happened. How the stranger at the fence had seemed so upset.

Like he could barely breathe for the weight of his losses. Whatever they were.

"I thought you might want to reach out to him." Ashley had finished the story and taken Landon's hand. "Maybe we could help him find the girl. Jenna."

Landon had stared at her for a long moment, like he was waiting for the punch line in a not-very-funny joke. "You're not serious, Ash."

Across the room, Kari had shrugged in Ashley's direction. "I tried to tell you."

Ryan had seemed completely confused. "You want Landon to reach out to some guy he doesn't know and offer to help him find a girl none of us has ever met?"

When he put it that way, Ashley felt ridiculous. "Never mind." She'd let the idea go for then. "You're right."

There was no point debating it. But no matter how hard she tried, she couldn't get the image of Brady out of her mind. What if they *could* do something to help? A couple times that evening Kari and Landon had asked her if she was okay. She'd told them she was. But later that night, Landon had pulled her close and apologized. "You were serious about that Brady guy." He searched her eyes. "Weren't you?"

Ashley had nodded. "Of course." She smiled, feeling the hurt in her expression. "I wouldn't joke about that."

"Hey." He hugged her and ran his hand along her back. "I'm sorry. Really, Ash." After a minute he'd looked at her again. "Let's pray for the guy. Then you can let it go."

Ashley had agreed, and together they prayed for Brady. That he'd find God and peace and yes, one day, that he'd find Jenna. Whoever she was.

The next morning, though, Landon had looked at her with the slightest bit of humor in his eyes. "I can't believe you took his letter off the fence." He shook his head. "And took a picture of it." He came to her and kissed her cheek. "That's my wife." His smile had been genuine. "One in a million, baby. No one like you."

He'd meant the words as a compliment. Ashley knew that. He always said he admired her courage. How she could have a tough conversation with anyone or help a complete stranger. But this time his attitude frustrated her. He'd seemed to be making light of the whole thing.

What if she wasn't supposed to dismiss the situation so easily? She had thought about asking Landon if he minded if she looked up the stranger. If she at least tried to help the guy. But she didn't ask. Mostly because she didn't want his disapproval.

Now it was Saturday morning and they were out on their rented houseboat, the culmination of the spring break trip. Landon and Ryan took turns driving the boat around the lake and then they headed for the quiet side of the shore, so the kids could swim. Everyone wore life jackets—even the adults. Landon's suggestion. So they'd set a good example for the children.

For now, the cousins were on the top deck with the men, in the observation area. And Kari was on a phone call with Ryan's mother, getting caught up with his side of the family. Ashley assessed the situation.

There couldn't be a better time.

She pulled her laptop from her bag and found a table near the back of the boat. They'd been so busy having fun she hadn't opened her phone, let alone her laptop. All she had was maybe ten minutes. And since the boat had Wi-Fi, it couldn't hurt to look. Guilt rattled her heart as she signed on to Facebook and typed in his name. There were several Brady Bradshaws but only one of them who could've been the man at the fence. She opened his page and saw she had the right one.

Firefighter. Oklahoma City.

A little snooping and she realized he'd been on the show *Survivor*. No wonder he looked familiar. He was also the June photo in a calendar of firefighters. Ashley looked at the image for a few seconds. There had to be a clue here somewhere. Then just as quickly she moved on. Never mind that. She searched his friends, typing in the girl's name: Jenna.

Nothing.

Of course nothing. She sighed. If Jenna was his Facebook friend, Brady wouldn't be looking for her at the memorial. She thought for a moment. It took no time to realize Landon was right. She had no leads, no last name. No possible way to find the girl.

Not unless she contacted Brady for more information.

She opened her photos and called up the picture of the letter again. His phone number was right there. All the information she might need was a mere text away. Then she could at least help the guy. Ashley stared at the number, and as she did she felt a hand on her shoulder.

A quick turn and her regret was immediate. "Landon!"

He looked from the laptop and phone to Ashley. Confusion clouded his face. "Didn't you hear me cut the engine?"

"No." She forced a laugh. "I was just . . . checking Facebook."

"Okay." Landon wasn't one to doubt her. Not ever.

Their marriage was something other couples dreamed about. But as he stared intently at her computer screen, the slightest hurt filled his eyes. "Brady Bradshaw?"

Ashley closed her laptop and clicked off her phone. She stood and faced her husband. "I'm sorry. I should've told you." She felt terrible. Landon didn't deserve this. "It's just . . . Honey, I want to help him." She took hold of his hands. "Is that crazy?"

For a while, Landon just looked at her. He seemed slightly irritated. "I don't know if it's crazy, Ash." He leaned in and gave her a quick kiss. As if he wanted to show her how much he trusted her. Like he was determined not to be angry. "How about you come swim with the kids?"

"Okay." She felt her muscles tense. Good thing they were alone. They didn't need an audience for this. "I might just reach out to him first."

"Now?" He still wasn't mad, but his patience was clearly unraveling. "The kids are swimming. We're on vacation."

"Exactly." Ashley tried to smile.

"I guess my question is why? Why look him up?" Landon worked the muscle in his jaw. "I thought we agreed to pray for him. Leave it at that."

"I know. But the more I think about it . . . Landon, listen." Ashley shifted so she could see him better. "If I can do something to help him, I should do it. Now."

"No." Landon let go of her fingers and took a step back. "Look, the guy's not exactly unattractive. That's kind of obvious." No question he was trying to stay calm. But frustration sounded in his tone. "You reach out to him, and . . ."

"And what?" Heat coursed through her body and her heart pounded. "What, Landon?" She uttered a single laugh, but there was nothing funny about it. "You can't be serious." Her anger took root. "You think I'm *hitting* on him?"

"Of course not." He lowered his voice. "But . . . those things start somewhere."

"Those things?" Now *she* was upset. "Really, Landon, that's ridiculous."

Suddenly she heard herself. What was happening? Why was she doing this? Fighting with the guy she loved more than her next breath? *Father, calm me. Please.* She closed her eyes for a brief moment and exhaled. "I'm sorry." She stared down at her chair, and then back at Landon. "That was rude."

He looked at her, like he wasn't sure what to say. The hurt in his eyes told her he was still struggling. "I'll let it go. I shouldn't have made a big deal out of it."

She still wanted to help the guy, but why right now? "It can wait. Or I can just drop it."

Landon drew a slow breath. He closed the distance between them and reached his hands out. "You don't even know him. If you contacted him, I guess you might find out more about the girl. But . . . I don't see how that would help."

"True." She gently wove her fingers between his. "I

really am sorry." Something bothered her. She had no choice but to voice it. "You . . . trust me, right?"

"Baby." They were only a few inches apart. "Of course I trust you." He took his time as he leaned in and kissed her. More tentatively this time. When he looked into her eyes he found her heart. "I'm sorry, too." The corners of his mouth lifted into a slight smile. "Let's go swim."

"Okay." She hugged him, brushing the side of her face gently against his. The situation wasn't worth talking about now. "I'm sorry again. I love you, Landon."

"I love you, too." He ran his thumb lightly along her fingers.

Ashley savored the feel of her hands in his, his cheek against hers. No one could ever understand her or love her, the way Landon did. "You're the best husband in all the world. Have I told you that lately?"

"Mmmm." He kissed her again. His words were a whisper, close to her neck. "You have the most beautiful hair. Has anyone ever told you that?"

Ashley felt her heart melt. Those words mattered only between the two of them. Words spoken long ago by dear Irvel, one of the Alzheimer's patients where Ashley worked when she and Landon fell in love. When all the world spun around the two of them.

The way it still did.

Ashley kissed him again. "Swim, right? Wasn't that it?"

"Yes." He hugged her and spoke in a whisper. "Until tonight."

She grinned. The private moment with her husband had turned everything for the better. The fact that even after getting frustrated with each other, they could still come together and be okay. The reality that Landon trusted her. He wasn't angry.

And later if she still felt compelled to help Brady, she would. Because this wasn't only about following God's lead in helping a guy find the girl he longed for. Brady might need a lot more than a girl named Jenna.

He might need God, Himself.

• • •

ASHLEY AND LANDON met up with the kids one deck down.

They had climbed out of the water and now all of them were sitting at the long table adjacent to the galley, eating sandwiches. Ashley saw the red cheeks on a few of the kids. "Let's do another round of sunscreen."

Janessa came running up. "Cole tried, but I need your help, Mommy."

Across the deck Cole shrugged. "I think she's good." He grinned. "But moms do a better job. That's what she said."

Moms do a better job. Ashley shot a quick look at Amy. Cole didn't mean any harm by his comment, but still it must hurt. Hearing something like that.

Ashley grabbed the sunscreen and rubbed it onto Janessa's shoulders and cheeks. Then she called Amy over.

"Aunts do a better job, too." She smiled at her niece. "Right?"

For a moment, Amy stood there. As if she wasn't sure she wanted anyone but her mom to help her. But very quickly a smile lifted her lips. "You're right. No one's better than you, Aunt Ashley!"

Tears stung at Ashley's eyes, but she refused them. Ashley had a feeling her niece's recent growth had a lot to do with her fascination with the Survivor Tree. Like the tree, Amy was determined to live. The thought of that warmed Ashley more than the sunshine.

After lunch the kids swam and paddled around in the rafts. Cole and Devin and RJ learned how to do flips off the back of the boat. They each had a floating ring and for a while they used those to play a slow version of water tag until they were laughing too hard to keep going. They returned the boat just before sunset, and after dinner the group headed back to the hotel.

But as they turned in that night, after Landon was asleep, Ashley couldn't settle her thoughts. What if she really could find this Jenna? Research was Ashley's specialty, right? Wasn't that something she'd known about herself for a decade?

And maybe if she connected with Brady, she could find out what he'd done to try to locate Jenna. Maybe Brady and Jenna were meant to be together, and maybe Ashley was supposed to help. Couldn't that be the reason she had gotten the chance to take a photo of his heartbreaking words?

Her thoughts kept her awake far too late.

Lord, is this from You? Is this something I should take on? She didn't exactly hear a clear answer, but she felt a sense all the same. As if God had arranged for Brady to be there at that exact moment. So Ashley could help him.

The next morning they set out early for home, and all the while Ashley found herself thinking about the firefighter. At one of the stops, while Landon was getting gas, Ashley went to the photos on her phone and read his letter once more. What could it hurt to reach out to him?

Whoever Jenna was, the guy had only shared his story with her. No one else understood him. No one else had the same heart as him. At least that was what Brady thought. By the sounds of it, Brady and Jenna were both survivors of the Oklahoma City bombing. But in what way? Had they been in the building, too, when their parents were killed?

Ashley closed her photo app as they hit the road again. She looked at Landon, his familiar profile and the joy in his eyes. Should she tell him she was thinking again about the letter, about helping Brady?

Landon must've caught her looking, because he met her gaze and smiled. "Perfect day for a road trip."

"Definitely." Her smile was quick. "It's been a great spring break."

"It has." He kept one hand on the wheel, and reached for hers with the other. "I love these years. While the kids are still young."

Her heart lurched. Probably best not to tell him now. Why ruin the mood with something harmless? She could tell him later, when they were home. Instead they talked about his job as the marketing director for the fire department. He was second in command now, but the understanding was that when the fire chief retired in a few years, the job belonged to Landon.

He'd come so far since the days when he had a constant cough, back when it looked like Landon might have a lung disease because of the months he'd spent in New York City at Ground Zero. Now his breathing was great. He still went in for an X-ray every year, but last time the doctor had told Landon his health had never been better.

Ashley was grateful to God. She had resisted Landon in her earlier years, back when she had rebelled against everyone who loved her. Now she only prayed for a long, healthy life with her husband. That they could be a source of faith and hope for their family and friends.

And maybe even for the stranger from the memorial.

• • •

THEY'D BEEN HOME two days when Ashley couldn't stand waiting another minute. She had to reach out to Brady. The idea of telling Landon first crossed her mind, but her husband was already in bed. He had an early breakfast meeting tomorrow. Once the kids were down for the night, Ashley settled into the living room sofa and stared at her phone.

Once more, she called up the photo of Brady's letter.

It was only nine o'clock in Oklahoma City. He would probably still be awake, so should she text him? She tapped her finger on the phone and thought for a minute. Of course she should text him. How else could she help the guy? Why wait?

Ashley dismissed the subtle feelings of guilt. No reason to feel sneaky or awkward. She would tell Landon tomorrow, once she'd made contact with Brady. Ashley didn't want anything weird here. Didn't want Brady thinking she had any motives other than to help him. So she wrote her text very carefully. Then she read it back to herself.

> Hi, Brady. You don't know me. My name's Ashley Baxter Blake, and I saw you at the Oklahoma City National Memorial on the anniversary. I watched you leave a note on the fence for someone named Jenna. I know this is strange, but I know you're trying to find her. Don't be angry, but I read the letter you left for her. I actually think there's a reason I saw you. I think God is telling me I'm supposed to help you.

Ashley smiled. Yes, that was the right way to word this. She kept reading.

> If you could tell me Jenna's last name, I'll see what I can do. I'm not sure why I feel compelled to reach out. But I'm very good at research and I have time to help you. I have a feeling I'll find her.

She thought about Irvel and Sunset Hills Adult Care Home. Also, the situation last year when Devin's teacher had mentioned she'd been trying to find her birth parents. The woman had tried everything. It wasn't until Ashley stepped in and helped that she finally located them. She still had photos from the teacher of that happy moment.

Time and again she was drawn into the lives of other people to make a difference. Helping people was her specialty.

She stared at her phone. The text needed just a bit more explanation.

> Anyway, if I can help at all, let me know. Just give me her last name and I'll see what I can find. And if there's anything else I can do, let me know. Until then, I'm praying for you.

The text was perfect. Exactly what Ashley wanted to say. When Landon came home tomorrow she'd let him read it. She already knew how it would go. He would smile at her and give a slight shake of his head. "You're an interesting one, Ashley," he would say.

Then he would pour himself a glass of water and watch her from across the kitchen. He would say something kind and understanding. Something like "I believe you're right, Ashley. Maybe God is using this situation for His good."

And if he didn't . . . well, if not then she would let the whole thing go.

She hesitated a moment longer, then she hit send. For the next hour while she washed the kitchen sink and counters and got ready for bed, she kept an eye on her phone. With every passing minute, she felt more foolish. What had made her think Brady would reply to her? Why would the guy trust a complete stranger?

By the time she climbed into bed she was sure of one thing: Landon had been right from the beginning. The guy didn't want her help.

Well, she told herself. *That's that. He isn't going to answer.*

Even still she would tell Landon about the text tomorrow, maybe while they watched the Reds game on TV.

She'd laugh it off with Landon and tell him he was right. "The poor guy probably thinks I'm a lunatic." She would utter a sad chuckle and she'd look straight at Landon. "Do you think I'm a little crazy?"

And Landon would give her an understanding smile and he would tease. "Ashley," he would say, "I married you because you're a little crazy. I like you that way."

Yes, that was how it would go. The whole thing would be over and she could get back to life without obsessing over a stranger's problems.

Ashley had barely finished writing the imaginary script for how tomorrow would play out, and had just turned off the lights when her phone dinged. She stared at it for a moment, plugged in by her bed. Then she picked it up. One new message. She pressed her thumb on the screen, and there it was.

A text from Brady Bradshaw.

Ashley's heart quickened as she opened it, but at the same time her hopes fell. His reply held no clue as to what he thought about her message, no words as to whether he believed Ashley could be of any help. His text said just this:

I don't know her last name.

9

The anniversary of the bombing had a greater hold on Jenna this April. She wasn't sure why, it just did. So on Friday after school when all her students were picked up and she'd finished her lesson plans for the next week, Jenna drove to Schiller Park.

The place had been one of her favorites since she'd moved to Columbus. Nicely kept with dozens of trees, all hundreds of years old. A path wound a little more than a mile around the perimeter, perfect for a walk. And today Jenna wanted nothing more.

She started near the statue of Friedrich von Schiller, the German poet. Clouds had gathered overhead, the air chilly for late April. She slipped her hands into the pockets of her rain jacket and stared straight ahead. Why was it so hard to move on? So hard to let go of what happened to her parents?

The answer was obvious. Healing was difficult. For nations and cities. But especially for people. She kept her eyes open, but gradually the images in front of her changed until she was no longer seeing trees and stretches of grass and park benches.

Rather she was seeing the Alfred P. Murrah Federal Building. After the bombing. Of course, Jenna didn't remember firsthand what it had looked like. Neither her grandmother nor she had ever driven by the ruins of what remained that spring. Her grandmother had been busy planning two funerals, and no one would've considered taking Jenna by the place where the building once stood.

It didn't matter.

On the fourth anniversary, Jenna's teacher presented a slide show of the devastation. Jenna must've seen pictures before then. But the photos that day were the first time she understood the scope of horror involved in the explosion. Watching the images, Jenna had started to cry, and when she couldn't stand to see another, she had gotten up and run from the room. After that, her grandmother never sent her to school on the anniversary again.

Staying home kept her safe from having to see reminders of the terrible reality of that day. It assured she wouldn't be sitting in class when a photo of her parents buried under rubble might randomly appear as part of a classroom discussion. But staying home left her with no one to talk to about that day. No one except her grandmother. And since her grandma had lost her daughter and son-in-law, the dear woman had no desire to speak about the tragedy.

Not with Jenna. Not with anyone.

Out of sight, out of mind. That was her grandmother's way of thinking. Which was why—when Jenna was seventeen—her heart had been nearly exploding for the chance to talk to someone about the bombings. The year she met Brady.

Jenna kept walking, slower now. She didn't think about Brady all the time anymore. Only around the anniversary. Sometimes not even then. There were years recently when she'd been so busy processing her miscarriage and then her divorce that she'd barely made time to find a quiet place to remember the anniversary at all.

The clouds overhead grew darker and the wind picked up. Jenna didn't care. She needed this time too much to worry about the weather. Besides, her coat kept her warm enough. She lifted her eyes to the sky as she walked.

The day with Brady had happened a month after Jenna's birthday. At first her plan had been to sleep in, get up around noon and get ahead on her homework.

But school had always come easily for Jenna, and she wasn't one to sleep late. She woke around seven that morning, took a shower and got dressed. By eight-thirty she knew where she wanted to go. The place she hadn't been to since her parents were killed.

The Oklahoma City National Memorial.

Once in a while she'd think about going there, heading through the gates and seeing the place dedicated to those killed. But Jenna had never seen any reason why she should go. Better to remember her parents as they were.

Happy and in love, sitting with her at the end of her bed, reading to her. *Love you to the moon and back, Jenna.*

As she headed out, her grandma had stopped her. "Honey? You okay?"

Jenna's answer was the same as always. "I'm fine." Then she hugged her grandmother and looked into her eyes. "What about you?"

And her grandma's tears had come. Just enough to wet her eyelashes. She shook her head, and her lips quivered. She put her hands alongside Jenna's cheeks. Her words took time to come. "I miss them. That's all, I just miss them."

Jenna used to feel jealous of her grandmother for that reason alone. She had more memories of Jenna's parents. For Jenna the memories were so distant, so dim that she was denied even that. The chance to miss them.

That day as she drove, Jenna hadn't even been sure how to get to the memorial. She got lost a few times, but finally she found the place. For thirty minutes she sat in her car and just stared at the entrance. She wasn't sure what she'd expected it to look like.

Certainly not like a park. Yet that was how it looked. Trees and grass, open and inviting. Jenna hadn't known where to start. She wasn't sure she would do more than sit in her car and look at the place from a distance. But something about it drew her inside.

Jenna paused the memory. She was still walking, but now she stared up through the leaves of the trees overhead, and suddenly she remembered another detail. In those first few minutes at the memorial, she had been struck by something deeply profound. What had happened to her parents didn't happen to her alone. It happened to the whole country. To everyone old enough to remember April 19, 1995. Of course, that had always been the case. But Jenna hadn't registered the fact until the moment she saw the scope of the memorial.

The significance of it.

She kept walking along the Schiller Park path, still slower than before. And as she did she gave herself over to everything about that distant memory. How the air had smelled of sweet jasmine planted near the pathway. The way the bronze walls stood, reaching to the sky with their time stamps.

9:01. That was the one Jenna could see from the parking lot. The minute before the bomb went off. The last minute her parents were still alive. With every step she took, every breath, the memory of her long ago visit came to life a little more.

Until finally she wasn't walking in Schiller Park at all. Rather, she was getting out of her car and crossing the memorial grounds. The sky had been cloudy that day, too, so Jenna wore a lightweight navy raincoat and a white knit beanie. She paid the admission fee and slipped through the gates unnoticed. The museum had displays with enormous photos of the horror.

Jenna didn't want to see any of them. That wasn't why she had come. She could go online anytime and see images of the bombing. No, she was here for one reason.

To honor the memory of her parents. To stand where they stood in their final moments on earth.

The empty chairs called to her first. They were each lit, translucent almost, one for every person killed in the attack. But almost at the same time she was drawn to another part of the site. The spot where most people milled about.

A stretch of fence that bordered one side of the grounds.

Jenna wandered that way and only then did she understand why so many people were there. The chain link was covered with cards and letters, photos and flowers. Things left in honor of those who died.

The entire stretch was quiet and reflective. Here, the memories were a living, breathing thing. Until that instant Jenna hadn't known the fence existed. That she could've brought letters or cards there in her parents' memory. Or that she maybe should've been visiting the site every year.

Jenna stepped back and took it all in, just watched the people around her. Some of them stood in one place and didn't move, not a step to the right or to the left, their gaze fixated on some object or photo, something written. Others walked slowly, reading the messages, caught up in the offerings.

Most people seemed to be by themselves. On pilgrimages of their own.

It was then, a few minutes after she'd found a spot

near the fence, that Jenna saw him. She thought he was older, twenty, maybe. Twenty-one. He was tall, tan with dark hair and muscled shoulders.

What's he doing here? she thought. Even now she remembered catching her breath as he walked closer. His attention was on the fence, as if he were looking for something. Or reading the letters left by other people.

Just as he was about to pass by, their eyes met.

Jenna wanted to look away. She'd been caught staring at him, after all, but she couldn't. She couldn't break contact with the stranger if her life depended on it. He slowed and then sauntered toward her.

"You're new."

She pointed to herself. "Me?"

"Yeah." He smiled, but it never reached his eyes. "You're new. I'm here every year. I've never seen you."

She shifted, captivated by him. "You mean . . . you know these people?" Her glance moved along the fence. The visitors were a mix of different ages. "Are you all . . . like from a club or something?"

He looked more intently at her. "You could say that."

Jenna wasn't sure what he meant, so she held out her hand. "I'm Jenna."

"Brady." His fingers felt warm against hers. He crossed his arms. "If you're here . . . today . . . something tells me you're in the club."

She looked at the fence. "What is it? The club?"

For a long time he said nothing. He slid his hands into his pockets and stared at the people around them. Like he was studying them. When he turned to her again the walls in his light brown eyes were down. Just a little. "Why are you here, Jenna?"

"I've never been." Her answer was quick. She didn't just tell people her story. Not so soon.

He nodded slowly. "That's it? You've never been?"

"Right." She tilted her chin and looked at him straight-on. "Why are you here?"

That's when he pushed up the sleeves of his cream-colored sweater. He held out his arms. "Look."

She took a step closer. At first she didn't see anything unusual. His forearms were as nice as his shoulders. Then she looked more carefully and there they were. Small lines etched into his skin.

"Touch them." His voice soothed the raw edges of her heart.

This was crazy. Jenna wouldn't typically touch strangers. But something about him drew her in. She ran her fingers lightly over the marks. Only then did she know the truth. They were scars. Her eyes lifted to his. "You . . . were hurt."

The dots connected all at once. She turned and looked at the place where the federal building had stood and then back to him. "You . . . you were in the building?"

He pulled his sleeves down and took a long breath. "Walk with me, Jenna."

She'd never met the guy. Never seen him before. But somehow he felt like a friend. Like she'd known him all her life. She walked beside him, both of them quiet. He led her up a set of stairs to a bench not far from a large tree. The image of the tree was familiar, its trunk and outstretched branches something she had seen before.

They sat on the bench and Brady sighed. "Me and the tree. We're the same." He turned and faced her. "We both survived that day."

Jenna felt the connection between them grow. "What happened?"

"You first." His eyes were kinder now. "Why are you here?"

From where they were sitting Jenna could see the field of empty chairs. She stared in that direction and took her time. If Brady had been here that day, if he'd been in the building when the explosion went off, then he would understand.

If anyone would.

She looked at him again. "My parents worked in the building. Different floors." Her eyes welled up. She hadn't expected to cry in front of him. "I . . . I lost them both."

Slowly, deliberately, Brady reached for her hand. He didn't say a word. He didn't have to. For a long time they stayed like that. His warm fingers around hers, his thumb soft against her skin. "Where were you?"

With her free hand, Jenna caught the first tear as it fell down her cheek. "With my grandma. I stayed with her while my parents were at work." She tried to smile, but it did nothing to stop her crying. "I was five."

That last part seemed to hit Brady harder than the rest of her story. "Five." He squinted toward the sky, then back at her. "I was five, too." His hand was still safe around hers. "I was here with my mom when . . ."

His voice trailed off. There was nothing rushed about their conversation. The silence was easy between them. Comfortable and achingly sad all at the same time.

Jenna waited. Brady's story would come eventually.

And after a minute it did.

10

Jenna had watched Brady, studying him. He was quiet for a long time, as if the train that held his memories only came by every so often.

He looked at the stormy sky again, or maybe to some far-off place he clearly didn't want to visit. He filled his lungs. "My mom and I were in line at one of the federal offices." He shifted his attention to her. "I was playing with this gray stanchion, this thick dirty cord that kept us in line, and my mom was telling me not to touch it. I'd get germs." He paused. "And then . . ." His eyes glistened, the memory alive again. "She came down to my level and smiled at me. Straight at me."

Jenna could picture it. Like a movie playing out in the space between them.

"She told me we were almost done." He sniffed and looked to the sky once more. "That's all I remember." He was still holding her hand, but he held up his other arm. "I woke up in the hospital with these cuts. That's it. My mom . . . she protected me from everything else."

He didn't have to say his mother didn't make it. Jenna already knew.

Brady pointed at the tree. "You know the story about that?"

"Not really." For the first time, Jenna wanted to know more about what happened that April 19. "I've . . . stayed away."

The empathy in Brady's tone was a connection Jenna had never felt before. Kind and understanding. The same hurt as her own. "I get that. Staying away." He searched her face. "You're still in the club. Whether you come here or not."

She nodded. The club. "The people along the fence. They all . . . they all lost someone?"

"That's what I tell myself." He looked over his shoulder back to where the people still stood. Some of them gripping the chain link. "I see lots of them every year." He turned to her again. "Why else would they be here?"

Jenna could think of a few reasons, but she liked Brady's explanation better. Wanderers, broken people. All of them survivors, one way or another. She motioned to the tree. "Tell me about it."

"The Survivor Tree?" Brady stood and helped her gently to her feet. Maybe because of the weather, there was no one else on the patio near the elm that day. Just the two of them, making their way to the tree trunk.

He still had hold of her hand. When they reached the tree, Brady put the palm of his other hand against the bark. "Every bit of this tree was ripped to shreds. Glass and metal. Who knows what else." He paused. "Its branches were sheared off." Brady glanced at her. "It even caught fire."

"It did?" Jenna pressed her free hand against the trunk, too. "You could never tell. It's so . . . strong." That was what surprised her most. The tree was easily the biggest and most beautiful at the memorial.

"Which is why I love this place." Brady pulled back and Jenna did the same. They faced each other. "If the old elm can be strong again . . . so can we."

"Yes." It was something Jenna desperately wanted to believe. But for that moment it was enough to be here with Brady.

For a second he looked like he might kiss her. But then he gave her the slightest smile. "Is it weird? That I'm holding your hand?"

"No." It wasn't just that he was the cutest boy she'd ever seen. Somehow holding hands here at the memorial with someone else who had lost his mom seemed perfectly normal. Better than normal. She felt the corners of her lips lift a little. "It's nice."

"Good." They walked down the stairs to the pond and found a low-slung stone wall. He released her hand as they sat side by side, facing the water. Close enough that his arm brushed against hers. He waited a minute. "I can't believe you haven't been here."

His tone didn't hold any judgment. Just surprise. If she'd known she might meet him here, she would've come sooner.

She glanced at him. “I can’t believe you come every year.”

“It’s my way . . . I don’t know.” He breathed in, deep and slow, and leaned toward the pond, elbows on his knees. “My way of keeping her with me.”

“Mmm.” Jenna let that settle for a minute. “I don’t think about this place.” She hesitated. “When I think of my parents, I guess I think about heaven. They . . . went there together.” Jenna smiled at Brady through fresh tears. “That makes me feel better.”

“I get that.” Brady looked past her eyes to her heart. “If they were anything like you . . . I wish I could’ve known them.”

“Me, too.” Jenna lifted her eyes to the sky. “Sometimes . . . I’m not sure what I remember is even real.” She shifted her gaze and let herself get lost in his eyes. “Tell me about your mom.”

Brady sat up straighter and took her hand again. “She was beautiful.” He was in no hurry. “Her smile was like the sun.”

Jenna kept watching him. It was sinking in, the fact that she and Brady had both lost their parents when they were five. Right here. On the same day. “Do you remember her?”

“Not like I want to.” Brady sighed. “Maybe that’s why I come every anniversary. I don’t want to lose her. The part of her I can still see and hear.”

They got up and walked to another bench, one near a grove of trees at the other side of the memorial. The clouds were darker still, and a cool breeze had picked up. They sat facing each other this time. He didn't reach for her hand, but it didn't matter. Their hearts were still connected. Jenna searched his face. "What about your dad?"

"I never knew him." The hesitation in Brady's eyes was gone now. Completely. "After my mom died, I lived with a friend of hers. Then the state moved me to foster care and I stayed in the system. One house to the next."

Jenna leaned forward. This time she took his hand in hers. "Even now?"

"Yeah." He looked at where their fingers touched. "It's fine. I'm gonna be a firefighter. I'll be on my own soon."

Her heart broke for him. She figured she knew the answer, but she had to ask anyway. "A firefighter? Because . . ."

"Yeah." He managed a quick smile. "Definitely." He saw all the way to her soul. "So some other little kid doesn't have to go through what I went through."

They talked about growing up in Oklahoma City and how every April 19 they felt alone. Like no one could understand what they were facing. "The bombing didn't just happen to the city." Brady removed his hand from hers and laced his fingers behind his head. He stared across the grounds of the memorial. "It was our tragedy." He glanced at her. "It's personal for you and me. It happened to us."

Us. Jenna loved how he said that. She took a quick breath. He might as well know the rest of her story. "I grew up with my grandma." She told him about the time her teacher had showed images from the bombing and how upset she'd gotten. "My grandma never made me go to school on April nineteenth again."

"But you never came here." Brady shifted so he could see her better.

"I think . . . somewhere in my childhood I allowed myself to believe a fantasy. That my parents were still alive. Living overseas somewhere like London or Rome. And one day they'd come back and we'd all be together again."

"So being here—"

"Yes." She had the feeling he knew exactly what she meant. What she was feeling. "Being here makes it real."

The breeze gusted now. Brady looked at the sky and back at her. "Storm's coming."

"Fitting." She tightened her jacket around her. "I used to fall asleep asking God just one thing. That in the morning I'd wake up and come downstairs and my parents would be there. Sitting at the kitchen table, sharing coffee."

Tears filled her eyes again. "They'd see me and we'd run to each other and I'd be in their arms. They'd kiss my head and tell me how much they missed me and everything . . . everything would be okay." She hesitated. "I prayed that till I was in middle school."

Brady let her story hang there for a minute. Blowing in the wind between them. Then he sat a little straighter. "We prayed the same thing, Jenna. I remember . . . I was six or seven . . . eight. Nine. Lying in bed, begging God that before I fell asleep my mom would walk into the room and sit on the edge of my bed. And just one more time she'd say, 'Love you to the moon and back, Brady. Love you to the moon and back.' "

A chill ran down Jenna's arms and legs. "Your mother used to say that?"

"Every night."

It was one more connection. "Mine, too." She paused, her tears spilling onto her cheeks. "After bedtime prayers. It was our special thing."

"They probably would've been friends, our moms." Brady seemed to think for a long moment, and gradually the hurt returned to his eyes. And something else. Anger or bitterness, maybe. "I remember the night I stopped praying. I told God if He didn't bring my mom back, then I was done talking to Him." He paused and for a moment his eyes grew harder. "I kept my promise."

"Me, too." The sad picture of the little boy he must've been was suddenly etched in Jenna's heart. "I don't pray anymore." The sameness of their stories was more than Jenna could take in. "I mean, I still go to church with my grandma. It would hurt her if I stayed home. But I guess I'm just . . . I don't know, frustrated with God." She looked straight at Brady. "Like why did He have to take *my* mom and dad?"

"And my mom." Brady took a deep breath and stood. The pain eased from his expression again. "Let's get coffee."

At that point, Jenna would've gone anywhere with him. No one had ever understood her feelings the way Brady did. They started walking. "So you don't go to church?"

"No." He made a sound more laugh than cry. "Hardly. The state says foster parents can't force us to do anything. Especially where religion is concerned."

"Makes sense."

Again Brady took her hand. This time he worked his fingers gently between hers. "Have you seen the commercials for that movie *Superbad*?"

"I think so . . . It looks, I don't know, not that great." She laughed, and he did, too.

"That's what I thought."

They left the memorial grounds and made their way down the street. The wind played with her hair. "Why did you ask? About that movie?"

"Because." He slowed his pace and stopped, facing her. With his thumb, he brushed her bangs out of her eyes. "You look like the actress in it."

She angled her head. "Thanks." Her smile came easily now. "I think. Right?"

"Definitely." He looked down, and then back at her. His cheeks grew slightly red. "You're very pretty, Jenna."

His words sent a rush through her. It wasn't the sort of thing she heard often. Not from guys who looked like Brady, anyway. Jenna tried to focus. "My grandma tells me I look just like my mom." She smiled again. More shy this time. "Dark red hair and green eyes like her. So I guess that's a good thing."

"Very good." Brady studied her for a few seconds before they started walking again. They got coffee from a small café and took the trip back to the memorial more slowly. Brady talked about the first year he came here. He was ten and one of his foster parents brought him. "That day I could really feel my mom with me again. Right beside me." Brady cast her a quick look. "After that I always asked someone to bring me here. My foster parents or my Little League coach. Whoever."

"Which is why you started recognizing people at the fence."

"Exactly." They stopped at a bench and sat down. For several minutes, neither of them said anything. They just sipped their coffee and listened to the wind from the coming storm. Jenna felt like she'd slipped into some other world. For the first time someone knew exactly what the hurt felt like.

Then the rain hit. Not the slow sort of rain that starts with a few drops and builds to a downpour. This one came over them all at once. Brady grabbed her hand and they ran with their coffees down the street and into the museum. By then they were drenched, and there—inside the building—they had nowhere to go, no way to avoid the photos mounted on the wall.

Brady let go of her hand and walked slowly to the first picture. A shot of the Alfred P. Murrah Building a few days before the bombing. Brady stood as close as he could, his eyes locked on the image. Jenna came up beside him. She blinked the rain from her lashes. At the same time they both seemed to notice something about the building.

The windows were lit.

Which meant her parents were somewhere in there. Walking around. Working. Putting in their time until they could come home and be with her. Princess Jenna. She narrowed her eyes and found the third and fifth floors. The places where their offices used to be.

"My parents . . . they would've been there that day." A chill came over her. Jenna wasn't sure whether it was from the rain or the reality of what she was taking in. "I can almost see them. Through the windows."

"Think about that, Jenna." He moved closer to her, the heat of his arm warm against hers. "How beautiful. It's like . . . they're still alive. At least in that picture."

She hadn't thought of it that way. More just the reality that if they could've gone back, if they would've known how little time they had . . . then maybe they wouldn't have gone to work that day . . . and maybe things would've turned out differently.

"What about you?" She leaned into his arm a little, her eyes still on the photo. "What do you see?"

"I guess I see what might've been." He examined the image. "That could've been us. Inside the building *that* day. Running errands on the sixteenth or seventeenth. But never on April nineteenth."

The possibility sank deep inside Jenna's heart. Her

parents hadn't known they had so little time. Nothing had warned them that if only they had taken that Wednesday off everything would still be okay. Their family would still be together. Same for Brady. There was no way for his mother and him to go back and do their errand another day.

So they'd be anywhere but the federal building that fateful morning.

Jenna drew a deep breath. "I have to go." Her grandmother would worry about her if she was gone longer than this. Rain still poured outside, so they were stuck in the museum. And Jenna couldn't bear the thought of studying the rest of the photos.

The destruction.

Brady nodded. He finished his coffee, tossed his empty cup and hers in a nearby trash can and shoved his hands in his pockets. The intimacy that had been between them earlier seemed to fade. They were strangers, after all. Two kids who had grown up with the same heartache, the same sad story.

But that was it.

He hesitated for a minute. "Hold on." A quick jog to the information desk a few yards away and he returned with paper and a pen. "Here." He wrote something on the sheet and handed it to her.

Brady. And beneath that, his number.

"You're in the club." He smiled, but his eyes were deep with sadness. "Call me. We'll come here together next year."

She nodded. The idea sounded good. Brady and her, the two of them here. Their heartache against the world. A smile tugged at her lips. "Okay."

Brady hesitated. "This is where you give me *your* number." He chuckled lightly. "So I don't have to wait a year to see you."

Her own laugh caught her off guard. "A year is a long time."

"A week's a long time." His eyes landed on hers and held.

She felt like she'd known him all her life. "Here." She ripped off a part of the paper and followed suit: *Jenna*. And beneath that, her number.

"Thanks." He looked at it and slipped it into his pocket. "I'll call you soon." His expression faded. "I will."

"Okay." She liked him. Everything about him. "Call me."

The museum was crowded, people trying to get out of the rain. Even so, Jenna felt like they were the only two people in the building. They were still facing each other. Jenna had a feeling their hearts would be connected, long after they said goodbye.

He took a step closer, his voice quieter than before. "I want to kiss you, Jenna."

She wanted that, too. But she couldn't say so. Instead she felt her grin warm her face. "I think we should wait."

"Yeah." He was teasing her now. Flirting with her. "Come here."

They were only inches apart. Jenna did as he asked

and for a second she thought he might kiss her anyway. Instead he pulled her into his arms. Not a lovers' embrace. But something more tender, deeper. Protective. Without any words, being held by him told her that after today she would never be alone in her missing, never be by herself in her sadness. She had Brady now.

She was part of the club.

• • •

RAIN FINALLY BROKE through the clouds and began falling over Schiller Park. As if God Himself were crying because of the memory she had just relived.

Brady hadn't written his last name on the slip of paper and Jenna hadn't noticed until she got home. She'd expected him to call her that day or sometime in the next week.

But he never did.

A week later she took his paper from the top drawer in the nightstand next to her bed and realized the rain had blurred the numbers. She could only make out a few of them. She threw the paper away and tried not to feel hurt. Their day together almost didn't seem real, anyway. He probably has a girlfriend, she told herself. Or he'd gotten away from the memorial and wondered why he'd given his number to a complete stranger.

Months passed and Jenna eventually put him out of her mind. Until the following April, anyway, when the anniversary came back around. But that year Jenna was sick on April 19. Too sick to get out of bed. She figured he had her number, and that maybe because of the anniversary he'd finally call.

But he never made contact.

Whatever the reason, Jenna clearly wasn't going to hear from Brady. And as time passed she told herself she was crazy to still think about him. She didn't even know his last name. The detail hadn't seemed important back then. He was going to call her that week. They had forever to figure out last names and logistics.

Instead, they missed whatever might have been. Though Jenna would always remember the magic of that single day.

The next four April 19 anniversaries, Jenna was in college at a small private university in Texas, so she never made it back to the memorial. She did, though, make her way back to Jesus.

Yes, God had a plan for her. She still believed that. A plan that included her teaching job in Columbus. But clearly it did not involve a dark-haired stranger from a lifetime ago. A guy she only knew by his smile and handsome face, his deep eyes and a name she would never forget as long as she lived.

Brady.

11

They'd been back from spring break for a week and this Saturday was one Ashley and the entire Baxter family had been looking forward to for a month. In a few hours, all of them were meeting at the Christian Kids Theater for a matinee performance of *Peter Pan*. Annie and Janessa and Amy were in the show. Amy was playing Wendy—her biggest role yet.

After the show, everyone was coming back to Landon and Ashley's house for dinner. Ashley checked the time on the microwave. Just after noon. She'd already dropped the girls off at the theater and three pot roasts with vegetables were cooking in her Crock-Pots—all lined up on the counter.

The show didn't start for another two hours.

Landon and the boys were fishing at Lake Monroe, so Ashley had something she didn't often have: time.

She still hadn't found Jenna, though she'd searched every way she knew how. No bombing survivors or grieving children by that name. Nothing in the Internet archives.

None of the survivor registries listed her name.

Which meant she must not have been in the building when the bomb went off.

Bottom line, Ashley needed more information. Sure she had Brady's cell number. But maybe if she revisited his Facebook page. Or found something on social media. Maybe then she'd know more about him and his story. Like why he'd been so short with her in his response last week.

Ashley grabbed her laptop and sat out on the back porch. The day was mild and breezy, the blue sky dotted with white puffy clouds. Spring had filled in green where bare branches were just a few weeks ago.

She turned on her computer and brought up Facebook. She'd seen his page before, that day on the boat, but only briefly. She still hadn't found the right time to tell Landon about her text to Brady. But it didn't matter. She hadn't texted Brady again.

Maybe Brady's social media would tell Ashley something new. Something about Jenna or the reason Brady felt so alone. He didn't have many posts on his page from what she remembered. But maybe she'd missed something. Ashley typed his name in the Facebook search bar: "Brady Bradshaw."

She closed her eyes. *Lord, why is this guy on my heart? If You want me to drop the whole thing, I will.* She took a slow breath and opened her eyes. She clicked enter and . . . there he was. Same as before. Brady Bradshaw. Firefighter. Oklahoma City. Dark hair and chiseled face. He didn't have sunglasses the way he had at the memorial. But it was him. No question. She scanned the page. Still not much here.

Okay, Ashley. Go slow. Look for clues.

She read the most recent post. It was from the anniversary. The picture was the fence, and there at the center of the image was his letter tucked into the chain link. *For Jenna.* Ashley could only read the girl's name because she knew what it said. Otherwise it would've been easy to miss. Just an artsy photo from the memorial.

But Ashley knew better.

It was a sign, of course. If Jenna were to look for Brady, and if somehow she were to find his Facebook page, then just maybe she would know. That every year since they met, Brady had come back to the site for her.

All for her.

The status wasn't long. Ashley read it. *Some years I wait a little longer at the fence. Just in case this is the year you join me.*

Chills ran down Ashley's arms. The guy was obsessed. Whatever had happened between him and Jenna, he wanted to find her more than he wanted his next breath. Or at least it seemed that way.

"Okay," she whispered. "So who are you, Brady?" She scrolled down the page. The older posts were about a fund-raiser the fire department was hosting. A little more reading and she figured it out. A firefighter had died working a fire a year earlier. The benefit was to raise money for his family.

She checked his photos. In case there might be something else, something from the memorial. Maybe a snapshot of the two of them eleven years ago. He didn't have many pictures. A few of the firehouse, and his rig. One of him with a couple fellow firefighters.

Another scroll down and there was the calendar image of him. He was August in the Oklahoma City Firefighters Calendar. This time Ashley studied the look on his face. He was smiling, but his eyes looked dead. Closed off. Whatever his story, it colored everything about his life. Even when he was supposed to be having fun.

Another page of pictures and there were a few of him much thinner, wearing only a scrappy pair of shorts. Super tan. From when he'd been a contestant on the TV show *Survivor*. Didn't make it more than a few weeks, by the look of it.

Ashley read every caption and post. There was no mention of faith or gratitude or the blessings of life. No signs of a deep friendship or close family members or a girlfriend. "He meant what he said in the letter," Ashley muttered. "He really is alone."

After half an hour on his page, Ashley understood him a bit better. Brady seemed dedicated to his job but otherwise without anyone important in his life. Not even God. She sighed, closed out of Facebook and took her laptop into the house. She set it on the kitchen table and looked at the pantry. Time to get the sweet potatoes in the oven. She was doing that when the boys got home.

They left their muddy boots by the back door and

came in like a rush of sunshine, talking all at once and laughing about something. As they entered the kitchen, Ashley saw they were all three drenched.

"Dad did it." Cole shook his head. He was still laughing so hard he had tears in his eyes. "We were in the canoe, almost back to the shore."

"And Dad sees an eagle." Devin leaned against the counter, catching his breath. "You know how Dad always thinks he can talk to animals?"

"His talent works with Toby." Ashley felt the afternoon get so much lighter. At the sound of his name, their one-year-old Labrador puppy came trotting into the kitchen. His paws were muddy, his coat as wet as the boys. Ashley took a step back and grinned at Landon. "So what happened?"

"I was calling the eagle." Landon shrugged.

"You know, Mom. 'Ca-CAW . . . ca-CAW!' " Devin slapped his knee. "Only Toby thought Dad was calling him."

"So the eagle flies off and Toby jumps to that side of the canoe and—"

Cole made a splashing sound and threw his hands in the air. "The canoe flips and we're all in the water. Just like that."

"Don't worry." Devin grinned. "We all had life jackets. Dad said that part would make you happy."

"So there we were. All your boys in the water." Cole patted Landon on the back. "At least we were close to the shore."

"Yes." Landon raised his brow at Ashley. "Guilty as

charged." He winked at the boys. "I still say the eagle would've come closer if it wasn't for Toby."

"I wanna hear more about it. But maybe go shower up first." Ashley laughed. "Another adventure for the books."

"Definitely." Landon leaned close enough to kiss her, all while keeping his distance so she didn't get wet. "I'll be back."

After he left she stared for a minute at her computer. She needed to tell him about texting Brady and looking him up again. She really meant to. But there never seemed to be the right time. Besides, Landon would understand. Ashley was sure.

She stood and followed him to their bathroom. While he showered she did her hair and makeup.

Thirty minutes later she was ready for the show, sitting at the kitchen table when Landon returned. The kids were still upstairs and they had time before they needed to leave. Landon grinned at her. "You look gorgeous." He walked over to her.

She stood. "You, too." Ashley hesitated. Her nerves were struggling. Everything was so good about this day. Why ruin it by— Before she could finish the thought, he came to her and kissed her again. This time with his body against hers.

"Mmmm." She loved moments like this. "I wish I could've seen the canoe flip." A giggle crossed her lips. "You're such a good dad, Landon." She brushed her cheek against his. "Did you catch any fish?"

"Four." He laughed. "Lost them all when the boat tipped."

Ashley winced. "A memory for sure." She put her hands on either side of his face. "At least we weren't counting on fish for dinner."

"Whatever's cooking smells a whole lot better." Landon put his hand gently against her cheek and searched her eyes. "What did you do? Besides miss us?" He pointed to her computer. "Email?"

"No." She hesitated. "Right. I was just going to tell you." Ashley took a step back and folded her arms. "I went to Brady Bradshaw's Facebook page again. Just, you know, looking for clues." She paused, gauging his reaction. "In case there was something more about Jenna."

"Oh." Landon's smile fell. He blinked, his expression frozen for several seconds. Then he slid his hands in the pockets of his black jeans. "I guess I thought you were past that." He leaned against the kitchen counter and searched her eyes.

"I was." She looked at the floor and then at him. "I mean, I was before. But I just . . . What if I can help him?"

"And why is that your job?" His eyes clouded. "The guy's a complete stranger, Ash."

"I know, but . . ." Frustration colored her tone. "Someone has to help him. I keep thinking maybe God wants me to do this. Have you thought about that?"

"No." Landon gave a single laugh. "God doesn't ask married women to befriend single men."

"I'm not *befriending* him." She shook her head and dropped to the chair nearest her laptop. "I can't believe you're mad."

His expression was a mix of hurt and anger. "So what'd you learn? That you didn't learn last time."

"I was looking for clues." Her answer was quick. Just short of snappy.

Landon nodded at the computer. "Open it up. Let's see the clues."

Ashley couldn't believe this. "You're really angry." Her disbelief came out as a solitary laugh. "Are you saying you don't trust me?"

"No." He took a few steps closer. "I want to see the clues."

"That's ridiculous, Landon." She thought about Brady's calendar photos. "I'm not going back to his page."

"Then tell me." His voice sounded harder now. "What did you find?"

Ashley hated this. She should've kept it to herself. Looking up Brady Bradshaw meant nothing. There was no reason for Landon to be upset. She released a pent-up breath. "Fine." She shifted in her chair so she was facing Landon. "He doesn't seem to have faith in God. No family or girlfriend. He's mostly about his job at the firehouse. Some firefighter calendar he was in and pictures of his time on the show *Survivor*."

"Calendar pictures?" Landon's eyes grew darker. "Do you hear how that sounds?"

"Okay, so I found nothing." This was getting worse. "I

was actually going to tell you I'm glad you never did the Bloomington firefighter calendar." Ashley stood and took a step back. The closeness between them a few minutes ago was gone. "It wouldn't have been fair to the other guys." She tried to smile. "You would've gotten the cover every time."

Landon didn't smile. "This isn't funny, Ashley." His tone was more hurt than mad. "I asked you to stop looking up the guy, but it's become . . . I don't know, an obsession."

"Landon!" She felt her own anger rising. "Because I want to help somebody, suddenly I'm obsessed?"

"You're not helping." Landon shook his head. "You're stalking. Or meddling. Something . . . but there's no point to it."

She felt her heart sink. Did he really think that? "Wow." She shrugged. "I don't know what to say."

Landon walked to the cupboard and grabbed a glass. He filled it with water and drank it, his eyes on Ashley the whole time. When he stopped for air he angled his head. "That's easy." His tone was more controlled now. "Tell me you'll let it go. You don't know him, Ash. There's nothing you can do to help him." He hesitated. "Let the guy figure out his own life."

"Let it go?" Determination gradually replaced the hurt. "I haven't found Jenna. I know you're mad but . . . I'd like to at least try."

"Are you serious?" He set his glass down. "How will you find her, Ash? Do you have special Internet powers?"

He clenched his jaw. "This Brady guy's been looking for her every year for more than a decade."

"What if . . . what if I text him?" She couldn't tell him that she already had. "Maybe he could point me in the right direction. Maybe there's something he's missed." She took a quick breath. *Let Landon hear my heart, God. Please.* "This isn't about Brady. It's about . . . doing what's right."

This time disbelief flashed in Landon's eyes. "Doing what's right, Ash? The right thing is to forget all about it."

From upstairs the sound of the kids interrupted the discussion. They were headed down, ready for the show. Ashley felt like running out the back door and finding her favorite spot. The rock by the stream at the far side of their property.

The last thing she wanted was to spend the afternoon with Landon. Not when he was so mad at her. What had she even done? She lowered her voice. "I want to be honest here, Landon. I'm sorry. I'm not . . . trying to hurt you."

He studied her, clearly still upset. "We can talk about it later." A quick turn and he left, headed toward the stairs. "Let's go." He switched to a pleasant tone as he called for the kids. "We need to leave."

Ashley stared at the floor. How did this happen? They should still have been standing here laughing about the incident with the canoe. Kissing and teasing and flirting. The way they were before.

Instead they were in the saddest, most rare place.

Stuck in the middle of a fight. And the craziest thing was even now, even still, Ashley wanted only to do one thing. The thing she absolutely couldn't do. Not until she and Landon were on the same page.

Contact Brady Bradshaw.

• • •

ASHLEY'S STOMACH HURT. The distance between Landon and her as their family arrived to the play still weighed on her. Landon had all his attention on the kids. He and Ashley hadn't even made eye contact since they left the house.

Once they found their seats Ashley spotted Bailey Flanigan Paul talking to another theater parent in the main aisle, several rows away. She needed a diversion so she got up. "Excuse me."

Landon stood and let her pass. But he didn't say a word.

A sigh worked its way through Ashley's troubled heart. She walked up the aisle and waited for Bailey to be free.

"Ashley!" Bailey hugged her. "I can't believe it's opening night!"

"And this auditorium." Ashley looked around. Bailey and her husband owned the theater and the entire city block. "The place is amazing. And the buildings around it. Better than ever."

"It's our dream." Bailey looked toward the front of the lobby. Her husband was holding Hannah, their little girl. She was ten months old now. Bailey nodded in their direction. "Brandon's the best dad."

"Makes life pretty amazing, doesn't it?" Ashley smiled. Landon was a wonderful father, too. She glanced back at the row where Landon was still sitting. She hated that they were fighting. They needed to figure this out when they got home. Ashley turned to Bailey again and tried to focus. "So Hannah's almost one."

"Time keeps flying." Bailey's eyes were soft. "Being a mom is the best." Moments like this Ashley wondered where the years had gone. It seemed just yesterday Bailey was a teenager, back when the Baxters and the Flanigans first became friends. Of course, in reality that was many years ago. Ashley had painted sets for CKT and Bailey had been one of the young actors. The Flanigans and Baxters were practically family, and Ashley couldn't be more proud of Bailey.

"Hey, guess who's pregnant?" Bailey's eyes lit up. She didn't wait for an answer. "Andi! She and Cody have tickets for today's show. They're in town to see her family."

The news warmed Ashley's heart. All through high school and college, Cody had been in love with Bailey. But the two were never meant to be. Meanwhile Bailey's best friend, Andi, had been secretly in love with Cody. Years of missed chances later, Cody and Andi were finally married. Beyond happy. "That's wonderful. They've been married almost a year, too. Right?"

"Exactly." Bailey's eyes lit up with her smile. Anyone could see that her happiness for her friends was as genuine as her beautiful heart. "They got married the same day Hannah was born. I'm thrilled for them."

Bailey caught Ashley up on the rest of her family. Her brothers were playing sports at Clear Creek High, where Shawn and Justin were both on the basketball team. Bailey's oldest brother, Connor, was still at Liberty University. "You probably know about Connor and Maddie." Bailey did a slight shrug. "On again, off again."

Ashley had heard. Maddie was her niece, Brooke's daughter. She'd been struggling with direction lately. Ashley wanted to get back to her seat, back to Landon. In case they could find at least a little breakthrough before the show started. For now, she kept her focus on Bailey. "Brooke says Maddie's at that age. Doesn't know what she wants."

Bailey smiled. "I think Connor knows. But he's being patient. He has some new girl at Liberty. Just friends, he says." She shook her head. "I keep praying for him."

"Brooke's doing the same for Maddie." Ashley hugged Bailey. "Again, just so proud of what you've done here. Your theater, the whole city block. It's the talk of Bloomington."

"Thanks." Bailey turned as Brandon walked up with their baby girl.

"Little Hannah!" Ashley touched the child's cheek. "She's beautiful."

"Thanks." A deep joy shone in Brandon's eyes. Like he couldn't have been more thrilled with life. "Good to see you, Ashley. Your whole family's here today."

"Of course. It's Amy's big night." Ashley remembered the main reason they were here. The other kids were in this show, but Amy was a lead. Tonight was her niece's debut as Wendy in *Peter Pan*. Ashley glanced at the stage. "I hope she's not nervous."

"A little. But she'll be fine." Brandon smiled and put his free arm around Bailey. "She's a natural. The perfect Wendy."

Bailey leaned into her husband, her eyes still on Ashley. "Amy's wonderful. You'll love the show."

"Can't wait to see it." Just then the houselights flashed. Ashley pointed to where her family was. "I better get going. We'll talk after."

She returned to her row and again Landon stood to let her pass by. Nothing more.

In front of them Ashley watched the Flanigans and their boys take their seats. Jenny and Jim waved and Landon lit up and returned the gesture. Ashley did the same, but as soon as the Flanigans were settled, Ashley watched the smile fall off Landon's face.

From the beginning, the show was even better than Ashley had hoped. Bailey was right. Amy was the perfect Wendy. Still, it was hard for Ashley to focus. Not once did Landon reach for her hand, even when the lights went down. But after a few scenes, Ashley stopped thinking about Landon and directed her full attention to the play.

When Wendy asked Peter Pan if he didn't miss having a mother and a father, Ashley got tears in her eyes. She wanted to lean her head on Landon's shoulder. This was a time when he would normally give her hand a soft squeeze. Instead the distance remained.

Ashley kept her eyes on Amy. What other little girl in the theater group could so personally understand the weight of missing her parents?

When the show ended, Landon walked over to the Flanigans. Ashley didn't join him. Pretending to be fine was exhausting. Instead she started slowly for the doors at the back of the theater. Cole and Devin stayed with her. As they went, Ashley saw Cody and Andi talking with Brandon and Bailey.

Despite her own sadness, Ashley smiled to herself. God was so good, allowing the four of them their own beautiful happily-ever-afters. Not what they had pictured once upon a yesterday. But more perfect than they could've imagined.

As they made their way to the parking lot, Ashley remembered dinner. Everyone was coming over to celebrate Annie and Janessa and Amy and the show. Even Dayne and Katy were in town with their little ones. Again on the way home Ashley and Landon barely talked.

It's going to be a long night, she thought. She kept her eyes on the side window most of the ride home.

The dinner was more fun than Ashley had expected. The joy of having her entire family around helped her forget for a while the trouble with Landon. The kids ran out back along the stream and looked for tadpoles in the pond. Ashley's dad and Landon stayed outside with them until it was nearly dark.

Ashley watched out the kitchen window and Kari and Brooke joined her. "Wasn't that just us?" Ashley looked at her sisters. "Running through that magical backyard. Pretending we were on some crazy adventure every afternoon?"

"Have you ever showed your kids the rock?" Brooke's tone was wistful as she stared at the kids. "The one with our handprints?"

Ashley grinned. "A few times." The rock sat along the stream at the edge of their property.

Now Ashley used it as a place to talk to God.

"I still love that spot." She looked at her sisters. "We used to hang out there all the time when we were little."

"Whenever life got hard." Brooke paused. "Remember?"

Ashley had taken her own children to the area years ago, but she wanted to show them again. Ashley sighed. "We definitely need to bring all the kids there. Maybe next time."

As they were sitting down to dinner, everyone complimented Amy on her work as Wendy. If anyone else noticed the similarities between Amy's character and her real life without actual parents, they didn't say so. There was also much praise for Janessa and Annie, both of whom were Tiger Lily's sidekicks.

The cousins sat at the kids' table a few feet away, and halfway through dinner Dayne and Katy updated everyone on their new movie. They were both starring in it, and though the film was slated for a limited theatrical release, Dayne still thought it would do well at the box office. "We're making it for under a million."

"The message is powerful." Katy glanced at Luke. "Right to life . . . and then it looks like our next movie will deal with religious freedom."

"Speaking of which." Ashley looked at her younger brother. "What's happening with Wendell Quinn, the principal of Hamilton High?"

It was a case Luke had taken on, one that thrust him into the national spotlight for a time. Luke set his napkin on the table. "Wendell is engaged to Alicia—remember her?"

"I do." Ashley grinned at Luke and then at Landon. "We figured that was going to happen. And he's still leading the voluntary Bible study for the students?"

"He is." Satisfaction shone in Luke's eyes. "God won that case, for sure."

"Yes." Reagan smiled at the others. "And Luke's home more. Only forty hours a week at the office." She put her arm around Luke's shoulders and kissed his cheek. "So life is good."

"Definitely." Luke kissed her on the lips and looked around the table.

Ashley was grateful for the things Luke and Reagan had figured out. Luke had let his dedication to law get the best of him last year. Too much time at work. Ashley could tell from her younger brother's eyes that he was doing much better.

The one thing Luke and Reagan didn't talk about was the fact that they'd run into Andi at the performance. Some time ago, during one of Andi's rough seasons, she had given birth to little Johnny. The father wasn't in the picture at all, and Andi knew she couldn't raise her son alone. Through a series of miracles, Luke and Reagan had adopted him.

Little Johnny knew he was adopted, but not necessarily that Andi was his birth mother. Apparently, all of them had agreed that Andi would only be a close friend whenever they all met up. Andi wanted it that way.

Less confusing for Johnny.

Before the show, Ashley had watched Andi drop down to Johnny's level to talk to him. After that, Andi and Reagan had spoken. Ashley could see they were smiling, but the moment didn't last long. Ashley would have to ask Reagan about it later.

During dessert Kari and Ryan updated everyone on Jessie's search for the right university. She and Cole were both looking at Liberty in Virginia. Ashley thought about how soon those changes were coming.

For now, though, there was just tonight and their time together.

When everyone was gone, Landon and the boys moved to the garage to clean the canoe and the fishing gear. Janessa and Amy were already asleep and Ashley was dying to talk to Landon. But in the meantime, she wanted to work on her sketch. She found her book and sat down at the kitchen table.

Ashley was lost in the drawing when Amy tiptoed downstairs in her nightgown. Her niece held a hand-painted picture. "I couldn't sleep." She set the picture down in front of Ashley. "I drew this. I thought you'd like it." She looped her arm around Ashley's neck and stared at her own artwork. "I think maybe I draw like you."

"Wow. That's beautiful, Amy." Ashley stared at the girl's drawing. She could hardly believe it. "Look what I was working on." She slid her sketchbook over so it was side by side with Amy's artwork. "When were you working on this?"

"The last few days." She looked at Ashley's illustration and then her own. "After we came back from spring break."

They'd been working on the exact same thing: the Survivor Tree.

Amy looked at her. "Are you going to paint yours?"

"I think so. People here don't really know about the tree. I think God let it live to symbolize what's possible. With Him."

"That's what I think, too." Amy gazed at her picture. "I'm glad you like it."

Amy was talented, for sure. What a privilege to help her niece discover gifts like this one. Ashley could only hope that somewhere in heaven, Erin and Sam were watching. "We'll have to frame it. Then you can hang it on the wall in your room."

"Near the bookcase."

"Yes, sweetheart. That would be perfect." She put her hands on Amy's shoulders. "You were very good today as Wendy."

"Thanks." Amy's face filled with tenderness. She kept her eyes on Ashley's. "I understand Wendy. All she wants is to go home to her mom and dad."

"Even though she's happy with Peter in Neverland."

Amy hesitated. "Yes." The hint of a smile lifted her lips. "Exactly."

Ashley hugged her close for a long while. "When you get to heaven one day, they'll be there."

"I know." Amy leaned back and looked at Ashley, her expression both innocent and sincere. "Until then, I do like it here. In Neverland."

Tears filled Ashley's eyes. She hugged Amy close again. "Sweet girl. I'll never be your mom. I'll never be good enough." She ran her hand along Amy's long blond hair. "But thanks for letting me try."

"Actually"—Amy shifted back and grinned at her—"you're very good at it."

Ashley put her hand alongside Amy's cheek. "Thanks, honey. I love you."

"Love you, too." Amy yawned. "I'm glad you like my painting."

"It's perfect." Ashley kissed the girl's forehead. "Just like you."

Amy left for bed, and Ashley stared at her computer a few feet away on the kitchen table. She closed her sketchbook. Brady Bradshaw was the only person she knew who could get a Survivor Tree sapling for Amy. Ashley hesitated, but just for a few seconds.

She could at least reach out to him one more time. For Amy. The sound of the boys' voices outside caught her attention. Maybe she should ask Landon first. Just get his opinion on the matter. But she couldn't do that. Things were already terrible between them. She needed to prove to Landon that she was only trying to help. She couldn't do that if she didn't do some good first.

Then Landon would understand.

The sapling gave Ashley the perfect reason to contact Brady. Once they talked about that, she could ask Brady about Jenna. She turned to her laptop and brought up his Facebook page again. A private message couldn't hurt anything.

> Dear Brady, thank you for responding to me earlier. I can see why you've struggled to find Jenna if you don't know her last name. I haven't found her yet. Is there anything else you could tell me? What high school she went to, or what university? What year did you meet her? Anyway, I know the chances are slim. But I'm praying that I find her. I still think there was a reason I saw you that day at the memorial.

Ashley read over what she'd written. Then she typed a few more lines.

> Also, on a personal note, how would I go about getting a Survivor Tree sapling for my 12-year-old niece? It's a long story, but the sapling is something she wants very much. They were gone by the time we got there that day. I'll wait to hear from you. Blessings, Ashley Baxter Blake.

A quick glance over what she'd written and she hit send.

She would tell Landon about it later.

12

The firehouse was active that day. An electrical fire in an old home on the edge of the city. A sweet widow whose cat was stuck in a tree. And a teenager with a shoe caught in a moving escalator.

All three calls had happy endings.

Brady sank into the sofa in the station's living room. He grabbed his laptop from his backpack and opened it. Now that things were slow, maybe he could catch up on Facebook. Like on most weekends, he needed to do another search for Jenna. In case she finally showed up on social media.

Where she hadn't been since he first started looking.

A sigh slipped from his lungs. The anniversary had been more than a week ago, but this year it had stayed with him. Like a bad cold he couldn't quite shake. He opened Facebook and immediately spotted the notification.

Someone had written to him.

Not too strange. People would find him from his time on *Survivor* or because of the calendar. There were the occasional offers on his page. Modeling agencies.

Casting directors. Girls. Most of them weren't legit. Especially not the women. Did they really think he'd strike up a relationship with them? Because of a private Facebook message?

Since meeting Jenna, Brady had dated a dozen girls. At least that many. He only remembered the names of a few of them. They were pretty or funny or interesting. But as soon as they learned about his mom, as soon as they discovered he'd been raised in foster care, something changed.

It wasn't their fault.

The blame was Brady's. He had an aversion to pity. When girls realized the details of his childhood, they looked at him differently. Like he was a project or a charity case. Whatever it was, Brady hated it. He didn't want sympathy.

He wanted empathy.

Sympathy felt sorry from the outside looking in. It knew nothing of a person's pain or experience.

Empathy lived it. The sorry feeling came from the inside looking out.

Which was why things never worked with the women he dated. Sure they were sad about his past. But they didn't understand it. And in the end it left a chasm too great to cross. A divide no bridge could span.

It was fine. Brady didn't need love. If he couldn't find Jenna, he would go on the way he had every year for more than a decade. Fighting fires. Serving the people of Oklahoma City. Working out at the local CrossFit gym. Maybe it wasn't the life he had hoped for. Not the life his mom would've wanted for him. But it was enough.

Brady opened the message and scanned to the bottom.

Ashley Baxter Blake.

Brady sat up straighter and stared at the screen. *Ashley?* She was the brunette from the memorial. The one who had randomly texted him a few days ago. She said she'd read the letter he'd written for Jenna. How she wanted to help. It had seemed harmless at the time, so he had texted back. He didn't know Jenna's last name, so what could the lady do to help? He had figured that would be the end of it.

So what was her deal? Why was she writing to him again? So bizarre. The woman was a complete stranger. So what was her interest?

He started at the top of the note.

> Dear Brady, thank you for responding to me earlier. I can see why you've struggled to find Jenna if you don't know her last name. I haven't found her yet.

He hesitated. Did she really think she could find Jenna? When he had been looking all these years? He kept reading. The woman wanted to know Jenna's high school or college and when Brady had met her. As if that would help.

Brady read the last few lines.

He felt his heart soften. Ashley wanted a sapling for her niece. Maybe that was what this was really about. He stared at the message. What had happened to the young girl that she wanted a piece of the Survivor Tree? Writing back made no real sense. But the part about the niece caught him by surprise. If he could help the child, he would.

"Okay, Ashley." He uttered the words under his breath as he hit the reply button. He kept his response brief.

> I don't have the information you asked for. We met in 2007, that's about it.

He hesitated, picturing Jenna the way she had looked back then. He could tell Ashley about that. The information couldn't hurt. He positioned his fingers on the keyboard again.

> Here's something. Eleven years ago Jenna looked like Emma Stone. Not sure if that helps. Also, I would like to help you find a Survivor Tree sapling for your niece. Are you coming back to the memorial next April? That's usually the only time they're given out. Was your niece related to someone who died in the bombing?

He looked at what he'd written and gradually felt his heart engage. Ashley didn't have to reach out. She didn't seem to have an ulterior motive. Just some sense about the situation. How had she said it? There was a reason. That was it. A reason she had seen him at the fence. Brady finished his note.

> Anyway, thanks for taking time to write. I don't think you'll find Jenna. But you mean well, and I appreciate that. Take care. Brady.

There. He hit the send button. It was still odd, a complete stranger trying to help him find Jenna. But he was touched by her kindness.

He searched through a few local websites. The downtown mission was hosting a fund-raiser next month. He sent a quick email to the organizer. Like last year he wanted to attend. Brady would act as a table host and get the word out about ticket sales.

Next he checked his email. A thank-you letter from the children's hospital, where he was also a regular volunteer. Brady didn't have his own family. So helping people gave him purpose. A way to do for children what no one had been able to do for him at that age.

Give them a reason to smile.

He read to the bottom of the letter. Would he be interested in coming in every week instead of every month? Brady felt the ache deep in his heart. Yes, he would be interested. Sick kids needed as much love as they could get.

Brady wasn't finished writing his response when the sirens went off. It took only seconds to know that the call was a big one.

"The structure is fully involved," the voice crackled over the radio. Then came other details.

The address was a warehouse on the east side of the city. The building sat adjacent to a retirement home, which according to the call was also ablaze. Trucks were being sent from every station in the area.

Brady was immediately on high alert. Fully involved was never good.

He'd been trained for moments like this. Trained to go from zero to a hundred in a few heartbeats. All around him firefighters were slipping into their gear, racing to get to the truck as fast as they could. Eric Munez, thirty-year-old father of three, jumped into the cab beside him. "Biggest fire of the month." Eric raised his brow. He and Brady had been working together for a long time.

"Biggest of the year." Brady was behind the wheel. He slammed the truck door shut. "Let's roll. We got this."

Wind whipped through the city. Brady felt it gust against the side of the rig. No wonder the fire was spreading. If they didn't get it out quickly, other buildings would ignite. The fire was in an area where structures sat almost on top of each other.

They reached the scene at the same time as four other trucks, from the lower east and central stations. All of them first responders. Even before they parked, Captain Jerry Cranston took charge over the radio.

"Checking the retirement home." Cranston ran up to a man who looked like the manager of the place. A dozen elderly residents milled about. Some leaning on nurses. Several in wheelchairs.

Cranston barked out orders for two trucks to get water on the residential building. The other three were to start on the warehouse. Brady and Eric's team was part of the latter group. The wind was fierce now, and already several other buildings were in imminent danger.

Even as Cranston shouted the instructions, Brady could see the threat. The warehouse was the tallest in the district. Four stories, easily. They could spray water from the ground, but they wouldn't gain control over the blaze unless they got on the roof.

The sound and heat from the fire were like something from hell. Brady squinted at Eric through the smoke, but before he could speak, Cranston gave the order.

"Munez, Bradshaw, get on the roof." He rattled off another four names. "All of you. Hurry. We need to take the life out of this thing."

Brady grabbed a hose from the truck and led the way as the six men scrambled up the ladder to the flaming roof. The most dangerous spot was the middle. Warehouse roofs were generally weaker and less supported than roofs on other buildings. Collapsed warehouse roofs killed more firefighters than almost anything.

The headsets inside their masks were all connected. Brady shouted over the line. "I've got middle." No way was he going to let Eric join him out there. He had a wife and kids at home.

Brady had no one.

Cranston must've agreed with the decision. "Munez, the rest of you, take the perimeter. Bradshaw, be careful. Don't go too far."

"Yes, sir." Brady trudged across the surface with the hose. Flames were whipping up and over the edges, lapping at the structures on the north side of the warehouse.

"Unit Three, hurry up. Those people don't have time!" Cranston sounded frantic.

Brady kept his eyes straight ahead. There was no time to look down at the ground, no time to see if the other team—Unit Three—had rescued the residents or not. Brady focused. Get the hose to the middle of the roof and he'd take out the heart of the blaze. He dragged the line further, toward the center.

"Bradshaw, that's far enough." Munez hung back near the roof's edge.

"A little more," Brady shouted over the roar of the fire. He could feel the spray from two additional hoses behind him. Munez had his back for sure. His friend wouldn't let him get caught too far out. He'd be okay.

His hose shook in his hands, the force of the water at its maximum level. Brady doused the flames but as he did he took another few steps toward the core of the fire.

The cracking sound was exactly what he didn't want to hear. It pierced the roaring blaze and wind and shook the building. Brady lost his footing and fell to his knees. The roof was collapsing! "No!" he shouted, desperately trying to reverse, to find his way to a safer spot.

Someone was pulling on his fire hose, dragging him back. Eric Munez. His friend had him. Everything was going to be okay. The last thing he heard was Eric's voice, telling him he was almost safe. Just a few more steps and then—

The roof gave way and Brady was tumbling down, forever down. Steel beams and sheet metal and flames engulfed him even before he hit the ground. This was it. Firefighters didn't survive these situations.

Something shot at his gut and a metal rod smacked against his head. Brady fought for oxygen, for a way to keep his face above the blazing debris. Smoke and searing air. That's what killed firemen who fell through burning warehouse roofs.

Stay awake, Brady. They'll come for you. He ordered himself to survive, to fight. Keep his head up. But as his body landed he was buried alive. The heat from earlier wasn't hell.

This was.

He clawed at the rubble, at the wreckage pushing him down. "Get me out! I can't breathe!" Panic pressed in on him, the weight of the roof more than he could bear. Why couldn't he draw a breath? Brady pushed hard at whatever was crushing him. There was no room for air. Just heat and flames and smoke.

Several thoughts hit him at once. First, he flashed back to the bombing. *This is what it was like for my mother. Her final moments.* She had gone from these terrifying seconds into paradise.

That wasn't all. He would never see Cheryl and Rodney Fisher again. Why hadn't he gone by their house more often? Taken them up on the offer of an occasional dinner.

I'm sorry. I should've cared more for them. How could I miss that? Regret burned hotter than the flames. *Give me another chance. Please . . .* He didn't know who he was talking to, who could possibly help him now. He tried to inhale, but nothing came. He was dying. This was it. *Please, get me out!*

His final thought was her.

Jenna.

Was it possible Ashley Baxter Blake had been at the memorial for a reason? Maybe Ashley really would find Jenna. As his heart felt ready to burst inside him, as the weight of the burning roof settled in around him and Brady lost consciousness, he realized the worst part of all. He had lost his only chance, even if Ashley found Jenna.

Because after today, he would never know.

13

The painting was developing beautifully, better than Ashley had hoped. Landon was at work and the kids were at school, but the hours were flying by. Ashley had set her easel up outside on the front porch. The sky was blue, the air warm.

No better day to paint.

Her pieces were still being sold at the gallery in downtown Bloomington. The shop owner had asked for more of her work. Lately, people from all over the country stopped in asking about Ashley's art. Her paintings were going for five times the price she'd originally set. Enough to put aside money for the kids' college tuitions. Since those days were fast approaching.

Ashley stared at the canvas. The Survivor Tree looked lifelike, its branches spread out over the patio. She was using a photo she'd taken at the memorial. Not everyone who saw it would know what it was. But some would. And for those people this image would be everything. To Amy it would.

Especially if she didn't hear back from Brady about the sapling.

Her heart drifted to Landon. The day after Amy's play she had told him about her text and Facebook message to Brady.

He had come in from the porch, looking to talk to her. When he walked through the door Ashley met him in the foyer. He looked physically sick. The slow way he walked, his resigned expression, the hurt and discouragement in his eyes.

Without saying a word she had come to him and slipped her arms around his neck. For a long time they stood there, clinging to each other. No words needed.

He leaned back enough to look at her. "I can't think or work." He'd searched her eyes. "I'm sorry, Ash." He paused. "Yesterday . . . I was wrong."

"I'm sorry, too. I just . . . I didn't see the problem." She had known even then that she had crossed the line. "A few days ago . . . I texted him. I didn't tell you, Landon. I'm so sorry." A quick breath. "And then . . . last night while you were cleaning out the canoe I private-messaged him on Facebook." She hadn't waited for his reaction. "That was wrong. I should've talked to you first."

The news had seemed to hit Landon like a round of pellets. Like hearing it wasn't comfortable. But he could take it. He swallowed and after a while he nodded. "You can do this, Ash. I won't stand in your way."

She had felt her heart melt. "Not if it's going to come between us."

"It's not, Ashley." He looked almost desperate. "Nothing could come between us." He placed his hands on the sides of her face and his words had gone easily to the deepest place of her heart. "Nothing. Not ever."

After that, Landon had listened patiently while she explained what she'd written to Brady and how she hoped he could help get a sapling for Amy.

Then Landon had taken hold of her hands, the two of them still standing just inside the front door. "I may never get this, Ash." He smiled and shook his head. "But I get you. The girl I married. Wanting to help someone, whatever the cost."

"Exactly." Tears had filled her eyes.

He kissed her and his lips lingered for a minute or more. The two of them finding their way back to north. "Help the guy find Jenna." He crooked his finger and put it gently beneath her chin. "If anyone can do it, you can."

"Thank you." She dabbed at a single tear. "I needed to hear that."

"But . . ." He had run his fingers lightly through her hair. "If this doesn't work out. If you don't find her in the next few days . . ." He paused, his eyes locked on hers. "Please, Ash, in that case let it go. Otherwise . . ."

"Otherwise?" Even now Ashley could hear the conversation playing in her mind. "Otherwise what?"

"Well." He had kissed her cheek and then her lips once more. "You're a very beautiful woman, Ash. You don't want to give him the wrong idea."

Ashley had smiled. "Deal." Landon was right. The last thing Ashley needed was a young firefighter pen pal.

So the two of them had come up with a reasonable

plan. Three days. Then she'd check to see if he'd written back.

Today was the third day.

A car pulled into her driveway and slowed as it came closer. Ashley stood. Her father! She loved afternoons like this when her dad stopped by unannounced. It was one of the joys of his retirement. Or at least his semi-retirement. He still taught classes and gave lectures at the hospital.

But he had freedom for times like this.

Her dad parked and walked up the path. He carried a flat of bright red strawberries. "Hi there!"

"Hi!" Ashley met him at the top of the porch steps. "What a surprise!"

He hugged her and held out the berries. "Farmers' market got an early crop."

"All this warm weather." Ashley took the fruit. "Wanna come in?"

"Let's sit out here." Her dad tilted his face to the sun, already making its way toward the horizon. "No place like this old porch."

Ashley smiled. "I've thought that since I was a little girl." She ran the strawberries inside and returned with two glasses of lemon water. "Here." She handed him one and they took the rocking chairs, side by side a few feet from her easel.

He glanced at her painting as he sat down. "Beautiful." He paused, really studying the piece. "You're so talented."

"Thanks, Dad."

His eyes were still on her work. "That tree. It looks familiar." He narrowed his brow. "An American elm, right?"

"It is." Ashley looked from the painting back to her dad. "It's called the Survivor Tree."

Slowly, he nodded. "Ahh, yes." He paused. "The Oklahoma City bombing."

"Right." Ashley took a sip of water and stared at the yard. The open fields and red oaks that dotted their property. She wasn't sure, but it seemed her dad was more interested than what might be normal. A quick glance his way. "We went there for spring break."

"Yes." Her father's tone said there was definitely something on his mind. "I talked to Kari yesterday. She told me about the young man. The firefighter you saw at the memorial."

Ashley braced herself. She resisted the urge to say anything biting. Really? Kari had talked to their dad about this? What was with everyone? Her days as the black sheep were a lifetime ago. That didn't mean she'd make a mess of things now.

Ashley took a slow breath. "Did she tell you about the letter?"

"Yes." Her dad searched her eyes. "I'm not worried, Ash. If that's what you're thinking."

She was quiet.

"That's not why I stopped by." He smiled and patted her hand. "Your faith in God . . . your love for Landon. Clearly you only want to help."

Relief spilled from her head to her heart. "Thank you."

"I do think you need to be careful." His expression was still warm. "You don't know this young man."

Ashley nodded. "I get that. I've told Landon all about it." She paused, searching his eyes. "Dad. It's fine."

"Okay." He leaned back in the rocker. "So you're trying to find the girl this young man is looking for?"

"Yes. Jenna. I don't have a last name." Ashley felt the weight of discouragement. "It really seemed God put me next to the guy for a reason. Like I was supposed to help." She shook her head. "But I haven't found her."

Her dad drank half the water in his glass. Then he set it down on the porch railing and stood. "Have you tried looking up her parents?" He turned and leaned against the railing.

Ashley was struck by his kindness. He really was only trying to help. Finding a reason to bring by some berries and talk a bit. "Her parents?" She settled into the chair. His question was interesting.

"They were both killed in the bombing. That's what Kari said." Her dad looked at her. "There were only so many couples in the building. I keep thinking maybe if you search that, maybe you'll find that one of them had a daughter named Jenna."

"Hmm." Ashley hadn't thought about that. She'd read the list of victims, of course. When she'd first Googled Jenna's name in relation to the Oklahoma City bombing. But she'd never thought to check the husband

and wife pairs killed in the bombing, and then look up their children. "You're thinking someone might have written about them?"

"Maybe." Her dad angled his head. His face was tan from his daily walks with Elaine. He continued. "The twenty-year anniversary was a few years ago. Everyone was doing stories on what happened. It's possible someone did a follow-up on the deaths of people with the same last name. The children orphaned."

"You're right." Ashley felt a surge of hope. "Why didn't I think of that?"

"You have a lot on your plate." Her father laughed. "Like four kids to feed and help with homework." He shrugged. "If I'd known her last name, I would've already looked myself."

"See?" Ashley laughed, too. "Now you know where I get it!"

"True." He paced to the spot in front of her easel.

Ashley appreciated her father's heart, his time. More than he would ever know. "I think there's a spiritual side to all this, too."

"For the guy?" Her dad turned to her.

"For both of them, maybe." Ashley stood and looked at her dad for a minute. "I guess we won't know until we find her."

"Until *you* find her." He chuckled. "I have a paper to write for the hospital administration. I'm presenting it next week."

"So here we are"—she smiled—"two fairly busy people. And we can't stop thinking about how to help a stranger." Ashley paused. "God's up to something. I have to believe it."

"Well." He breathed deep and glanced at her easel once more. "I'll let you get back to your painting." He grinned at her. "Just thought it'd be better to talk about this in person."

Ashley understood what he meant. If he had texted or called, she might've misunderstood him. She could've assumed he was doubtful about her intentions. But that wasn't the case at all.

He only wanted to help.

The way he always did.

She hugged him and kissed his cheek. "Tell Elaine I said hi." She stepped back and smiled. "And thanks for the berries. The kids will love them."

"Elaine's making shortcake back at home." He shook his head, his eyes sparkling. "She made enough for the neighborhood."

"I have an idea!" Ashley laughed. "Why don't you and Elaine join us for dinner? Landon's grilling, and Elaine can bring the shortcake."

Her dad nodded. "Sounds like a perfect night. I'll talk to Elaine." He paused at the bottom of the stairs. "I love this, Ash. Being so close. Having time with you and your siblings."

"We love it, too." She waved and watched him leave, waited as his car moved along their paved drive to the road.

As soon as he was out of sight she went inside, found her laptop and brought it back out to the front porch. Why hadn't she thought about looking up Jenna's parents? Like her dad said, there were only so many couples killed in the bombing. She Googled the list of victims.

She went through a full search of the surviving family members of couples killed in the tragedy. Then she came to Bill and Betsy Phillips. "Bill and Betsy Phillips." Ashley whispered their names as she typed them into the search line. Then she typed "survivors."

Suddenly she was looking at a headline.

WHERE ARE THEY NOW? CHILDREN ORPHANED BY THE OKLAHOMA CITY BOMBING.

Ashley felt her heart skip a beat. Could Bill and Betsy be Jenna's parents? The article was in *The Oklahoman,* still online after a decade. She opened it and began to read. The first part of the article led to a section titled "Life After the Bombing—Bill and Betsy Phillips." Beneath that was a list of their surviving family members, including a daughter named Elizabeth Jenna Phillips.

Elizabeth *Jenna* Phillips?

Ashley felt the porch begin to spin. Her heart pounded as she read this part of the story.

Elizabeth Jenna Phillips was just five years old when her parents went to work that April 19 and never came home. She lived with her grandmother for the rest of her school years.

Ashley kept reading. The article was heartbreaking,

detailing the jobs the little girl's parents had held, and how long they'd worked at the Alfred P. Murrah Building. But nothing more about the child.

In a rush, Ashley switched to Facebook. "Elizabeth Jenna Phillips," she typed. Four matches came up, but none were younger than forty. She searched again with just "Jenna Phillips," but again, nothing.

She was so close. Ashley tapped her fingers on the table. "Come on." There had to be something. *Please, God, lead me to her.* Ashley took a deep breath and tried again. This time she Googled "Elizabeth Jenna Phillips" and "Oklahoma City Bombing."

The results that came back were slightly different.

Top of the list was an article titled ORPHANS OF OKLAHOMA CITY—TWENTY YEARS LATER.

Ashley couldn't read the story fast enough. The opening paragraph explained that in honor of the twenty-year anniversary the paper was doing a series of profiles on the victims and their surviving family members. How life had changed when the bomb exploded through the Alfred P. Murrah Federal Building.

"Dear God, thank You," Ashley whispered. Her hands trembled as she scanned the article for the names Bill and Betsy Phillips. The two weren't quite thirty years old when they reported for work at the federal building in downtown Oklahoma City that April 19, 1995. Betsy on the third floor, and Bill on the fifth.

Ashley could picture the couple saying goodbye to their little girl, heading off to work. Parking across the street and climbing out of the same car, headed to their separate jobs. They couldn't have known it would be the last time.

Ashley kept reading. Both Bill and Betsy were killed when the bomb went off, but their only daughter, five-year-old Elizabeth Jenna, had survived. Safe at home with her grandmother, who had moved to Oklahoma City a year before the bombing. Otherwise she might've been in the daycare when the attack happened.

Apparently the child went by the name Jenna. Her grandmother once said even though her daughter and son-in-law had missed seeing Jenna grow up, they would've been grateful she survived. Grateful that she had been raised by her grandmother. The girl had eventually finished school and married.

Married? Ashley closed her eyes. Brady was going to be heartbroken. She couldn't imagine being the one to tell him the news. That is, if this was her. And Ashley believed it was.

She opened her eyes and kept reading.

This part of the feature finished with *Elizabeth Jenna Phillips—now Davis—graduated from college in Texas and is currently a teacher in Columbus, Ohio.*

That was all there was. The article ended with a section on the memorial, the husband-and-wife team who designed it and how many visitors came through each year.

Ashley's head was spinning.

She stared at the screen.

She couldn't believe it! This was the best and worst news. She'd found Brady's girl, but she was married. She was Jenna Davis now. A teacher in Columbus. At least it seemed that way. Ashley wasn't sure what to do next. She started to set the laptop down, to head inside the house, but then she stopped herself.

Where was she going? She couldn't call Brady out of the blue. Besides, she hadn't actually found Jenna. But she'd most likely found more information than Brady had discovered in all these years.

All because of her father's suggestion.

Her hands were shaking so hard she could barely type. Facebook. She needed to look there first. In case Jenna Davis wasn't the one Brady was looking for. She entered "Jenna Davis" in the search line and several names appeared. One of them lived in Columbus.

She clicked it. "God, You're amazing." She whispered the words, her eyes glued to the young woman's profile page as it came up. Jenna Davis. Teacher at Martin Luther King Junior Elementary School. Ashley enlarged her profile picture as big as she could make it.

The photo was of Jenna surrounded by twenty children. Ashley hesitated. If this was Brady's Jenna, married and living in Columbus, at least he'd have closure. Maybe that's what she was supposed to bring to the situation. A reason for Brady to let go. She scrolled down Jenna's page.

Ashley kept reading until she saw something that stopped her cold. It was a status she'd posted on Christmas Eve.

A status that changed everything.

Beneath a Christmas photo of the front door of what must've been Jenna's house she had written this: *Thankful that with God, I'm not alone this Christmas. I never will be.*

Alone? Ashley blinked a few times, trying to understand. Another five minutes of searching her time line and Ashley was sure. Jenna was divorced. Whatever had happened, the young woman seemed to have faith and hope. At least according to her Christmas post.

Ashley hurt for Jenna, for everything the girl had been through. Losing her parents when she was so little, and then losing her husband. Whatever the situation. Yet, she appeared to be making it on her own. She seemed to enjoy teaching.

Assuming this was the same girl Ashley had been looking for, what did Jenna think about Brady?

Did he ever cross her mind? Or had she forgotten him after their one day together? Ashley looked more closely at Jenna's face. The sweet girl-next-door look. But even still the hurt was there in her pretty green eyes.

Ashley took a deep breath. What to do next? Suddenly she remembered her message to Brady. All this time she'd been on Facebook studying Jenna's profile and she hadn't thought to check her in-box. She glanced at the icon on her screen and sure enough, there was a message.

She opened it and immediately she saw who it was from.

Brady Bradshaw.

And something else. The letter was longer than two

words. She started at the beginning. He said he didn't have much information except the year they met. She closed her eyes, picturing Brady finally deciding to trust her, to open up. Even a little. She blinked and kept reading. He described Jenna as looking like Emma Stone. And yes, he said he would try to help find a sapling Survivor Tree.

A few clicks and Ashley had Jenna's picture back up. This had to be the same girl Brady had met that day. No question Jenna looked like the famous actress.

Ashley wanted to shout for joy. She'd done it. She had actually found Jenna. She went back to Brady's letter and felt her heart melt a little. The tough guy had a soft side. Clearly. Otherwise he wouldn't have been touched by Amy's request. She found her place and finished reading. He closed by thanking her but he added that he didn't think she'd have much luck finding Jenna.

How surprised would he be when she reached out to tell him that she had actually found the girl? And yes, she still looked like Emma Stone. Ashley tapped the keyboard, and then absently she pulled up Brady's profile. In case he'd included something else about Jenna.

Instead, it took her a few seconds to grasp what she was seeing.

Someone had posted a link to a Go Fund Me page: "Help with Expenses for Brady Bradshaw." "What?" Ashley leaned forward. Her heart was pounding again. What had happened?

She clicked the link and struggled to catch her

breath. Brady Bradshaw was in intensive care in an Oklahoma City hospital after falling through the roof of a warehouse during a huge fire two days ago.

Two days ago? Ashley checked the time and date on the private message he'd sent her. Then she Googled his name and details about the fire. He must've gotten hurt just after sending her note.

And now . . .

She found the most updated article on the Web. It had been posted a few hours ago. DOCTORS LOSING HOPE FOR OK CITY FIREFIGHTER IN ICU.

"No!" The word came out as a cry. How could this be happening? *Dear God, please let him live.*

Suddenly Ashley knew what she had to do. Columbus was less than four hours away. She needed to pray for Brady Bradshaw and she needed to find her way to Martin Luther King Junior Elementary School. The only way to have this conversation with Jenna was in person. When she helped someone, she gave it everything she had. No Facebook message. Not this time. Driving to see Jenna was the right thing to do. Ashley was convinced. She would tell Landon when he got home.

Then first thing in the morning she would set out for Columbus.

14

Minutes into lunch, one of the other teachers gave Jenna a message. Someone was waiting for her in the main office. A woman. The teacher shrugged one shoulder. "Might be a parent, but I've never seen her before."

"Thanks." Jenna hadn't been very hungry. She wrapped up the rest of her sandwich and slipped it back into the staff refrigerator. Then she made her way through the hall to the office.

Before she opened the door she saw that her coworker was right. The woman waiting wasn't someone she'd ever seen before. Jenna stepped inside and approached her. "I'm Jenna Davis." She smiled. "Are you looking for me?"

The strange woman's eyes filled with tears. "Yes." She held out her hand. "I'm Ashley Blake." She looked around. Like she didn't want to say too much here, with the staff in earshot. "Can we . . . go outside?"

Jenna felt her stomach drop. Who was this Ashley woman and how come she was here? Had something happened to Dan in London? If so, this was no time to tell her. He'd been out of her life too long for anything about him to be urgent.

Or maybe she was a lawyer. Maybe someone was suing her. For reading *Noah's Ark,* perhaps. But then why would the woman have tears in her eyes? None of it made sense.

Jenna stuffed the possibilities into the corner of her mind and led the woman outside. There was a bench in front of the school. The clouds overhead meant they could talk without wearing sunglasses.

Jenna sat first and Ashley took the spot next to her. Jenna shook her head. "I'm sorry . . ." She tried to sound confident. "What's this about?"

With kind, concerned eyes, the woman looked straight at her. "Are you Elizabeth Jenna Phillips? Was that your maiden name?"

Jenna felt the blood leave her face. "Yes. That's me."

"That's what I thought." Ashley seemed relieved. "I had to come talk to you in person. It's about Brady Bradshaw. From Oklahoma City."

Brady Bradshaw? Jenna's heart skipped a beat. Could this be . . . was Bradshaw his last name, after all these years? Jenna's breathing was suddenly jagged and her heart pounded in her throat. What in the world? "How . . . how do you know Brady?"

"I don't know him." The woman seemed flustered. "It's a long story. I'll try to make it quick." Ashley glanced at the building. "I know you have to get back to class."

"Yes." Jenna felt like she might pass out. What did the woman know? And what was so important that she needed to come here in person? "Please tell me."

The story was as unbelievable as meeting this strange woman. So unbelievable it had a ring of truth to it. Ashley had been at the Oklahoma City memorial on the anniversary of the bombing. She'd stood at the fence next to a random stranger, a guy with dark hair and a world of hurt on his face.

"He left a note in the fence. For you." Ashley pulled her phone from her purse. "I took pictures."

"You did?"

"Yes." Ashley hesitated. "I don't know if you believe in God, Jenna. But I do. My family does. And in that moment . . . in that moment when I saw the letter in the fence . . . I felt like God put me there to help. However I could."

Jenna's heart was still pounding. "Yes. I believe in God. Very much so." She leaned closer. "Can I see the picture? The letter?"

Ashley pulled up the first photo. "This is how it looked on the fence. When Brady left it there."

Jenna tried to focus. Was she dreaming? Could this really be happening? Someone had found Brady after all this time? She squinted at the photo, then used her fingers to make the image larger.

Sure enough, there it was. Written across the front of a scrolled-up letter. *"For Jenna."* She brought her hand to her mouth and stared at the screen. "He left that there? For me?" Jenna looked at Ashley. "Just a few weeks ago?"

"Yes. My family was visiting for spring break." Ashley shook her head. "Look at the next photo. Please, Jenna."

She scrolled to the right and there it was. A photo of the letter, opened. And at the bottom, his name and number. Brady Bradshaw. Jenna couldn't catch her breath. She exhaled. *Relax. You have to relax.* In twenty minutes she needed to be back in the classroom. She couldn't fall apart.

Ashley handed over the phone, and again Jenna made the image larger. As she did, she read every line of the letter.

Dear Jenna,

Like I do every year, I wrote you a letter. In case you come to the memorial today. In case you want to find me as much as I want to find you. Every year I do this, I leave you a note in case. Anyway, here I am again, eleventh year in a row.

Jenna closed her eyes for a few seconds. Eleven years in a row? He'd been there every year, looking for her? She found her place and kept reading. He said that again he had come to find her, because every year wound up the same. No response to his letter. Next he had a question for her. One that hit a place in her heart she had ignored for so long.

Don't you remember, Jenna? What it was like having that one day together?

"Yes," Jenna whispered. "I still remember." She was so lost in the letter she forgot she was sitting next to the stranger. She kept reading.

His letter said that he'd lost her number, but he'd thought it would be easy to find her. And how after all this time he still thinks about her.

The truth is, I don't think about anyone but you. I'm a firefighter in Oklahoma City. It gives me purpose. But I'm alone. I'm always alone.

Tears filled Jenna's eyes and spilled onto her cheeks. She looked up at the sky, warding off the sobs building in her heart. *Brady, I'm so sorry. How could I have missed this?* All these years. She steeled herself against the heartache and read the rest of the note.

It was the hardest part. He wrote how he was waiting for her and he'd be back again next year. On the anniversary.

And one of these days, Jenna . . . one of these days you'll be here. I'll find you. I have to believe that. Remember what you said? Our hearts are the same. And so they are. Always. Brady Bradshaw.

Jenna was shivering, but it had nothing to do with the cool afternoon. She handed the phone back to Ashley. "I . . . I can't believe this."

"I looked you up on Facebook. I . . . don't know your situation. You're divorced? . . . Your last name is different. But I figured it might be you. And if it was . . ." Ashley hesitated. "I thought you'd want to know."

Jenna felt the familiar sinking feeling. "I'm not married. My husband, he left me a few years ago. He's . . . moved on."

A genuine look of sadness filled Ashley's eyes. "I'm sorry. Really."

"Me, too. But I'm not alone. I have my faith." A supernatural strength resonated within her. The way it did whenever she remembered her situation. "That's what matters."

Ashley's face grew serious. "There's more, Jenna." The color seemed to drain from her cheeks. "Brady . . . he's hurt. He's in ICU at a hospital in Oklahoma City."

"What?" Jenna stood and paced away from the bench. Her legs shook. How could any of this be happening? "How did he get hurt?"

"In a fire a few days ago." Ashley slid to the edge of the bench. "He's fighting for his life." She hesitated, as if she wasn't sure what to say next. "I knew the only way to tell you any of this was in person."

Jenna hadn't even asked the woman where she was from. "How far did you drive?"

"I live in Bloomington. My husband is a firefighter. Maybe that's why . . ." Ashley's voice trailed off. "I don't know. I had to come find you."

Ashley went on to explain that she'd been in touch with Brady and even though he hadn't been able to find Jenna, Ashley had a strong belief she could. That she might somehow connect them. Even if their lives had moved on.

"And now . . ." Jenna sat back down on the bench beside Ashley. "Thank you. Can you please . . . would you send me those pictures?"

"Definitely." Ashley took Jenna's cell number and texted her the photos.

Jenna looked at them again. "Do you know what hospital he's at?"

"The article said Oklahoma University Medical Center." Ashley looked like she didn't want to say whatever was next. "The last I read, they were concerned. He might not survive."

The face of Brady Bradshaw filled her heart and soul. Jenna closed her eyes for a short while. When she opened them she had to blink back tears to see Ashley clearly. "Thank you. For coming." She shook her head. All of this was so crazy. "I can't believe you'd drive so far."

"Brady's waited more than a decade." Ashley's smile was as kind as it was sad. "The least I could do is take a day to come find you. Especially if . . ."

If he didn't make it. That's clearly what Ashley didn't want to say. Jenna hung her head and tried not to fall to the ground weeping. Brady had been alone all this time, thinking about her, missing her. Why hadn't she ever gone back to the memorial?

So what if he hadn't called her? If she could change things she never would've been so hasty. If she could go back to her seventeen-year-old self, she would've called him or figured out a way to meet up with him somewhere. Anything to see him again.

Ashley checked her watch. "I need to go." She paused. "Can I . . . pray for you? For Brady?"

"Please." In that moment Jenna knew she would've been friends with Ashley Blake. If she had more time to get to know her, or if they lived in the same city. She reached out her hands and took hold of Ashley's.

With heads bowed, Ashley prayed. That Brady would be healed of his injuries and that somehow Jenna and him might find the friendship they'd started years ago. And she prayed that God would help them both in whatever the coming days held. Then she thanked God for helping her find Jenna. Just when it mattered most.

They both said amen, and stood. Without hesitating, Jenna hugged Ashley. "You're the nicest person. Thank you for coming." Again, Jenna could barely breathe. But this time it was out of fear. Fear that she might miss the chance to see Brady.

Jenna looked at her phone. "I need to call the hospital." She hesitated. "Is it okay if I text you? To tell you how he's doing?"

"I'd love that." Ashley smiled. "My husband and I will pray." They shared another hug and Ashley walked off to the parking lot.

For a minute Jenna dropped back to the bench. If not for the hard slats beneath her legs, she'd have to wonder. None of this felt real. As if she'd blink and be in bed. Waking up from the most amazing, terrifying dream. She knew where Brady was, and that he hadn't forgotten her.

But only in time to learn he was fighting for his life.

And in that moment she made a decision. She was going back to Oklahoma City this summer anyway. To take her parents' pictures and precious items and make their part of the memorial right. While she was there she would see Brady. That is if he was still . . .

She picked up her phone and searched the number for the OU Medical Center. A minute later she was talking to a nurse. No, she wasn't family. Yes, she knew him well. She closed her eyes and prayed God would understand the stretched truth.

She had known him well eleven years ago.

Finally the nurse came back on the line. She couldn't

give specific details, but she could say this: Brady was still in a coma.

Tears filled Jenna's eyes as she hung up. God was working in this. He had to be. Hadn't Jenna just been praying for their paths to cross? Whatever Brady faced, Jenna would find him.

Suddenly an idea hit. This was the first Wednesday in May. Next week was the last of the school year. She scrolled through her contacts and called another number. A long-ago friend of her mother's. Yes the woman was home this summer, and yes she had two spare bedrooms.

"Come for as long as you'd like, Jenna." The woman sounded as friendly as Jenna remembered. And just like that she had a place to stay.

Back in the break room, she mentioned it to her teacher friends. "I found the woman my mom used to work with in Oklahoma," she told them. "I'm thinking of taking an adventure. Driving there for the summer."

A few of her friends looked less than happy for her. "An adventure? To Oklahoma?"

"Sure." She wasn't ready to talk about Brady yet. What would she say? "I've been planning it for a while. I want to add pictures and special things to my parents' memorial. I've never done that." She paused. "Anything's an adventure if you make it one."

"Sounds like a second-grade lesson." One of them laughed. "Whatever, Jenna. When you come home after a few days give us a call." She looked at the other girls in the room. "We're spending a month at the lake."

No chance of that. In Jenna's mind it was settled. When the school year was behind her, Jenna would pack her things and head for Oklahoma City. And as soon as she possibly could, she would find her way to the OU Medical Center and a boy she had met in 2007.

Brady Bradshaw.

• • •

ASHLEY DROVE HOME from Columbus in disbelief. Brady had looked for Jenna since they were seventeen. Now, because of her dad's brilliant idea, Ashley had found her in less than a few weeks. Whatever had happened in Jenna's personal life since that long-ago day at the Oklahoma City memorial, she still cared about Brady.

That much was obvious.

The whole way home Ashley prayed for the two, that Brady would recover and they'd find their way together. Even for just one more day.

So neither of them would have doubts about what might've been.

Ashley parked in the driveway just before the kids were scheduled to get home. She'd had her phone off while she drove but as soon as she turned it on she saw the text from Jenna.

Brady was being moved out of ICU. He was still in a coma, but he had turned a corner.

"Oh, dear God, thank You." Relief washed over Ashley as she made her way inside.

That night after the kids had finished their homework and headed to bed, she found Landon in the kitchen, doing the dishes. She had told him only that the day had been a success and that she'd give him the details later.

This was the moment.

Ashley came up behind Landon at the sink. "You're the most amazing man." She worked her hands around his waist. "Have I told you that lately?"

"Yes." He turned in her arms and faced her, his hands still wet with sudsy soap. He dried them on his jeans. "Tell me again."

"You"—she kissed him on the lips—"my Prince Charming, are the most amazing man I know."

"Mmmm." He returned her kiss. "You're my favorite princess. In case I haven't told you lately."

She laughed lightly. There was nothing like the love she felt for Landon, the love they shared. "You wanna hear about it?"

"Must be really good." He took the dish towel and gave her a light smack with it. "Otherwise you wouldn't have made me wait."

"Walk with me." She took his hand. "Outside. It's a pretty sky."

This was something they'd done a lot of when they were dating, when they were still figuring out whether they'd find a way to make things work. Tonight was the perfect time to talk under the bright sky. Especially since they were good again, since the fight was behind them.

Once they were outside, they walked to the stream behind their house. Along the way Ashley caught him up on what had happened. "God was ahead of me at every turn. I found Jenna, no problem." Ashley raised her brow. "Of course, at first I think she thought I was some crazy person. But when I said Brady's name, her expression changed. From that point on I had her attention, for sure."

"She's not married anymore? You're sure?" Landon looked concerned. Understandably. He and Ashley had agreed this wasn't something to do if Jenna were still married.

"Her husband left her." Ashley let that sad detail sit for a moment. "We prayed before I left. And by the time I got home she'd texted me. Brady's out of ICU."

For a long time Landon only looked at her in the moonlight. He slid a piece of her dark hair behind her ear. "You realize we're having a conversation about perfect strangers." He smiled at her. "As if we know them."

"Yes." Ashley made a nervous face. "It's true. This sort of thing could only happen to me."

"Absolutely. But I'm glad I stepped out of the way. Because you were right, Ash. God wanted to use you. I believe that." Landon's smile dropped off. "Sounds like the accident was serious. Keep me posted on how things turn out."

"I promised her we'd pray. You and me."

"Okay, then . . . let's do it." Landon pulled her into his arms and prayed out loud. For a couple of people they didn't know named Jenna and Brady, and that Ashley would always be drawn to help people.

Even total strangers.

15

Brady wasn't sure if he was in hell or not. His head throbbed and he couldn't speak. Whatever had happened to him, he couldn't move his arms or legs. Couldn't turn his head from side to side.

Still somewhere deep in his subconscious he had the slightest sense that maybe he wasn't in hell. Heaven, either. Just possibly, he might actually be alive. Not because he felt himself getting better.

But because he kept seeing Jenna in his dreams.

Like a favorite movie on replay, the memory would start at the beginning. The day he and Jenna spent together. Brady couldn't take a deep breath. Everything was numb, and the pain throughout his body consumed him. Even so, images from years ago were taking shape in his heart once more.

Brady felt his head sink deep into the pillow. Then he did what he'd done every time Jenna filled his mind and heart.

He let the memory come.

• • •

HE'D ALWAYS THOUGHT of them as part of a club. The wanderers who made it to the memorial every April 19. The ones who walked along the chain-link fence alone and without words of any kind. All of them had lost someone.

Brady never asked who, never talked to anyone at the memorial. Even when he saw the same people year after year. He never spoke to a single person until 2007.

The year he met Jenna.

He was reading the offerings left on the fence when he spotted her. Golden dark red hair, beautiful green eyes. A face that took his breath even with the sorrow written into her expression. He was about to walk by, wouldn't have interrupted her moment.

But just as he was about to miss her, their eyes met.

They exchanged names, and he showed her his arms. Proof he'd been in the building that terrible day. At one point he asked her to feel his scars. She did, and her touch was the softest thing he'd ever felt.

He could still feel her fingers against his skin.

She had no reason to trust him, but a connection happened between them. They spent an hour at the Survivor Tree, and all the while he could feel himself drawn to her. And his attraction gradually turned into something deeper.

She told her story and when she finished, when they realized they had been only a couple of five-year-olds when the bomb went off, Brady had reached for her hand. And for the first time in all his life he felt something he'd never felt before.

He felt complete.

Her hand was made for his, and gently he ran his thumb along her fingers. For a minute or so he didn't say anything. He didn't want to ruin the quiet understanding between them. Like they were both still just two kids missing their parents.

Jenna's expression was different than any Brady had ever seen. And somewhere along the course of the day, Brady knew what it was. Empathy. The empathy he had missed every day since. Jenna's eyes held a kindness and understanding, the sort that could only come from someone who had been through it. She was another grown-up five-year-old who had lost everything that April morning.

As the day played out, the weather changed. It grew colder and they took a walk. All the while Brady wanted just one thing: for the day to never end. One of the best parts of their time together was the conversation they had before they walked to the coffee shop across the street from the memorial. They agreed that people talked about the bombing like it happened to the city.

When really it happened to the two of them.

Personally.

Then they got deeper still. Jenna admitted how she used to imagine that her parents were traveling somewhere far, far away and one day they would walk through the door and they could all be together again. Brady admitted that he had thought something similar. They talked about how they used to pray that God would return their parents, that life might miraculously find its way back to what it once had been.

Before the bombing.

That's when they discovered something else they had in common. One more connection. Both their mothers had come to their rooms every night and said the words "Love you to the moon and back."

After that he was hooked. He might only have been seventeen, but he knew he wanted Jenna in his life as long as he lived.

Then Brady shared something else he hadn't shared with anyone before. He told her about his disconnect with God. Jenna felt the same. She said she was frustrated with God. Why would He take her parents?

Brady would never forget the walk back to the memorial. The wind was in full force and he took her hand again. When he eased his fingers between hers, the feeling sent chills down his arms and legs. She looked just like Emma Stone, only prettier. Jenna was definitely prettier.

Brady couldn't remember everything else they talked about. But he would remember the feel of her hand in his as long as he lived. Finally the clouds had broken open and it started pouring. They ran into the museum to get out of the rain and there they found their way to the picture.

The one before the bomb went off.

They talked about how Brady and his mom could've

run errands another day, and maybe her parents might've stayed home from work that April 19.

And then it was time for Jenna to go.

Brady still held her hand, still had his fingers between hers. They swapped numbers and he promised he would call. He had to call. He was sure he would.

No one had ever connected with his soul the way Jenna had.

They promised at least to talk when the next anniversary came around. But then Jenna smiled at him. "A year is a long time."

"A week's a long time." They were standing so close. He wanted to kiss her, but it wasn't the time. He stared at her number. "I'll call you soon. It'd be nice to get to know you." He felt his smile drop off. "Outside the club, I mean."

"I'll never forget today." Jenna took a step closer to him. "You're the only one who knows just how I feel."

"You, too." He couldn't keep from telling her how he felt. He practically whispered the next words. "I want to kiss you, Jenna."

She looked like she wanted that, too. But she only smiled. "I think we should wait."

"Yeah." He could feel himself flirting with her. "Come here."

They were only inches apart. Jenna did as he asked and it took all of his willpower not to kiss her. Instead, he took her in his arms and held her. The hug wasn't something passionate.

It was deeper than that.

Like two people who'd been lost and now were found.

• • •

THE DREAM WAS fading, at least it felt that way. Brady could see light through his closed eyelids. He could hear sounds. He still couldn't lift his head or turn it, couldn't move his hands or feet or shift his position. And he certainly couldn't talk.

Someone was saying something about levels or numbers, vital signs. Something Brady couldn't make out. It was a guy and he was still talking. "Brady? Brady, can you hear me?"

He tried to close his eyes more fully. He didn't recognize the voice of the man. Why would he be talking about numbers? Where was he, anyway?

Then another voice spoke closer to him. A woman's.

"Brady . . . can you hear me?"

The sound worked its way through his consciousness and straight to his heart. *Jenna? Jenna, is that you?* Only his words didn't come out very loud. They didn't come out at all.

The voice came again. "Anyway, it's me. Jenna. I've been living in Columbus, Ohio. Teaching."

Brady tried with everything in him to sit up straight and open his eyes. Tried to shout that yes, he could hear her and yes, he knew who she was. He was dreaming still, of course. He had to be. Jenna wasn't in his life except when he dreamed.

But for some reason in his dream he couldn't move.

"You're probably wondering how I found you." It sounded like she was crying. She sniffed. "You know that woman? Ashley Blake. She found me, Brady. She drove all the way to Columbus and found me at my school." Another pause. "I came here as soon as I could."

Jenna was still talking, but Brady couldn't make out the words. Ashley Blake? Ashley had found Jenna? That could only mean one thing.

Maybe he wasn't dreaming after all.

16

Jenna hadn't been to the Oklahoma City memorial in eleven years. Today was as good a time to go back as any. She'd been in town three days, and this morning her mother's friend, Allison Wessel, made her breakfast. They chatted for an hour before Allison headed to the inner city medical clinic where she worked.

Talking to Allison was like getting a glimpse of what it might've been like if Jenna's mother had lived. Allison had worked with Jenna's mother. Same floor. But on April 19 she had taken the day off.

A random doctor's appointment saved her life.

Before she left for college, Jenna used to stop by Allison's house once every few weeks. Jenna always had the feeling she was visiting with her mother. Never mind Allison's brown skin and deep brown eyes. In the woman's presence, Jenna was home.

Back then they would share coffee and catch up on Jenna's schoolwork and friendships and dreams. Usually they'd end up laughing about something, and then before Jenna would leave, the conversation would turn to Jenna's mother.

"It should've been me," Allison would sometimes say as they hugged goodbye. "I wasn't married. I didn't have a little girl waiting at home."

"No." Jenna would shake her head. "You can't say that. No one should've died that day."

Now, Jenna had a clearer understanding. It was her parents' time. They loved God. They believed in Jesus. They had gone home to heaven together. Period. Whenever she was tempted to doubt God or spiral into a whirlpool of whys, Jenna would remember Romans 8:28. The meaning stayed with her every day. *In all things God works for the good of those who love Him*. No matter what dark alley her thoughts sometimes took, that truth remained.

God was working good out of what had happened.

Even if sometimes Jenna didn't see it.

She kept the radio off as she drove. Her friendship with Allison Wessel was one good thing that had come from her parents' death. The woman hadn't believed in God before the bombing.

Now she talked about Jesus like He was her personal friend.

The connection between Jenna and Allison had returned the moment Jenna walked through the woman's door. Allison had hugged her and looked long at her face. "I'm glad you're here."

"Me, too." Jenna embraced her again.

Allison's kindness had made it possible for Jenna to come to Oklahoma at all. She wouldn't have had enough money to stay in a hotel for more than a few days. But now she had all the time in the world.

The whole summer.

Which gave Jenna this day to see the memorial and then return to the hospital. She'd been there every day since getting into town. Brady was still in a coma. Because he had no next of kin, the doctor deemed it necessary to share Brady's progress with her.

His doctor had said Jenna was the only person other than his fellow firefighters and a sweet older couple who had been by. The only ones who had seemed to care.

Brady had two broken legs and a fractured spine. His right calf and thigh were seriously burned and he'd been fighting pneumonia since he was admitted. His lungs seemed to be healing, so that was good. Apparently, his helmet had protected his face, but not necessarily his head.

"Brain damage is possible," the doctor had told her yesterday. "He may never wake up. These things are hard to diagnose until he's conscious."

Jenna had decided to stop asking questions. Instead she spent most of her time at the hospital praying. Because only God knew what the future held for Brady Bradshaw.

She reached the memorial and parked several rows from the front. The anniversary had happened nearly a month ago, but still the place was busy. Jenna had read about the fascination. Oklahomans came because they wanted to pay their respects. Make a statement that something like the bombing would never be ignored.

The victims would never be forgotten.

But it wasn't just Oklahomans who made their way to the memorial. Some were like the woman Jenna had met at school, Ashley Blake. A visit here was part of a road trip or a spring break. Jenna sat in her car and stared at the gates. The towering walls that stood adjacent to each other at one end of the memorial.

She wore her key today. The one with *9:03* engraved in it. Yes, healing had begun then. But healing could take a while, that was the thing.

The past pressed in around her, pulling her from the car. She took a bag from her backseat, the one with her parents' pictures and personal items. These were the reason she'd planned the trip, after all. She stepped out of the car.

A cool breeze drifted over the parking lot. Jenna wore a long-sleeve lightweight sweater and dark jeans. A wide-brimmed hat and sunglasses would keep the moment private.

Which was how she wanted it.

Her first stop was her parents' chairs and then she walked over to the Survivor Tree. Every step of the way she caught herself thinking not so much about her parents, but about the boy who had made her part of the club. At the bench next to the tree, Jenna sat and closed her eyes.

Without her faith, she wouldn't be here. It had been the biggest part of her healing.

Run to Jesus, she had told herself over the years. Stop

trying to live life without Him. And along the way, she had become a new person.

Free. Whole. Ready to live again.

Yes, she would always miss her parents. She would wonder why they had been called to heaven so soon. But she wasn't angry with God. She loved Him.

He was with her, every day of her life—even when she was mad at Him. And one day she would see her parents again.

Jenna drew a quick breath. Had Brady ever returned to God? Was he still determined to keep his distance?

She held a map of the memorial grounds, and she stared at it. There she saw something she'd missed the day she'd met Brady. On the east end of the memorial were several slabs of concrete from the original structure. Etched into them were the names of more than six hundred people who had been in the building and survived.

Brady's name. She had to find it. She walked closer, right near the gate that read 9:01. And there, in alphabetical order, were the names of those who—like the slabs of concrete—had withstood the blast.

It took seconds to find his name.

Lord, would you heal Brady, please? Breathe Your strength through him by the power of Your Holy Spirit. I can't believe this is it for him. He needs You, Lord.

He had lived through the most terrible thing once.

He would live through it again. She had to believe it.

On her way into the building, Jenna stopped in the victims' room. There she met up with a volunteer who took the items from her bag. Along with photos she gave the woman an engraved key chain from her parents' fifth anniversary and the bookmark her mom had treasured, the one with the quote from *Little Women*. Her dad's Bible and some dried flowers. An old penny dated the year her parents married.

Small things, but still important.

The lady assured Jenna that her parents' memorabilia would be placed in two separate side-by-side glass boxes for visitors to see.

"We'll have it put together by the end of the week," she said.

Jenna looked again at their pictures and she could feel the memories come to life.

She might've only been five years old, but she remembered them both. She could still hear her mother's voice, feel her arms around her daddy's neck. She could see their eyes, the way they looked into hers. Yes, she was glad she'd come today. Glad she'd brought the items for her parents' part of the memorial. However sad, it was important that people know who Bill and Betsy Phillips were. Proof that her parents had lived and mattered. A way for everyone who passed by to see something of who they had been.

Before she left, Jenna found the glass box for Sandra Bradshaw—Brady's mother. Inside was a photo of a woman and a little boy—clearly the two of them. Next to it was what looked like a copy of a child's drawing of the moon and stars. Beneath the image, in childish writing, the words *To the Moon and Back—Brady Bradshaw—Age 5*. Jenna felt her heart breaking.

A final look at the other glass boxes and photos that lined the walls of the room and Jenna took a step back. *God, remove me from this place. I've had all I can take. I want to be with Brady.* She turned and walked back to her car. Something told her she needed to hurry, that her voice was important to him. Not just that, but her faith, too.

Because if Brady ever needed God it was now.

• • •

SOMETHING WAS DIFFERENT about Brady. Jenna could tell as soon as she entered his hospital room. She put her things down and stood at the side of his bed.

"Brady, it's me. I'm back." A quick pause and she searched his face, his arms, his bandaged right leg. Looking for any sign of movement. There was none. "Brady, it's Jenna." She studied his still handsome face. "If you can hear me, move your fingers. Open your eyes."

There was a sound at the door and Jenna turned. A man wearing an Oklahoma City Fire Department shirt stood there. Clearly another firefighter. He stepped inside, hesitant. "Hi." His eyes moved to Brady and then back to Jenna. "I'm Eric." He walked in and shook her hand. "Eric Munez. I work with Brady."

Jenna introduced herself. She paused. "You're probably wondering why I'm here." She could sense that much.

"He didn't . . . mention you." Eric looked like he felt bad making the admission.

She wouldn't have expected Brady to talk about her to his work friends. He hadn't seen her since they were seventeen. The fact that he'd written her a letter every April 19 and left it at the memorial was far more than she'd ever imagined.

She took one of the chairs near Brady's bed and motioned for Eric to take the other. "It's a long story."

He seemed willing to listen, so for the next ten minutes she told him about meeting Brady and how the impact of that single day had remained. For both of them. "When I heard he was here"—she looked at Brady. He still hadn't moved—"I had to come."

"Wow." Eric leaned forward, his elbows on his knees. "Brady never talked about it."

"I'm guessing he didn't marry?" Jenna had visited Brady's Facebook page, but there was no relationship status listed.

"No." Eric took a deep breath and stood. He walked to the side of Brady's bed and stared at his friend. "Never married. Barely dates." Eric looked back at Jenna. "His whole life's his work."

Jenna knew Brady's injuries were caused by the fire. But she didn't know more than that. "Do you know how he got hurt?"

"Yeah." Eric nodded. His eyes grew distant. "I was on the roof with him. At the edge." He clenched his jaw and exhaled. "He took the middle . . . the most dangerous spot . . . so I wouldn't." His eyes met hers again. "I have a family. He doesn't. If something happened he wanted it to happen to him."

Her heart melted. "That's the Brady I met years ago."

"He shouldn't be here. Falling through a roof like that, he never should've made it." Eric turned and leaned against the bed rail, facing Jenna. "God has a plan for Brady. That's what I keep telling him."

"He must." Jenna looked at Brady. "His doctor keeps saying it's a miracle he's still here."

"I begged God for his life." Eric sighed. "Brady's a hero. Heroes shouldn't die fighting fires."

"All firefighters are heroes." Jenna believed that.

Eric nodded. "Brady's different." He told her how Brady served Oklahoma City a dozen ways. At least. The downtown mission, the children's hospital, whenever there's a project benefiting just about anyone. "Brady's there."

Jenna was about to ask if Brady believed in God, whether that was part of his motivation to help others. But before she could find the words, there was a stirring in the bed.

Jenna was on her feet. Eric turned and watched Brady. He was lifting his fingers. Just the slightest wiggle, but still it was something.

"Brady . . . hey, man, can you hear me?" Eric took hold of Brady's hand. "You're crazy, Bradshaw. You never shoulda gone that far out to the middle."

The slightest groan came from Brady. Jenna walked

to the other side of the bed and waited. She didn't want to confuse him. And since Eric's was a voice he was familiar with, she kept quiet.

Another moan came from Brady's lips. This time Jenna watched him squeeze Eric's hand, just enough for them to know. He could actually hear Eric's voice. Over the next hour neither of them left the side of his bed.

Brady's doctor came in, checked his vitals and confirmed the obvious. He was waking up. "Take it slowly." The doctor nodded at both of them. "He'll want to hear your voices, but he'll be very tired. I'll come by every few minutes to check on him."

Again Jenna didn't want to say anything. *He wouldn't know my voice if I was the only one in the room*, she thought. Now that he was stirring she wondered why she was even here. The shock of seeing her might be too much. If she'd been alone with him, maybe. But for now she would wait.

Another hour passed and Brady seemed to grow agitated. He was trying to open his eyes, trying to form words. At least it seemed that way. Finally, just as Eric was getting ready to leave, Brady spoke. "Wh . . . where?" His voice was a raspy whisper. But the word was clear.

"Brady." Eric bent over the bed, their faces close. "You're at the hospital." Tears filled Eric's eyes. He was a tough-looking firefighter, built like a tank. But here he was just a guy pulling for his friend. "Can you hear me?"

This time Brady nodded. The motion was clear and undeniable. "Wha . . . happened?"

Jenna stood a few feet away. Tears filled her own eyes. This was the answer she'd prayed for. However long the journey ahead, at least Brady understood what his buddy was saying.

Eric clearly didn't want to tell Brady too much. He wiped his tears, his voice strong. "You're okay, man. You're going to get through this."

The effort of trying to talk must've been too much because Brady fell asleep again. It was just after two o'clock. Eric had to leave, but he gave Jenna his number. "Call me if he wakes up more than this. I want to be here."

She nodded and thanked Eric. Thanks to him she now knew more about the years she'd missed with Brady. She sat by his bed and pulled up the photo Ashley Blake had sent her. The one with his letter.

God, I don't know what You're doing. But I can feel it. Please . . . give Brady a miracle. Give us both one.

Exhaustion came over her. Sitting here watching Brady was taking its toll. Wondering what he'd say when he woke up again, or if he would wake up at all. Jenna was about to leave, head back to Allison's house for a nap, when Brady started moaning again. He turned his head a few inches in each direction, clearly agitated.

No one else was in the room, so Jenna took hold of his hand.

A rush of memories came over her, the way his hand had felt eleven years earlier. His skin was rougher now. Firefighter hands. But they were as warm as they'd been that far-off spring day.

Jenna stared at him. Should she speak to him? Now that he was coming to? She held her breath and decided she had to say something. Brady wanted to find her. It mattered to him. Maybe it would give him a reason to fully wake up if he knew she was here. "Brady . . ." She could feel her heartbeat in the hollow of her neck. "Brady, it's me. Jenna."

His restlessness suddenly stopped. He went still and then just as quickly he began to move again. And this time, finally, his eyes blinked open. Not all the way, but enough to squint at her. He turned his face in her direction and blinked a few more times.

"Jenna." Her name on his lips was unmistakable. "H-how?"

Every word took all his energy. Jenna could see that. Tears blurred her eyes. "Brady, I'm here. I found you."

His eyes closed again, but he knew. She was absolutely sure he knew. Not because he was able to look at her or say her name. But because of the way he squeezed her hand and ran his thumb along her finger.

Just like he'd done more than a decade ago.

17

Brady had been awake for two weeks.

He was still in the hospital, but earlier today they had moved him to rehab, four miles away and closer to his fire station. Though he had some swelling in his brain, miraculously he had no permanent damage. So it was time for him to get serious about his recovery, his doctor told him. Brady was all for that.

He had a reason to live now.

Jenna was helping him get set up in his new room. Eric came by every few days, and the Fishers, too. Cards and balloons from his other firefighter friends lined the shelf in the corner of the small space. A window spanned the area adjacent to his bed, and a television hung on the opposite wall. The place was very much like a hospital room, except instead of heart monitors and IV stands there were exercise machines. Pulleys for stretching and pushing and teaching Brady how to move again.

Brady watched Jenna, the way she moved, the efficient way she had of putting his things in their proper place. Everything about her was familiar. Not because they'd spent so much time together, but because he had memorized every detail about the hours they had shared.

He would never forget them.

"You're supposed to be sleeping." She smiled over her shoulder at him. "The doctor said, remember?" For a moment she studied the room. Then she took the chair by his bed. "You'll need your strength."

I need you, he wanted to say. But he kept his thoughts to himself. He didn't want to scare her. He leaned back into the pillow. "I'm not tired."

She took hold of the arms of the chair and watched him. "The doctors forgot they were dealing with Superman."

"Exactly." He laughed and winced at the same time. Any movement of his chest still hurt. He began to cough and with the energy it used to take to finish a two-hour workout, he pushed himself higher up in the bed. When he'd caught his breath he used the button on the side of his bed to move to a sitting position. "Okay." He gasped. "Sorry." He steadied himself, refusing another wave of coughs. "Maybe not Superman."

A smile lifted the corners of her lips. A seriousness came over her. "You are to the people in that retirement home." She stood and came closer, poured him a fresh cup of water and handed it to him. "Eric says the whole place would've burned down if you hadn't held the hose on the middle for so long."

"I don't know." Brady closed his eyes for a long moment. He was more tired than he wanted to admit. Again he looked at her. "Better me than him."

"He said you'd say that." She angled her head, studying him. "You need anything?"

There were a hundred ways he could answer her. But he only smiled and shook his head. "I'm okay."

"You need more water."

"True." He swigged back half of it and then looked at her again. "Thank you, Jenna." Her name on his lips still was more than he could believe. "You don't have to stay."

"I'll leave soon. I'm in town because I pulled together photos of my parents for the memorial. Photos and a few personal items. I'd never done that before."

"Oh." He felt the slightest disappointment. She wasn't here for him, after all. "Glad you did. That's important."

"Right now, what's important is you." She leaned toward him, her eyes dark with worry. "We need to get you walking."

Brady stared at her. He couldn't talk. Couldn't do anything but look at her. Not because of his injuries, but because he felt like he was caught up in some beautiful dream. Her being beside him, the two of them so close like this . . . none of it made sense.

"You're really here?" He held out his hand. She looked the same as when she was seventeen, but more beautiful. She had a confidence that hadn't been there before. "I keep thinking I'm dreaming."

She slid her fingers between his. "I'm here, Brady."

He was still on medication for pain, and his mind wasn't fully clear. Details about the accident were gone, probably forever. The swelling in his brain meant that some days he still struggled to remember his address. But even if he were completely recovered it would be difficult to comprehend that a stranger named Ashley Baxter Blake had actually found Jenna.

And even harder still to believe was the fact that Jenna had come to him. That she had stayed these last few weeks. He'd had surgery on his legs and now both of them had been fitted with metal rods. His spine had been fused to help his back heal and he'd had a skin graft operation for his right calf.

But she was here. That was all that mattered.

His doctor had said there was no telling how well he'd walk or if he'd walk. Firefighting was almost certainly out of the question. Brady didn't believe a word of it.

Jenna had found him. Anything was possible.

"You're a miracle." She released his hand and took a step back, toward the door. "You look so much better than you did. Even a week ago."

He couldn't stop watching her, couldn't stop staring into her eyes. "You texted Ashley, right?" Sometimes he felt like he was repeating himself. But he tried not to let that bother him. This part was critical. Ashley needed to know. "You told her I'm okay?"

"I did." She leaned forward. There was no end to the concern in her eyes. "You want something?"

"The last eleven years back." He smiled and forced

himself to relax against the bed again. "But no food. Thanks." He checked the clock on the wall. "You leaving?"

"In a bit. I told Allison I'd make dinner." She hesitated. "I'll get a cup of coffee and come right back. At least for an hour or so." She moved closer to the door. "We still have a lot to catch up on."

"I like it." He watched her go. Their conversations had been in fits and starts. When they weren't being interrupted by a doctor or a therapist or a nurse drawing blood, he'd been sleeping. But every day he was a little more awake, more able to carry on a conversation.

Brady closed his eyes. No one had thought he'd live through the trauma. But here he was. Coughing every few minutes, still working to clear his lungs, still fighting to prove the doctors wrong. Now that he'd lived, they were worried about his future.

Not Brady. He was sure he'd beat the pneumonia and walk again. Convinced he'd fight fires once more and live the way he'd done before the accident. The only thing that worried him was losing Jenna.

He'd gotten the basics about her last eleven years. She'd finished college and moved to Columbus to teach. There she'd met and married some jerk named Dan who walked out on her. Brady clenched his jaw.

If only he'd found her years ago. He opened his eyes and stared out the window. Or if he'd run into Ashley Blake sooner. Outside the sky was cloudy. Rain hit the window and ran down toward the world below. How could any guy walk away from Jenna?

She returned with a coffee and sat in the chair near him. This time they talked about Jenna's school, the kids she taught and how much she loved it. "I'm connected. I have my friends and my church." She slid the chair closer to his bed. "My students. Life is good."

Brady listened, taking in every word. This wasn't the first time she'd talked about loving her life in Ohio. Her work and her church. Brady felt a piercing fear. The old Jenna had loved Oklahoma. She didn't believe in God and she hadn't had her heart broken by a guy. Was Jenna too different now? He didn't dare think about the possibility. Back then they'd had everything in common. Now he wasn't sure.

Best not to think about it. He could fall through the roof of a burning building and survive near death on a dozen different levels. But if all this was only leading to another terrible goodbye, Brady wasn't sure he could stand it. He took another sip of water. "Did you ever think about making a life here?" The question had come before, Brady was pretty sure. But he couldn't remember her answer. And he had to know.

"I didn't." Her reply came as quickly as the sadness that filled her eyes. "I couldn't . . . you know, drive by the memorial every day. Hear about the bombing every April." She shook her head. "I needed a life away from this."

He nodded. "I guess for me . . . it was too late for that. It already defined me. What happened that day." He paused. "It still does."

"I get that."

An older nurse came in then. "You need to sleep, Mr. Bradshaw. Your first rehab is in two hours."

"I'm not tired." He grinned at the woman.

She cast a wary look at Jenna and back at Brady. "I see that." Patience didn't seem to be her strong suit. "Either way, I need you to sleep."

Jenna took the hint. As soon as the woman was gone she stood and reached for Brady's hand once more. "Work hard this afternoon." She smiled, her eyes locked on his for a long few seconds. "I'll be here tomorrow."

"Okay." He savored the warmth of her touch. If only he could freeze time, hold on to this moment forever. "Thanks again. For being here."

She smiled at him. "I'm glad I found you."

He grinned. "You did actually talk to Ashley Blake, right? She's not an angel?"

Jenna laughed, and the sound filled the room like the most beautiful song. "Yes. I texted her. She and her husband are praying for you."

"Well, then." He was procrastinating; doing everything he could to keep Jenna beside him a minute longer. "You better go."

"I better." Her eyes sparkled. He had the feeling she didn't want to leave, either.

He sighed. "Bye, Jenna."

"Bye, Brady." She released his fingers, took her bag and headed for the door.

With everything in him, he wanted to get out of bed,

take her in his arms and ask if she felt the same way he did. He certainly hated seeing her go. But the nurse was right. Rest was the only way he'd be able to work hard enough to walk again. And he had to walk again.

So he could do the other thing he'd forever wanted to do.

Take Jenna Phillips on a date.

18

As May became June, Jenna could feel herself falling. Her summer in Oklahoma City was like something from a movie. The sound of Brady's voice, the way she felt when he watched her. Some afternoons she could barely breathe for the effect he had on her.

Her new life had taken on a different kind of routine. When she wasn't with Brady, she and Allison would share breakfast on the weekends and sometimes they'd work in Allison's garden or take a trip to the library. Other times they'd sit at the neighborhood pool and talk. But only when Brady was busy.

During the week Jenna would find a few minutes to talk to Ashley, catch her up on how Brady was doing. The two of them had gotten close. Jenna could tell they were going to be friends, just like she had believed that day when Ashley came to her school.

Just yesterday Ashley had asked about the future, whether Jenna saw any hope for her and Brady.

"That's tough." Jenna felt comfortable sharing this. Ashley seemed to understand the situation better than almost anyone. Even Brady. "We're very . . . different. Especially in our faith."

Deep conversations happened between Ashley and her nearly every morning.

Then, in the afternoon, Jenna would head to the rehab facility.

Brady worked hardest when she was there, Jenna was convinced. Each morning the therapist would teach him the day's routine, and when Jenna arrived she'd cheer on his practice. She'd go home for dinner and then return for another few hours with Brady.

Today Jenna parked in her familiar spot and headed into the facility. If things went right, this would be Brady's first day on his feet. They'd gotten him up several times already, but with a lift and only to keep his circulation going. This would be Brady's big test, the chance to see the full extent of his damage and just how far he had to go to walk again.

Jenna knew something was wrong as soon as she entered his room. He was sitting on the side of the bed, his shirt off, his muscled back to her. Sweat glistened on his arms and shoulders and his head hung in defeat. He sounded out of breath.

Should she leave or find his therapist? Maybe he didn't want her to see him right now. She stopped and was about to turn around when he must've heard her. He looked over his shoulder and the muscles in his jaw flexed. He shook his head. "Go, Jenna." His voice was tight, like he was speaking through clenched teeth. "I can't see you now."

"Okay." Jenna stepped out of the room and walked to the nurses' station. She waited until Brady's therapist, Kyrie, spotted her.

The woman was from Kenya, a strong, no-nonsense type. Today, though, her face was marked with compassion. She motioned for Jenna to follow her down the hall and when they were out of earshot, Kyrie turned to her. "It was a rough morning for your friend."

"I see that." Jenna felt her heart start to pound. "Did . . . did you get him on his feet?"

"I tried." Kyrie narrowed her eyes. "It didn't go well. The combination of pain and muscle atrophy. The rods in his thighs." She shook her head, clearly discouraged. "I have to be honest, Jenna. Some people never regain use of their legs after an injury like his."

Please, God, no. Jenna could feel the blood draining from her face. She turned and took a few steps in the direction of Brady's room and then back toward Kyrie. "Brady has to walk again." Tears welled in her eyes as she looked at the therapist.

"I feel the same way."

Jenna's head was spinning. Walking was all Brady talked about. That and how happy he was that she was here, that they'd found each other again. She managed to speak. "Is there a way . . . some sort of test to know? Whether he'll walk?"

"Not at this point." Kyrie sighed. "He has feeling. It's really a matter of whether he can tolerate the process."

Tolerate the process? Jenna wanted to laugh at the woman. Of course Brady could tolerate the process. He had fallen through a burning roof. He had lived his whole life in foster care with no one to love him. And he had waited for her eleven years without giving up.

Jenna forced herself to sound polite. "Ma'am. Brady can handle anything."

"Well then." Kyrie nodded toward his room. "Maybe he needs a little encouragement."

"From me?" Jenna thought about how he'd looked, how he had asked her to leave. "He sent me away."

"They all do at first." Kyrie stood a little straighter, more hopeful. "You say he can deal with anything. So go back in there and get him on his feet." She patted Jenna's arm. "I'll be right back to help."

A sick feeling came over her. In the weeks since she'd been in Oklahoma, she hadn't once seen Brady down. Never experienced a single moment of the utter defeat she saw in him today.

Jenna steadied herself and walked toward Brady's room. With every step she found a new level of determination. If he needed someone to push him, she was up for the task. She reached his room and walked inside. He was still sitting on the side of the bed facing the window, his shirt still off. But his breathing was more normal and he wasn't as sweaty.

Again he turned to her, his expression a mix of despair and frustration. "I said go, Jenna." He faced the window again. "I can't . . . I can't have you see me like this."

"Like what?" She set her bag down and walked to him. So she was right in front of him. "Kyrie says you need practice."

He lifted his face to her. Tears pooled in his eyes and his lip quivered. "Practice?" He laughed, but it was more of a cry. "Jenna, I can't put weight on my feet." He shrugged his bare shoulders. "My legs won't work."

"They will." Jenna was acting. All she wanted to do was run out of the room and let Kyrie take over. She was scared to death he might be right. But Brady needed her strength, not her fear. "Come on." She held out her hands. "I'll help you."

Jenna heard someone at the door. She looked up to see Kyrie. The woman had her hands on her hips. "You can do this, Brady. Use your thighs."

"My thighs?" He was shaking now. As if just the thought of standing again was more than his body could take. "I don't have thighs, Kyrie. I have metal rods. Remember?"

"Okay, so you're bionic." Her voice didn't hold a drop of compassion now.

Jenna understood. Brady needed tough love. Otherwise he wouldn't push himself to the next level. She still stood in front of him, arms stretched out toward him.

"You got the prettiest girl in physical therapy willing to help you." Kyrie clucked her tongue. "Use your metal rods, then. And push from your heels. But get that specimen of a body up." She raised her voice. "Now, Brady. Do it now."

Anger flickered in his eyes and Jenna watched it catch, watched it burn through his whole being. He gritted his teeth and took hold of both Jenna's hands. Then with an effort that took Jenna's breath, Brady pushed off his heels until his body began to rise from the bed.

"Good." Kyrie came a few steps closer. She nodded, emphatic. "That's it, Brady. You got this."

Once Jenna had watched a documentary on a woman who had gotten lost in the jungle and nearly died of malaria. That was how sick Brady looked now. Every inch of him was shaking and sweat streamed down his face.

"Breathe." Kyrie stayed back far enough to let Jenna do the assisting. "You gotta breathe, Brady."

A rush of air came through his clenched teeth, his face red from the exertion. When he was almost fully upright, he hit a wall and dropped back to the edge of the bed.

"There. See." Kyrie gave a firm nod. "Don't tell me you can't, Brady. You're one of Oklahoma City's finest." She had a fervor in her voice. "You most certainly can and you will." She turned to Jenna. "Next time don't let him fall back to the bed. I want him on his feet for three minutes. Then he can rest." She pointed at Jenna. "And don't you do the work. You're just there for support."

Clearly satisfied, Kyrie smiled at Brady. "Again, Mr. Bradshaw." She headed toward the door. "Come on. Again."

Kyrie left the room and Jenna stared at Brady. His sides were heaving, and he looked ready to pass out.

"Is she kidding?" Brady's eyes found hers. The anger was still there, but something else now.

Hope.

Jenna grabbed a towel from the shelf in the corner of the room. She could hardly wipe the sweat from his body. But he needed help. She handed him the towel. "Where's your shirt?"

"Drenched." He took the towel and ran it over one arm and then the other. His movements were slow and shaky. "I've never been so tired."

Jenna thought about what Kyrie wanted. She found her confidence and stood in front of him once more. "Let's try it again."

Brady ran the towel over his forehead and then tossed it on the bed. He searched Jenna's face. "You're serious?"

"Kyrie's serious." She forced a determined smile. "You ready?"

He laughed, his breathing still fast from the previous attempt. "Do I have a choice?"

"Apparently not." She held out her hands.

He gripped her forearms, and she could feel him trembling. "You sure you want to do this?"

She wanted nothing more. "That's why I'm here."

Brady positioned his feet, his heels and he clenched his jaw. His determination was like a physical force. Gradually, one inch at a time, he lifted off the bed until he was upright. Jenna's breath caught in her throat. "You're doing it . . . You're standing!"

As soon as she said the words, she felt his body give out. This time, though, instead of dropping to the bed he leaned into her. His chest pressed against her, his body hot and shaking. He hung his head, clearly embarrassed. "I'm sorry. You don't have to do this."

"It's okay. I want to help." A million thoughts fought for her attention. He was taller than she remembered and somehow he smelled amazing. Which didn't actually make sense. Maybe it was his shampoo or the lotion they used to keep his skin from chafing while he lay in bed.

Whatever it was, Jenna could barely focus. She could feel him breathing, feel his heartbeat against her body. He struggled with his balance, but he remained close to her. "How long?"

Jenna hadn't been keeping track. She swallowed, trying to find her own stability. "A minute. At least a minute."

Finally he looked down and stared into her eyes. But only for a second. Never mind the hardship he was working through or the fact that this was merely an exercise. The attraction was absolutely there for both of them.

Like all he wanted to do was kiss her. And all she wanted was for him to do it.

He steadied himself, easing back some so he was bearing his own weight. "Longest minute of my life."

And mine. She kept her thoughts to herself. She glanced at the wall clock and the second hand. "One more to go."

He looked at her again. His arms and body still shook, and he was sweaty all over. But he managed to find a smile. "I have a question."

"Go ahead." She braced herself so he could lean against her if he needed more support.

"So . . ." His eyes searched hers as he blinked a sweat drop from his lashes. A single laugh slipped from between his lips. "How am I supposed to think about standing . . . when all I want to do is kiss you."

She felt the heat in her cheeks even before he finished his sentence. "I was sort of thinking the same thing."

For the next ten seconds she was sure he was going to kiss her. But his strength was giving out. "Jenna . . ." He was breathing harder, the strain pushing him to the edge. "I have to believe . . . there will be a better time."

She laughed and lost her balance. He dropped back to the bed and she narrowly avoided falling on top of him. Instead she landed beside him. Despite his exhaustion they were both laughing now. Laughing so hard that they fell back onto the bed, side by side.

Kyrie walked in then. "The goal is to be standing." She gave them a stern look, but her tone told them she was teasing. "Let him rest for ten minutes."

"Yes, ma'am." Jenna scrambled to sit up. She wondered if Brady's heart was beating as hard as hers. Whatever was happening between them, she couldn't stop it.

"You're right about one thing, Kyrie." Brady was still lying on the bed. He grabbed the towel and wiped his arms and chest and face again. Then he shot a teasing look at the therapist. "She kept me on my feet longer than you did."

"I figured." Kyrie shook her head and left the room. "Ten minutes. That's it."

And so it continued. Every ten minutes for an hour, Jenna would act as support for Brady as he practiced standing. And every time he seemed to do all he could to keep from looking at her. They weren't going to kiss. Brady was right, of course. This wasn't the time.

But Jenna made a note to bring him a few new T-shirts tomorrow. She could only take so much.

• • •

AS JUNE PLAYED out Brady proved everyone wrong, even himself. Two weeks after checking into the rehab facility, with Jenna at his side, Brady took his first steps. After that there was no stopping him.

Kyrie explained it best. The body remembers. Once Brady started working the muscles in his legs, his memory took over. That, and the fact that Brady had been in top physical condition at the time of the accident, meant he would get stronger every day.

The third week of June, Brady was discharged. Jenna was there when it happened.

His doctor told him the good news. Brady's legs were strong, his lungs were fully functioning and the swelling in his brain had completely subsided. "You're healed, Brady. Someone must've been praying for you."

The doctor's mention of prayer was the only moment that day when Brady looked indifferent, irritated almost. Before they left, Kyrie scheduled outpatient therapy a few times a week. "It'll be a year before you feel like you did prior to the accident." She smiled at him. "Keep working, Brady. Every day." Then to Jenna, "You stay on him. He'll get there."

There was nothing but joy between them as Jenna pulled up the car and loaded his things. Brady made it to her passenger door without any problem. Fifteen minutes later, she walked with him into his apartment and suddenly his eyes lit up. "The letters!" He motioned to her. "I'll be back."

He returned with a manila envelope and then he nodded to the living room. "Sit with me." He took her hand and they sat side by side on his sofa. "I want you to read them."

Jenna took the envelope and opened it. Inside were the letters he'd written to her. One every year since they met. "I wish . . ." She looked at him, deep into his eyes. "I wish we could go back and live those years again."

"Me, too."

She read one of the letters while he watched her. The sound of their heartbeats filled the inches between them. "Thank you. For these." She stood. "I have to go, but I'll read them later."

"Okay." He looked relieved. "I'm just glad you finally have them."

They walked to the door and before she left he took her in his arms. This time he didn't need any help keeping his balance. He ran his thumb along her cheekbone and seemed to get lost in her eyes. "Jenna." His voice fell to a whisper. "Will you . . . go out with me tonight?"

She wanted to tell him yes, of course. Being out with him was something she'd dreamed about ever since that day in rehab, when they had almost kissed. She was about to respond when he moved closer.

"Before you answer . . ." He ran his hands down her arms. Jenna could smell the mint on his breath, feel the heat from his body. He framed her face with both hands. "I need to thank you. For helping me." He searched her eyes. "You're the reason I'm here."

Jenna had never felt more attracted to any guy in all her life. She grinned at him. "I loved it." This was intoxicating, standing here in his embrace. The way his strength had returned. Her voice was barely audible. "The first day on your feet was the best."

"What a mess I was." He chuckled under his breath and his eyes found a place in her heart that was his alone. He eased back some and his laughter faded. For a long time he only looked at her. Straight to her heart. "Even so . . . I'll remember it forever."

She felt her breathing pick up. "You told me we needed . . . a better time to kiss."

"Exactly." His voice fell to a whisper, his fingertips soft against her cheeks, a mix of strength and tenderness. "Like now."

And in slow motion the moment she'd longed for was happening. His lips found hers and the kiss was more wonderful than anything she could've imagined. Despite the time they'd spent together at the hospital and rehab center, Jenna was almost certain she was dreaming.

He drew back a few inches. His eyes told her he felt the same way. "I've dreamed of this as long as I can remember." He kissed her again, and she knew. She would be his forever. The kiss was everything they'd both thought about and hoped for. Not since she'd arrived in town.

But since they were seventeen.

19

The Baxter family's Fourth of July picnics at Lake Monroe were always epic and this year figured to be another memorable one. Everyone had set up their tables and blankets near the grassy shore, and now Ashley and Cole were trying to organize what had become their latest tradition. The one Ashley loved best.

A sand castle contest.

Each family was responsible for building a single sand creation. Their dad and Elaine would create one, too, so in all there would be six entries. Cole had come up with a voting system. It was a complicated but effective idea: each person could choose two sand castles, a first and a second place.

Every first-place vote was worth ten points, and a second-place vote was worth five. Also, you couldn't vote for your own sand castle.

Once Cole was done explaining the rules Luke yelled out, "There will be a test on this later, in case some of you weren't paying attention." He pointed to a few of the younger kids and then he chuckled. "No, really. You can help us grown-ups."

Everyone laughed and Cole set a timer. One hour to build the best sand castle. Dayne and Katy and their kids were there, too, and this year they'd brought a dozen different-shaped buckets and turret molds and shovels. Kari and Ryan provided each team with a box of decorative seashells.

When Devin saw the supplies he announced that the news should cover the competition live.

"It'll probably come to that at some point." Ashley's dad chuckled.

"Yeah." Brooke put her arm around Peter. "Then the Olympics."

"For now, though"—Cole looked at the families—"it's just us. Best sand castle competition ever."

The setting sun, in part, dictated the time limit. Landon leaned close to Ashley seconds before the starter went off. "This is us, baby. It's our year."

Ashley nodded. "I can feel it."

Cole gave the countdown. "Five . . . four . . . three . . . two . . . one!" He raised his fist. "Start your castles!"

Ashley loved her family, every wonderful crazy person in the mix. The groups dashed to the supply pile and found what they needed to start building. The way Ashley saw it, her family had the edge. They had the most kids and they had Cole. Who had been planning the Blake Family Castle Idea since May.

The idea was a secret, of course. But now that the time had come, there was no more hiding. They were about to build Aslan, the lion from Narnia. Cole huddled the family together. "I didn't know about the seashells." He couldn't have been more serious. "I think we just won."

"Why?" Devin's expression went blank.

"Because." The answer was clearly obvious to Cole.

Ashley looked from one boy to the other and Janessa did the same thing.

"Okay." Landon looked at the setting sun. "Tell us about the seashells! Time's a-ticking."

Cole lowered his voice. "We'll use them for the mane."

"That's it." Amy clapped her hands. "You're right. We just won!"

Ashley smiled to herself as they got busy. She was in charge of building a short castle-type wall around the spot where Aslan would sit. Landon and Janessa would dig the mote around the outside of the wall.

And Cole, Amy and Devin would work on the lion.

"Plus"—Cole was now working furiously, building a smooth platform for Aslan—"we have two artists in our family." He grinned. "Mom . . . and Amy."

Ashley caught the way his compliment hit Amy. The look on her face as she basked in her cousin's praise was priceless. Ashley shared a quick glance with Landon. He smiled.

He had seen Amy's reaction, too.

The whole family worked so hard and so fast that the hour flew by. As the minutes ticked down, Cole gave warnings. Finally time was up. They were all out of breath, talking and celebrating and covered in sand.

Ashley put her arms around Landon's waist as they surveyed their work. Landon chuckled. "It's actually pretty amazing."

"It is." Ashley grinned. Aslan looked very much like a lion, and sure enough, the seashells made his mane look beyond majestic.

"Of course"—Landon kissed the side of her head—"Cole's right. It isn't really fair that we have two artists on our team."

"True." She gave him a sheepish look.

Each team took a turn revealing what they had created. In the event it wasn't obvious—which for some was the case.

Luke and Reagan's family had made the White House. Though Tommy admitted that he got confused and tried to do the Lincoln Memorial halfway through.

"Our team was definitely a little unclear." Luke laughed. "But it looks good. Whatever it is."

Kari and Ryan and their kids had created an all-sand football stadium. "It's supposed to be Clear Creek High." Kari took a bow. "We think we nailed it."

The Kensington Palace replica was done by Brooke and Peter and their girls. "Because it's supposed to be a castle." Hayley clapped and high-fived her older sister. "Right, Maddie?"

"Yes, that's right." Maddie linked arms with her and waited.

Dayne and Katy's family had made a theater, complete with rows of seats—each topped with a seashell.

"Very nice." Cole nodded. "When it comes time to judge, don't forget the little touches." He winked at Landon. "The details all matter. Speaking of which . . ." He motioned to Ashley. "Mom . . . tell them about ours."

Ashley took a quick breath. "Ours is Aslan of Narnia."

"Are you serious? The eyes look like they're real." Brooke put her hands on her hips. "Ash, how can we compete with you?"

"The eyes weren't mine." Ashley beamed at her niece. "They were Amy's."

"Way to go, Amy." Tommy clapped for her.

"And don't forget the seashell mane." Cole stepped back so everyone could see it. "Papa, it's your turn."

Ashley turned to her dad and Elaine. They were down the beach a little bit, and Ashley and the others didn't see their creation right away. But now that they all walked closer, Ashley knew what it was before her dad said a word.

"It's the Baxter house." He put his arm around Elaine's shoulders. "The place where it all began. The house that will always be home."

"Talk about details." Ashley stared at the house. She stooped down and looked more closely. "Seashell shutters. That's brilliant."

Somehow her dad and Elaine had even managed to capture the front porch and the basketball hoop in the driveway.

For a long time, the adult kids stood around, staring

at the design. Tears filled Ashley's eyes and when she looked up from the sand house she saw she wasn't the only one.

"How can you look at that and not see a million memories?" Kari folded her arms. "Dad, Elaine . . . it's beautiful."

"It was his idea." Elaine smiled. "I thought it was a good one. Especially today."

Elaine was very deep and this was a perfect example. She might never have lived in the house, the one Ashley and Landon called home now. But Ashley's mother had lived there. And since she had started the Fourth of July picnic tradition, it was only right that her memory carry on.

Even in a sand castle.

"And instead of a moat it has a pond and a stream." Devin cheered, both arms in the air. "That's amazing, Papa! Way to go, both of you."

Cole gave Devin a look. "It's a competition." He lifted his hands and let them fall again. "Probably don't sway the votes to another team."

Everyone laughed and Cole handed out scoring sheets along with a quick refresher on the intricate voting system. The whole group walked around choosing a first and second place.

"No comparing notes," Cole directed. "This is serious stuff!" Even he chuckled at his words.

Ashley loved that he could poke fun at himself. He

came by his competitive nature honestly. But at least he knew when to back off. Ashley couldn't always say that for herself.

Voting was simple for Ashley. She wrote her name, made her picks and handed her sheet to Cole. She was also careful to take pictures of each of the sand creations. The only way any of them would remember exactly what they'd done here today.

Landon made his selection quickly, too. Same with Kari and Ryan. The four of them walked up the hill to the nearest picnic table while the others were still deciding.

Landon and Ryan sat on top of the table while Ashley and Kari used towels to brush the sand off their arms. Kari was still laughing. "We might just be the most fun family on earth."

"Absolutely." Ashley dropped her towel near a pile from earlier in the day. Then she sat on the bench and leaned back against Landon's legs.

Kari did the same, resting on Ryan's knees. Only then did she turn to Ashley. "So whatever happened with that guy you met at the memorial? Brady, right?"

Ashley had kept Landon up on the latest, but she and Kari hadn't talked about it since the day she found Jenna and learned Brady had been injured fighting a fire. Ashley looked over her shoulder and grinned up at Landon. "It's all good news, right?"

"It's a miracle." Landon shook his head. "I mean really. I have to admit, I thought maybe Ashley had gone off the deep end on this one." He sighed. "But wait till you hear."

"Yeah, I wondered, too." Ryan leaned forward. Both he and Kari were listening intently.

Near the water the rest of the family was finishing up their selections. Some of them were headed up the hill already. Ashley needed to make the story quick. "So you know how I went to Columbus and talked to Jenna in person?"

"Naturally." Kari nodded. "Like any sane person would do."

"Yes. Right." She laughed at herself. The whole story was pretty crazy. "Well, so, Brady was still in a coma and Jenna could hardly wait to go see him."

"She left work?" Ryan looked confused. "I thought she was a teacher."

"School was getting out the next week." Ashley's tone grew more excited. "So she moves to Oklahoma City for the summer because she knows someone who lives there."

"She moved?" Kari's eyes grew wide. "I can't believe it."

"Right, and then Jenna stays by Brady's bedside in the hospital until he's well enough to be transferred to a rehabilitation center." Ashley looked back at Landon and he pulled her gently up to sit next to him.

"Sounds familiar, right?" Landon looked at the others and back at Ashley. "I wouldn't have survived if you hadn't been sitting there all those days, Ash."

She felt sick at the memory. Landon had been fighting a house fire when he found a little boy, overcome by the smoke. Landon had saved the boy's life, but in the process nearly lost his own.

Ashley let the memory linger for a few seconds before she continued the story. She looked from Ryan to Kari. "So then he gets to rehab and it doesn't seem like he'll be able to walk again. Because his legs are a mess and his spine's fractured."

Ashley felt Landon shudder beside her. He took a deep breath. "Such a tough job, fighting fires."

"Absolutely." Ryan put his hands on Kari's shoulders. "You're all heroes."

"It's true." Ashley kissed Landon's cheek. "So get this . . . Brady learns to walk. But only because of Jenna. Because she won't let him give up." She finished the story with the news Jenna had shared with her this week. "And now they're dating!"

"They are?" Kari stood up. "I can't believe this."

"Not because of Jenna." Landon reached for Ashley's hand. "Because my wife won't take no for an answer."

Dayne and Katy had come up the hill. Katy looked pensive as she stood next to Dayne. "Sitting at a hospital bedside while someone you love fights for his life. A little close to home." She looked at her husband. "Right?"

"Definitely." Dayne looked at Ashley. His memory was there for all of them. The time Dayne's car had been run off the road by paparazzi. The day he almost died. Dayne drew a deep breath. "Anyway . . . back to you, Ash. Talking about that firefighter you're helping?"

Ashley smiled. "Yes." There were no secrets in a family like theirs.

Cole was running up the grassy embankment, and behind him the rest of the family followed. "The votes are in!" He jumped onto the center of a picnic table. "I'm about to go from sixth to first place."

"You mean last place?" Maddie was clearly teasing. "Come on, Cole. Someone has to be last."

"Besides, there's always next year." Ashley's dad raised his brow. "Losing is a part of life. Even when it's all in fun."

Everyone agreed.

"Okay, here goes!" Cole looked to the bottom of the sheet of paper. "In sixth place we have Uncle Luke and Aunt Reagan's family."

"Yay for the half White House, half Lincoln Memorial!" Tommy started giggling and in a few seconds he was doubled over laughing. "Still . . . sixth place isn't bad. And first place for originality!"

Ashley savored everything about the moment. Her family was hilarious. And yes, this was the best Fourth of July picnic yet.

As the laughter quieted, Cole found his announcer voice again. "And in fifth place, Uncle Ryan and Aunt Kari's family with the Clear Creek Football Stadium!"

A round of applause showed the appreciation. Landon leaned over to Ryan. "Don't tell the team."

Ryan grinned. "Don't worry!"

Jessie, their oldest, shrugged. She looped her arms around her brother and sister. "It was the best sandy football field on the lake. That's for sure!"

More laughter and then Cole revealed fourth place going to Dayne and Katy and their kids, and third place to his own family's creation. "Aslan of Narnia!"

Ashley was proud of Cole. He had dreamed about this contest for weeks and worked on figuring out a scoring system. She would've guessed they finished first by the enthusiastic way he ran up the hill with the results. But evidently he had taken the message to heart. This was about the family having fun.

Not about winning.

Besides—as her dad had said earlier—losing was part of life.

Second place went to Brooke and Peter's family, and the sand replica of Kensington Palace. Hayley jumped around and hugged Maddie, then her mother. She was one of the happiest people any of them knew. She might as well have won the Olympic medal for sand castle building.

"Which means, first place goes to . . ." Cole did a faux drumroll on his knees. "Papa and Grandma Elaine for the Baxter house."

Ashley smiled, her heart full. Was there ever any question?

A round of high fives and congratulations came from the others. Ashley watched her dad hug Elaine and kiss her. The two of them had married several years after Ashley's mother died. Elaine was a very special woman, for sure. In fact, not long ago for a school project Cole had met with Ashley's dad so he could tell the love story between him and Ashley's mom. Cole's Grandma Elizabeth. Elaine was not only supportive of the project, she encouraged it.

It was evident today that nothing about that project had harmed her dad and Elaine in the least. Ashley was glad. She loved seeing her dad so happy.

"Let's take a look once more at all the sand castles." Ashley's dad led the way down the grassy bank, Elaine at his side. "Before the sun goes down."

Just then a couple of ski boats sped by not far from the shore. They weren't doing anything dangerous, really. But Ashley watched as the boats kicked up a wake and then zipped off across the lake.

"The wild ones come out on the Fourth." Landon shaded his eyes from the setting sun.

Before anyone could say anything else, a series of waves reached the shore and washed up against the winning creation.

Cole ran toward it. "Wait!" He was a few feet away when the house, weak from the wave, melted into a pile of mushy sand.

For a few seconds all anyone could do was stare. Then Cole glanced back at his papa. "All that work . . ."

Ashley looked at her dad, but he was smiling, his eyes deep with nostalgia. "Isn't that just how it is, though? You build something here on earth thinking it'll last forever." He drew a slow breath. "When really it's the people who last. The souls of people. Their faith and their God. That's what endures."

"True." Ashley walked up to the collapsed house and took one of the seashells. She studied it for a few seconds. "All of that and something else." She smiled at her dad and held up the shell. "The memories."

Kari joined her and took a seashell from the pile, and then Ashley's other siblings did the same thing. Because whether it was a sand castle or Kensington Palace, their dad was right. Time would take the things they treasured here on earth.

Even, one day, the Baxter house.

Which was why, at the end of a day like this, Ashley was grateful. Not only that her family enjoyed celebrating the Fourth of July this way, but that each of them loved Jesus. Because one far-off day on the shores of heaven, the sand castle contest could involve the entire family.

Not just the ones here today.

20

This summer was easily the most beautiful of Brady's life, and yet he had the worst feeling. The sense that life with Jenna wasn't just beginning.

It was ending.

Brady tried not to think about it, tried not to read into some of her comments or expressions. She had read every letter he had ever written to her, and they'd talked about them. Each one seemed to draw the two of them closer.

In fact, their good times were better than Brady ever imagined they might be. But so far Jenna hadn't wanted to discuss what they were going to do next, after summer. Sometimes at night he'd lie awake remembering every wonderful thing that had happened since she'd walked back into his life, and then the fear would hit.

Summer was almost over.

School had a start date, first full week of August for teachers. When that day arrived, Jenna would be there. Not in Oklahoma City with him.

That much was certain.

Columbus was a thousand miles away. A thirteen-hour drive on a good day.

That wasn't all.

Lately she'd been mentioning her faith more often. It was becoming the religious elephant in the room. Eleven years ago they were the same, raised with their parents' faith but certain God had forgotten them. He had taken away the people they cared about most, and He hadn't answered any of their prayers since.

Back then they agreed on every point.

Now, though, Jenna spoke like someone who definitely believed in God. She talked about wanting to know God's will and several times she had referenced her certainty that God had great plans for His people.

Whatever that meant. Because how could God's great plans include what happened at the Murrah Building?

Brady gripped the wheel of his pickup. He was five minutes from the place where Jenna was staying. Today they were doing something new. Riding bikes together. Kyrie thought it would help his recovery to use his upper leg muscles. A bike ride through the park had been Jenna's idea.

When he didn't think about her increasing penchant for faith or the fact that summer was fading, Brady put his concerns out of his mind. Their chemistry was crazy amazing, and even though Jenna seemed careful not to spend time at his apartment, she clearly felt as much for him as he felt for her.

Brady pulled up in front of Allison's house and hurried out of his pickup. Not because he was late. Because it felt so good to be able to move. To order his legs to take a stretch of sidewalk at a fast clip—the way he had done all his life—and for his body to follow through.

He still hurt, still woke up each morning stiff and achy. Kyrie said that was to be expected. But the more he moved throughout the day, the better he felt. And every day he could move a little more.

Jenna opened the front door before he reached the top of the steps. "You're getting around so well." She shut the door behind her and joined him on the porch. "You're the hardest worker I know."

This was something else he'd noticed. She never invited him inside. They'd hung out every day for the past few weeks, and yet they'd been alone only a handful of times.

And almost never lately.

Brady let it go.

"I found the perfect park." Jenna moved to the edge of the porch. "Fifteen miles of paths and they rent bikes right near the parking lot."

"Sounds good." He took Jenna's hand as they walked back to his truck. If this summer was all they ever shared, if he had to live the rest of his life without knowing the sweet look in her eyes or the feel of her lips against his then he would at least have the memories of these weeks.

The feel of her fingers between his.

He opened the truck door for her and before she stepped inside, he pulled her into his arms. "Is Allison home?" His voice was softer than before. Full of a desire he could no longer avoid.

"She's not." The want in Jenna's eyes mirrored his own. But again she stopped short of inviting him in. "Brady . . . I can't . . ."

"Shhh." He put his finger to her lips, and then, like he was dying to do, he kissed her. "I missed you."

This time she kissed him and when she finally stepped back, her cheeks were red. "I missed you, too." But as soon as she said the words the look in her eyes changed.

There it is again, he thought. *What is it?* He walked to the driver's side and climbed in. Every move made him aware of his healing injuries. But nothing hurt more than her hesitancy or doubt. Whatever it was.

Forget it, Brady. He started the truck and pulled away from the curb. She was here. She was real and she was his. There was nothing to fear. He forced himself to relax.

The radio was on. Country music. Something by Thomas Rhett. He turned it down and glanced at her. "I used to pretend you were in the car behind me." He grinned. Anything to hold on to the good between them. "Did I ever tell you that?"

"No." She turned in her seat so she was facing him. "Like I was driving behind you?"

"Yeah." He looked straight ahead again. "I couldn't find you. So I let myself believe you were there." He raised his brow in her direction. "Does that freak you out?"

She laughed. "I mean, it's sad, but no." A quick pause. "Of course, if you actually *saw* me in the car behind you I'd have to wonder."

"It never got that bad." Not quite true, but Brady liked the easy banter too much to be too honest now. There were definitely times when he looked in his rear-view mirror and saw her. His imagination was that strong.

"I have to say, I never pretended you were in the car behind me." Jenna looked relaxed, happy.

"Never?" He mouthed the word in her direction. Then he feigned a knife through his heart. "Ouch." Another glance in her direction. "And the mall." He allowed a quiet laugh. "I pretended we were shopping in different stores. That we'd meet up for lunch, but then . . ." His laughter faded. "Lunch never came."

Jenna watched him, her expression tender again. "I never got to the place of seeing you where you weren't." She didn't look away. "Every time I remembered that day, I was sure there was a reason you never called. Like you had a girlfriend. Or maybe you'd just moved on like the rest of the club."

He nodded a few times. "The club." They were almost at the park. "I stopped looking for familiar faces after you didn't come back the next year. Since then . . ." His voice trailed off. "I guess I haven't thought much about the club."

They reached the park and Brady found a spot at the back of the lot. More walking. Better for his recovery.

He'd been worried about getting on a bike. Before the accident, his workouts were hours at a time. He could've biked up the side of a mountain. Thirty miles would be a cooldown.

But now, he wasn't sure he'd find his balance, or if his legs would move the way they were supposed to. Also it was hotter than it had been all month. Hot and humid. Some days Brady still felt his energy drop off, sometimes without warning.

Not that it mattered. He would get through this bike ride no matter what toll it took on him. Clouds gathered in the distance and Brady remembered that thunderstorms were forecast. Maybe they should cut the ride short.

Jenna looked up. "Glad we're starting now." She didn't say what she was probably thinking. That the worst thing would be for them to get caught in a storm. A slippery path could make even the simplest ride hazardous.

They rented bikes from a booth near the parking lot. Jenna climbed on hers first, and Brady stayed behind her. If he couldn't work the pedals he didn't want her to see him fall. He clenched his teeth, his determination fierce. His first attempt was a fail. He slid off the seat, his legs on either side of the frame.

Then in a single motion he tried again and he was on, his feet and legs working just as they should. Jenna looked back. "You've got it!"

There was a humiliation in realizing that anyone was celebrating the fact he could ride a bike. Especially Jenna.

But in this situation Brady didn't care. He might as well have won gold in the Olympics. He was riding a bike! Nearly three months ago he had almost died. And now he was pedaling through a city park with Jenna.

Life was good.

They rode four miles of path before taking a break. Jenna's idea. Brady had water bottles in his backpack and he grabbed one for each of them. She took a long sip. "How do you feel?"

He looked at her, searched her face and her eyes. "Perfect."

"Good." She drank more water, put the lid back on and handed him the bottle. She seemed to notice the storm moving closer on the horizon. "Maybe we should turn back."

"Another couple miles." He breathed in deep. "I've never felt so alive in all my life."

He wanted to kiss her again, take her in his arms and get back to the bike ride later. But today couldn't be about that. He wanted to know her heart, her thoughts. What she wanted for tomorrow and next month and ten years from now.

The conversation they both seemed to keep avoiding.

Brady led the way this time. His legs didn't hurt, and by the end of the next few miles he had forgotten about the rods in his thighs or the approaching storm or the fact that the summer was waning.

After a while, they reached a grove of flowering dogwoods and black walnut trees. They stopped their bikes and climbed off. Only then did Brady realize he was breathing too hard. *Exhale. Just exhale.*

"You okay?" Jenna walked her bicycle beside him and leaned on the seat. Her eyes clouded with worry. "We should go back."

"No. I'm . . . fine." *Another few out-breaths*. There. He felt the panic subside. He could fill his lungs with air again. "I'm a little rusty. That's all." He wanted to talk about something else. "I love trees. I always have."

"Me, too." Jenna lifted her eyes to the branches overhead. "Ever since that first time at the memorial."

"Yeah. Who knew so much heart and emotion could come from an elm."

"Mmmm. True." Jenna smiled at him. "I see the branches like arms, lifted to heaven. Praising God. Because the creation can't do anything else." Her eyes were flirty, her tone carefree. This wasn't one of those moments, where she almost seemed like she was testing him, his faith.

But the comment rubbed Brady like sandpaper. Did she really believe that? Trees had no choice but to praise God? He clenched his jaw. The idea was ridiculous. He looked at a grove of oaks up ahead. *Calm, Brady. Don't ruin the moment*. He forced himself to relax. "You know what I see when I look at a tree?"

"Tell me." She tilted her head back.

The wind in her hair was a vision that for a long moment left Brady speechless. He took a deep breath and tried to focus. "I see *The Swiss Family Robinson*. A mom and dad, a couple imaginative brothers. All of them shipwrecked together, making the most of it." He paused. "I saw that movie a dozen times when I was in middle school. I had the same foster family for three years. It was their favorite film."

"I remember it." Jenna looked up at the highest branches. "I loved how they survived together."

"Yes." He caught a few glimpses of her, face lifted toward the sky, understanding how he felt about something as simple as *The Swiss Family Robinson*. How did she do it? Whatever his heart felt, hers felt, too. Even now. More than a decade later. Still, there was a part she wasn't connecting with. "Don't you get it, Jenna?"

"Get what?" She looked at him.

"God didn't let our families survive together. So how could the trees be praising Him?"

She looked hurt by his remark, but before she could say anything the first clap of thunder hit.

"Come on." He took a few steps and climbed back on his bike. "Now we really do need to get back."

Lightning split the clouds as they turned around and set out. Ten minutes later the sky opened up and rain poured hard and intense around them. Brady had to yell to be heard over the sound of it. "There!" He pointed to a picnic shelter twenty yards ahead.

Wind whipped against them as they pedaled the last few feet to cover. They pulled their bikes under and rested them against the wall. Brady was breathing hard, the effort taking its toll. Jenna was out of breath, too.

Both of them were drenched.

Brady leaned against his bike and faced her. He laughed, but it was more out of desperation. His legs shook and he wondered if he might collapse. "I've . . . got nothing left." The storm raged outside, but they didn't have to yell now.

Worry changed Jenna's expression. She pointed to a picnic table. "You need to sit down."

She was right, but he couldn't move, couldn't take a step. "It's . . . okay."

The handlebars were pressing into his back, and suddenly Jenna seemed to notice. "Here . . . let me help." She moved the bike so he could rest against the wall.

His breaths were shallow and fast, his body struggling to get oxygen. *Relax . . . inhale.* She stepped back, watching him, clearly concerned. He followed his own orders and after a minute or so his breathing steadied.

"The wind's crazy." She looked suddenly afraid. "It's not a tornado, right?"

With his remaining energy, he pulled his phone from his pocket. His hands trembled as he checked his weather app. He clicked on the radar and saw the banner across the bottom. SEVERE THUNDERSTORM WARNING. He stared at the sky and put his phone away. The clouds were blacker than before. "No tornado. Not yet, anyway."

Lightning crackled on either side of the shelter. Thunder shook the ground and Jenna jumped. "That was close." Her teeth chattered, her hair wet against her face. "You think . . . we're okay here?"

His energy was coming back. Just enough for him to realize what was happening around him. She was scared. If she needed protecting, he was the guy. He found his footing and held out his hands. "Come here." He willed himself to find the strength to hold her. "I've got you, Jenna."

She slipped her arms around his waist. "I'm afraid."

"I know." He ran his hand along her back. "I'm here."

He could feel her heart beat, her breath against his neck. The storm was getting worse, fierce hail and pounding rain battering the roof and sides of the shelter. It felt like dusk, the clouds were so dark now. Before he could check the radar again, the alert on his phone buzzed. "Hold on." He took his phone from his pocket again and read the notification. "Tornado warning."

"Brady!" She was more panicked, more afraid. Her eyes locked onto his. "What do we do?"

"We'll be okay." He would keep her safe, whatever he had to do.

In the distance sirens began to sound, their haunting rhythmic cry filling the air, mixing with the whistling wind and hail. Brady still felt shaky. The weakness wanted to consume him, but he fought it. Jenna needed him. His eyes darted around the shelter.

At the same time the wind grew stronger, howling and almost drowning out the wailing sirens. Brady needed a plan. There were four picnic tables under the covering. The table in the back corner was probably the safest. "Come on." He took her hand and led her to that one. "Get under it."

They scrambled to the ground and he made sure she was under the table before he took refuge beside her. She was shaking, and Brady realized the temperature had dropped. Twenty, thirty degrees maybe. Classic tornado weather.

A sound like a barreling freight train came next. Brady had to yell to be heard. "Hold on to me!"

Jenna did as he asked. She grabbed his waist and held on like her life depended on it. For all Brady knew, it did. He wrapped his arms around her body and clung to her.

"Jesus, help us!" Jenna cried out the words.

And even there, hanging on to each other beneath a picnic table in the middle of what seemed like a tornado, Brady felt the name grate against his soul. *Jesus*? She was crying out to Him now? The flicker of a thought ran through his mind.

Why would Jesus help them? He hadn't helped their parents.

Stop, he told himself. *Focus*. The most important thing was protecting her. The shelter started to shake and suddenly sections of wood pulled away and disappeared.

Jenna buried her face in Brady's chest. She was still praying, at least it sounded that way. It was too loud to hear her. Brady put one hand over her head and the other tight against her back, holding her as close as he could.

Next it was the roof. The half by the entrance collapsed in a sudden ground-shaking crash. Their bikes were buried in the rubble.

Right where they had been standing.

Jenna had her eyes closed, her face still pressed against him. She didn't know yet what had almost happened. The storm roared overhead and then, gradually, the sound began to lessen. More thunder and lightning, but the tornado sirens stopped.

He breathed against her hair, holding her. That was close. Way too close. Adrenaline continued pumping through his arms and legs. "It's okay." His heart still raced. "It's over."

They climbed out from under the table and Jenna held on to him again. Only then did she see the collapsed roof and their bikes, somewhere under the debris. "If we hadn't . . ." She turned and eased her arms around his waist. "If you hadn't . . ."

She didn't have to finish her sentence. If they hadn't gotten under the table, they could've been killed. Brady had responded to storm scenes where people had died in lesser situations.

A ton of roofing and brick and wood collapsing over them? He shuddered. "I'm glad we moved when we did."

"It all happened so fast." She stepped back and held on to his forearms. "I mean, ten minutes ago we were riding our bikes and now . . ." Tears shone in her eyes. "Brady, we could be dead."

The storm was passing, leaving only the subsiding wind and rain and an occasional rumble of thunder. Never mind the broken pieces all around them, all Brady could see was her face. Her unforgettable green eyes.

"Jenna . . ." He eased his fingers along her cheeks and into her wet hair. His voice grew quiet. "I wasn't going to let anything happen to you." He allowed himself to get lost in her. "Not ever."

Like the tide against the shore, they came together. The attraction, the chemistry between them was stronger than the storm. Brady's kiss came in a rush of passion and intensity, more than before. Everything about it was like a dream. Before, Jenna had always seemed so careful when they kissed.

But here, now, there was none of that. Nothing could've stopped the moment. The kiss grew until it felt almost desperate. This was Jenna, in his arms. The one he'd looked for and longed for half his life.

Finally he drew back, his breathing fast. He released his hold on her and looked at the scene around them. Beyond the damaged shelter a few trees were down. Nothing like the destruction Brady had seen from other Oklahoma tornadoes. But bad, all the same. He reached for her again.

"We need to go." Fear returned to her eyes. "We need

dry clothes. And you're not supposed to be out this long."

Brady nodded. She looked so beautiful. All he wanted to do was live in this minute forever. He would've stayed here all week if it meant not letting go of Jenna. But she was right. His adrenaline had worn off and the tired feeling was back. They were both drenched as he took her hands, and that's when he noticed it. Something in her touch was different. Like her heart had pulled away in a matter of seconds.

Brady knew deep in his gut that the change had nothing to do with the storm or their soaking wet clothing.

He hugged her again, but it didn't last as long. He studied her eyes, her expression. There was no time like now. He tried to draw a deep breath and failed. It didn't matter. He had something to say. "Can we talk? Before we go?"

Jenna relaxed, and nodded. "Okay." The concern was definitely there. Concern or hesitation. Something. "We should."

He wanted to kiss her again. But he wanted answers more. "Something's different. With you . . . with us."

She didn't deny it. She only looked at him, straight to his soul.

"Why?" The thudding in his chest came harder, faster. His legs felt weak. "What's . . . going on?"

Jenna placed her hand against his cheek. "Summer's

almost over." She shrugged one shoulder. "I'm going home soon."

Panic wrapped its fingers around his throat. "Jenna . . . I spent years looking for you." He forced a single laugh. "You think my feelings are going to change because summer's over?"

She lowered her hand. This time she eased her fingers between his, but she focused on a spot on the floor. When she looked up, there were tears in her eyes again. "We . . . whatever we have . . ." She shook her head. "It isn't going to work."

He needed to sit down. "I'm . . . sorry, I . . ." His legs buckled and he dropped to the picnic bench.

"Brady!" She was instantly beside him.

He hated this. Hated his weakness. "I'm . . . okay."

"You're not." She put her arm around his shoulders. "We can talk about it later."

He couldn't let his body beat him. Not now. He gripped the edge of the bench. "I'm fine . . . we can talk—" Dizziness swept over him. He was wet and shivering. He closed his eyes and hung his head. "Jenna . . ."

"What can I do?" She sounded anxious again. "Should I call someone?"

"No." He was light-headed, trying to grasp what she was saying, why she was willing to let things fall apart just because school was starting. The thoughts chased each other around his mind, making the dizziness worse. He was so thirsty. More than ever in his life. "Water. Please."

He could feel her get up, hear her take a few steps. But then she stopped. "It's all buried. We have nothing."

Brady drew a few breaths. Deep as he could get them. What was he supposed to do? The last thing he wanted was a crew of paramedics running down the bike path, trying to rescue him. He was fine. He had to be fine.

He was still hanging his head, still trying to stop the rotating. An idea hit him. Something that couldn't hurt, given the situation. He tried to concentrate. Tried to stop the dizziness twisting his insides. *God, if Jenna is so sure about You, fine. If You're real, get me out of here. Give me the energy to get up. Make my head stop spinning. Then I'll know.*

"Brady?" She was still worried. "Can you hear me?" Jenna was sitting beside him again.

Thirst was still an issue, but he wanted to answer her. He blinked and his eyes opened. He blinked again.

The dizziness was gone.

He sat straight up and felt his heart skitter into a strange rhythm for a few seconds. What was this? How could the faintness be gone seconds after he asked God to prove Himself?

Coincidence.

Brady breathed deep and this time he felt his lungs fill with air. The way they were supposed to. His energy was returning, that was all. Random perfect timing.

He put the thought out of his head and turned to Jenna. "That was weird." He tried to smile. "It hit so hard."

"Like the storm." Her face showed how worried she was. "You okay?" She had her phone out. "I can call for help."

"No." Brady stood. His balance was almost perfect. "I'm not dizzy anymore." He looked at the sky. It was still stormy. "We should go." He reached for her hand and they made their way through one of the gaping holes in the side of the structure.

At the same time a park truck drove up. The driver saw Brady and Jenna and stopped. "Everyone okay?"

"Yes, sir." Brady felt well enough to walk on his own. As he made his way toward the pickup he noticed something. His shaking legs, his shallow breathing. The weakness and spinning. All of it was gone. Brady pointed to the collapsed shelter. "We rented bikes, but . . . they're buried." He looked at the driver. "Could you please give us a ride back?"

The man dropped them off at the parking lot, where the bike stand was also in a heap of rubble. Brady opened the door for Jenna, but he was too tired to help her into the truck. It took him nearly a minute to walk around the front of the rig and climb inside.

On the drive home, several times Jenna urged Brady to see the doctor.

"I'm okay, Jenna." It was the truth, at least physically. If she wanted to worry about anything, she should worry about his heart. About both their hearts.

After that they drove in silence. Not his choice. This wasn't how he wanted the day to finish. But she didn't seem to feel like talking. He wanted to hear more about what she was thinking, and why she thought this beautiful thing they'd found had to end.

As they pulled up to Allison's house, Brady didn't walk her to the door. Jenna seemed in a hurry, and she said something about needing to get out of her wet clothes.

Brady's desperation mixed with panic. This couldn't be the end. "Tomorrow?"

Jenna nodded. "Yes." She watched him for a long moment. "Ten o'clock?"

"Ten."

"Thank you." She hesitated before climbing out. "For saving my life today."

He tried to find a lighthearted smile. But it wasn't possible. "It's what I do."

She nodded, never breaking eye contact. Then she managed a little wave and mouthed her next words. "See you."

Brady wanted to scream. Why did they have to end the day now? Like this? She could've come to his apartment and they could've watched a movie or played backgammon. He wouldn't push things physically, if that's what she was worried about. They could've sat at the table and talked for all he cared. Anything but spend the evening alone when she was right here.

When it was still summer.

But she was already walking toward the house. He sighed, frustration taking jabs at him. "See you, Jenna."

She was too far away to hear his words. She waved once more before she went inside, and with no choice left, he drove home. He could feel her pulling away. Like some dream, destined to end too quickly, their time together was almost over.

Sure, she could tell him why tomorrow. They could work out the details and come to an understanding. But that wouldn't change the fact.

Jenna was leaving.

She was going back to Ohio and that would be that. When he was home, he stretched out on his bed and stared at the ceiling. That whole talking to God and his symptoms going away was nothing. Brady was strong. His body was fit. He would've gotten better with or without his challenge to God.

If God were real, this wouldn't be happening. He never would've allowed them to find each other, only to take Jenna away again.

Brady blinked back tears. Once Jenna was gone, he would fall back into his same routine. He could already see it: working and volunteering and trying to make his way past April 19, 1995, 9:02 A.M. But this time missing her and longing for her wouldn't last eleven years. Brady was sure.

It would last the rest of his life.

21

Jenna was grateful Allison had her Bible study that night. She couldn't have stayed up chatting, pretending everything was okay. Not when her heart was breaking. Allison would've seen through her façade and asked her about it.

And Jenna wouldn't have known what to say. She was still processing the answers herself.

But by the next morning when Brady picked her up she couldn't run from the truth anymore. She had the answers, and they weren't good. She wore the key necklace today, the one she'd had engraved years ago. The one she would give to Brady, no matter how much her heart was breaking.

If only he shared her faith. If only he had found his way back to Jesus. Every day Jenna had tried to gauge Brady's interest in God. She would talk about something being a blessing or she would refer to how the Lord was working in her life. Every mention of anything spiritual only irritated him. Confused him.

Jenna could tell. His eyes gave him away. Since yesterday's storm, Jenna had replayed over and over the promise she'd made to God. The promise she'd made to herself. Brady was nothing like Dan, but the fact remained: Brady was determined to spend his life far from the Lord. He had alluded to that just before the tornado.

Which meant one thing.

She had to keep her word. Even if walking away from Brady Bradshaw was the hardest thing she'd ever have to do.

From the moment Brady picked her up, his steps were sure, his face alive with energy. Not the broken guy from yesterday's storm experience, for sure. As she climbed into his truck, she ran her fingers over the engraved numbers on the key. She had no idea how he would take the news. She would have to tell him sometime today. Later. So they'd have at least a few good hours.

He smiled at her. "Hi."

"Hi." Her heart hurt. The subtle smell of his cologne mixed with the leather from the seats. She returned the smile, but the whole time she could feel the sadness coming.

If only he didn't take her breath away every time they were together. She stared at her hands for a moment. *God, change his mind about You. Please, get his attention.*

Before he pulled away from the curb, he glanced at her necklace. "I like that. A key." He seemed so much stronger today. "It's different."

"Thanks." She looked out her passenger window. *Dif-*

ferent. The word lodged in her soul. That was the problem now. As much as they had in common, when it came to what mattered most they were different.

Their plan today had been set since the beginning of the week. They had decided to go to the memorial. Brady wanted to see about getting a sapling from the Survivor Tree for Amy, Ashley's niece. And Jenna needed to see her parents' memorial boxes. The way they looked with the photos and items she'd brought from home.

Still, the whole day seemed like a last-ditch attempt to Jenna, on both their parts. Maybe if they spent a day at the place where they had met they would figure out a way past their differences, a way around the logistics.

And they'd never have to say goodbye.

Before they reached the memorial Brady stopped at the coffee shop, the one they'd visited together all those years earlier. On the way in, he put his hand ever so lightly at the small of her back. The feeling was electric. One thing was sure. No matter what happened after today, Jenna would never forget him.

Never love anyone the way she loved him.

Everything about being back in the café put Jenna's heart on high alert. She had to fight to keep from drowning in Brady's presence. The way his voice soothed her soul, the feel of his arm against hers as they waited for their drinks.

Since Brady had been well enough to get around he had teased Jenna that she was a coffee addict. "It's a teacher thing," she always told him. As for Brady, he had given up coffee his first year as a firefighter.

Now, though, when she ordered a caffe breve, he stepped up beside her, his eyes sparkling. "Make it two, please."

"Yes, sir. Two." The guy behind the counter entered the order.

Jenna looked at Brady, confused. "Two?"

"One for me." He elbowed her gently in the ribs. "I gotta broaden my horizons a little, right? Get out of my box."

Something in his tone made her laugh, and he started to laugh, too. And Jenna realized something. They hadn't done much of this recently. Between his injuries and rehab and the desperate feeling that they were running out of time, they hadn't laughed.

The exhilaration and joy that came with it felt wonderful.

When their coffees were ready Jenna put a cardboard sleeve on her cup and Brady did the same. He winked at her. "You're the expert."

"Definitely." She loved this, the way she felt around him. She couldn't help herself. That was the problem: this feeling, the way she fell into his gravity, could never be enough. She would keep her promise to God, no matter what.

Even if it meant losing him.

As they walked out of the coffee shop, Brady put his arm around her. The touch of his fingers against her shoulder sent chills down her. If she stayed another week, no matter what her convictions, Jenna was certain of one thing.

She'd never go home.

As soon as they were in the truck, Brady took his first sip of coffee and started to make a face. But then his eyebrows raised and his expression relaxed. "What in the . . . Are you kidding me? No wonder I gave it up."

"What?" She laughed. "You mean because it's so good, right?"

Another sip and Brady sank back in his seat. "This is amazing." He pointed at her, his eyes sparkling. "When I'm addicted a month from now, it'll be your fault."

"Guilty." With everything in her she wanted to stay here, hold on to the moment. Forget about the conversation that would come later. But even as she laughed again, she knew. There was no way to save what they had found.

They reached the memorial ten minutes later, and the place was nearly empty. As they walked onto the grounds, Brady stopped. He looked around and breathed deep. "I can't believe you're here. The two of us like it was that day."

The smell of jasmine filled the air, the summer sun warm on their skin. "I remember everything about it." She faced him. This couldn't go on. Jenna had to say something. "Brady . . . we need to talk."

He searched her eyes, and gradually his smile faded. A dozen thoughts seemed to flash in his expression. Was something wrong? How could she ruin a perfectly good day? Didn't she know how he felt about her? Without a single word, Jenna could see it all. But he said only "Sure."

They didn't have to talk about where they would go, which of the benches they would sit on. Without a word they started walking toward the Survivor Tree. They still had their coffees, but with his free hand, Brady took hers.

She didn't resist. There were only so many hours like this left.

They made their way up the stairs and sat on the bench closest to the tree. For a few minutes they stared at it, drinking their coffee. Lost to yesterday.

When they finished their drinks, Brady took both cups to a nearby trash can. With his every step, her every heartbeat, Jenna could feel the sorrow build. If only there were some other way.

Brady returned and sat facing her. He put his arm up along the back of the bench and watched her. He seemed in no hurry. "What's on your heart, Jenna?"

So much. She wanted to grab his hand and run as far away from here as she could, to a place where Brady's eyes could finally be opened to God. Or where she could break down and cry for a hundred days.

The last thing she wanted was to tell him the truth.

She didn't look away. First things first. "Brady . . ." She drew a shallow breath and pushed ahead. "I have to leave tomorrow morning. I found out last night. We have a mandatory teachers' meeting Monday."

His expression was something Jenna had seen before. When she was in high school some kid had walked up and sucker punched a boy. Jenna was right there, headed to lunch. She saw the whole thing. The approach, the swing. And the way the other kid looked after the hit.

Pale and shocked and in pain.

The way Brady seemed now. He fell forward a little and shook his head. His voice was quieter than before. Like he couldn't get enough air to fully speak. "No . . . warning?"

"I'm on call after the first of August." She exhaled, desperate for things to be different. "Today's the fourth, Brady. The only reason I didn't leave sooner . . . was you."

He stood and paced a few feet toward the tree and back again. "I thought school starts in September."

"Not in my district." Jenna felt her stomach tighten. If only that were all she had to tell him.

Brady took his seat again. "So that's what this is all about? The way you . . ." He glanced around, like the words might be swaying from the branches of the old elm. "I don't know, the way you've been different this week?"

She stared at him, into his eyes, willing him to understand. "That's not why."

This time he didn't say anything. He just waited, his eyes on hers. Didn't move. Didn't blink.

"Brady . . . every time I mention God, you get mad.

Things get tense." She wasn't finding the right words. "It's not like you don't let me talk about Him. But you just . . . you don't believe, do you?"

Shock and anger painted broad strokes across his expression. "I can't believe you're asking me." He shook his head. "You already know the answer, Jenna. It's practically all we talked about the day we met."

"Exactly. That was a long time ago, Brady. I've changed since then." Jenna didn't mean to raise her voice. But the memorial was still nearly empty. She needed him to understand how difficult this was for her. "I hoped you had, too." Tears clouded her vision. "I prayed you had."

Brady looked sick to his stomach. He released a sound that seemed part disbelief, part heartache. "You've gotta be kidding me." He stood and walked to the tree again. For a long time he stayed there, facing the trunk, his back to her. A couple times he seemed to grab a deep breath, probably struggling for control.

The ground could've opened up and swallowed her and she wouldn't have noticed. All she could feel was her world falling apart. Tears ran down her face. *God, why? Please, would You help us? How am I supposed to leave?*

With all her heart, Jenna wanted to go to him. But what would that do? She couldn't take him in her arms and kiss him, couldn't comfort him. The truth was there now, out in the open for both of them to see.

Goodbye wasn't far off.

Finally he returned to the bench. His eyes were red and damp. "Come on, Jenna." He held out his hand. "Let's go see your parents' memorial boxes."

She took his hand and all of her senses were fixed on that one feeling. The warmth of his fingers between hers. "Okay." It was time. This was why she'd come to Oklahoma City. She would see the project through, even as her heart was breaking.

They stood and walked into the museum, through the building and into the area with the individual glass memory boxes. The moment they entered the room, Jenna saw the one for her parents.

Brady stayed with her as she went up and put her hand over their names. Neither of them spoke. Not for a long time.

"Tell me." Brady's voice was soft, kind. "Why these things?"

Jenna fought the tears gathering in her eyes. She steadied herself. "The little Bible in the corner, that was my dad's. He kept it in the kitchen."

Brady listened, his eyes on the objects in the glass boxes.

"He had his own personal Bible." She managed a smile. "It's in the top drawer of my dresser. But that one"—she pointed to the small leather-bound book—"that was the one he'd pull out during dinner."

"While you ate?" Brady's tone was kind, his frustration with God seemingly on hold for now.

"Yes." She turned to him. "The Psalms tell about the

Word of God being like honey. My dad used to say a few minutes in the Bible was like dessert."

"Hmm." Brady's expression grew softer. "Must have been a good dad."

"He was." She looked at the box again. "That bookmark was my mom's. She loved to read. Her mother gave it to her when she was a little girl."

"Must've been hard to let it go." Sadness crept into Brady's tone. "For the memorial." He moved closer. The heat from his body warmed her.

She told him about the other items. The key chain and a dried flower her dad had given her mother the day Jenna was born. The pictures didn't need explaining. They showed the reality of Jenna's former life. Happy couple. Happy little girl.

All of life ahead of them.

There was one more piece, one more truth he had to hear. She looked deep into his eyes. "Every day without my parents I want to remember . . . that God alone lets me live in the healing. I'm a survivor because of Him. Because He has my parents safe in heaven and one day . . ." Her voice broke. She blinked back the new tears. *Let him hear this, please*. "One day I'll be with them again. And when that time comes, I want the people I love . . . to be there, too."

Quiet fell over the moment. She didn't want to move on from here. What could she say? There was no way around the goodbye ahead.

Brady broke the silence first. "My mom . . . she believed." He looked from the glass box to Jenna. His voice fell to barely a whisper. "Look where it got her."

Jenna understood. Without a different view of the heartache in the world, it was impossible to understand how a great and loving God could allow tragedy on earth. Scripture offered a chance to make sense of it all. But it was never easy. Even for her. She breathed in, thinking of a way to respond. "She's with Him now. She's having the happiest time, so happy we can't even imagine it."

He considered that for a long moment. Then he did a slight shrug. "I don't know, Jenna. I'm not sure."

"I am." Her answer was quick. "You know what your mother is doing right now?" She didn't wait for his response. "She's praying for you. That you'll see each other again one day."

Brady flexed his jaw. Whatever he was thinking, he didn't speak it.

They walked together to his mother's glass memory box. "To the moon and back." He put his hand over the top of the container and his gaze seemed to fall on the page with the childlike artwork. "I drew that for her just before she died."

Tears filled her eyes again. "I'm sorry, Brady." She paused. "For both of us." This would probably be the last time Jenna visited the memorial. She didn't like thinking of her parents here. She liked thinking of them in heaven.

With Brady's mom.

He released her fingers and turned to her. His eyes were full of love and hurt. "Why, Jenna?" He seemed to search for the place in her soul where the answers lived. "Why is it so important that I believe?" He put his hand on her cheek, his fingers in her hair. "I love you. Isn't that enough?"

She couldn't breathe, couldn't turn and run. Couldn't do anything to stop the way her heart was breaking. Brady Bradshaw actually loved her after all this time. The whole scene felt like something from a dream, except for one thing. This wasn't a beginning.

It was an ending.

And suddenly nothing could've kept them apart. She closed the distance between them and said the only words that mattered in this moment. "I love you, too, Brady." Tears spilled from her eyes. "I always will." She struggled to speak. "I always have."

"Then why?" His voice was broken, as if he was completely unable to make sense of what was happening.

She had no words. Not now. Not here. Brady leaned in and in a blur of the most wonderful, most gut-wrenching seconds, he kissed her. Here, in the exact spot where he had almost kissed her years ago. Like they'd come full circle.

Their tears mixed and the taste was salty on her lips.

Another kiss and then Jenna pulled back a few inches. "Brady . . . I can't." She stared at the ground and then at him. "Please . . . can we leave?"

His hand was still on the side of her face. But gradually his expression showed the beginning of defeat. He nodded, searching her eyes. "Okay."

They were headed toward the door, when Jenna saw the wall. The one with the time stamp engraved on it. Suddenly she didn't want to leave. Not yet. Not until she'd explained herself a little better. "Wait. I want to show you something."

"Jenna . . ." He stopped and crossed his arms. Like he couldn't stand to draw out this terrible goodbye for another minute.

"Please, Brady . . . it's important." She led the way outside to the survivor wall, the one she'd visited last time she was here. Even if he'd seen it a dozen times, she wanted him to see it again.

When they were standing in front of the cracked slab of concrete, she pointed to his name—engraved with the others who had lived through the bombing. "See."

Brady looked confused. "What? My name?" He shrugged. "So?"

"So . . ." She turned to him and searched his eyes. *Please, God, let him get this.* "You're a survivor, Brady. It says so right there in that piece of the building. God let you survive." She paused, letting the weight of this hit him. "And He did that for a reason."

She felt the key around her neck and in that instant she knew what she had to do. She looked around and spotted a bench nearby. "Can we sit here . . . for a minute?"

"Why?" He took a step back. "I mean, Jenna . . . what's the point?"

She felt terrible. All she wanted was for him to kiss her again. But there was no way back. She would do this one last thing for Brady, then she would say goodbye. Forever. Because of her love for God she'd found the superhuman strength to do something she wasn't sure she could ever do.

Push Brady away.

She found her voice. "After all we've been through . . . I can't leave without giving you something."

He stared at her for a minute, looking like he had just lost his best friend. "Okay."

This was hard for him. Hard for both of them.

His hesitation didn't last long. With a slight sigh of what seemed to be resignation, he reached for her hand once more. It was one thing to stop him from kissing her, but she wouldn't resist him taking her hand. When their fingers were together, their hearts were, too. That had been true from the beginning.

Jenna sat on the bench and Brady did the same. Their knees and shoulders were touching. She took a slow breath. "Do you remember what the time stamp on the wall stands for?"

"The 9:01?" He clearly knew the memorial grounds well. "There are two walls, Jenna."

"Not that one." If only she could fix the brokenness inside him. "We can't go back to 9:01. None of us can." She hesitated. "I'm talking about the other wall."

Brady nodded slowly and looked at the wall at the other end of the pool. "I know it." He sat a little straighter, almost as if he were squaring off with the wall. Like the two of them were enemies somehow.

After a long moment he shook his head. "I never got there. 9:03."

Give me the words, God, please. Help him hear me in his heart. She held her key necklace and looked from it to Brady. "You said you liked my necklace. Look at it."

A quick hesitation and then gently he took the key and stared at it. The realization hit him all at once. She could see it in his eyes. He nodded slowly and lifted his face to hers. "The minute healing began." He looked at the key again. "You live in 9:03. Life after the bombing."

"Yes." She blinked back her own tears. The story needed to be shared. "I had returned to God before I met Dan. I met him at church, so I thought he believed the way I did. The way my parents did." She caught a tear with her fingertips and tried to focus. "But in the months after we married, I found out he didn't. He only pretended to believe in God."

Brady was listening. His expression held a layer of sympathy that hadn't been there before.

The sun was hot overhead, but Jenna barely noticed. "Dan stopped going to church with me, stopped wanting to talk about the Bible." She could picture herself back then, married and alone. "I thought he might be having an affair with one of our neighbors. But before I could figure it out, he was gone." She blinked back another wave of tears. "I never heard from him again."

For a while Brady said nothing. "I'm sorry."

"It's okay." She sniffed and shook her head. "I've been over him for a long time. I'm at peace." This was the part she wanted him to understand. "But after he left, I made God a promise. I said I'd never fall in love with an unbeliever again. Never."

Brady's understanding was instant. He released her hand. "So that's it." He nodded and folded his hands. For a long moment he stared at the ground. Then he looked at her. "I get it." His hint of a smile didn't reach his eyes. "You made a promise to God. So I'm not the guy."

He looked off, but after a few seconds he turned to her again.

"Jenna, I would do anything to keep you here with me." He leaned closer, looking into the deepest places of her soul. "I would say anything." He hesitated. "But I will never lie to you." The hurt in his eyes intensified. "I don't believe. I can't."

His words were like so many bullets. But she ignored them. There was something she had to do.

The key was still between her thumb and forefinger, her eyes on his. "This is called a Giving Key. It's meant to be given away." She paused. "I bought it because I hoped . . . I prayed . . . that one day we'd find each other and . . . and you'd believe in God again." She wiped another tear.

He seemed to feel the news to his core. Any slight smile faded, and he clenched his jaw. "I'm not there, Jenna. I'm sorry."

Her tears came harder now. With her fingertips she dabbed beneath her eyes. "I understand." *Composure,*

Jenna. You can't break down. She drew a deep breath. "I see that now."

"And it's why you and I . . ." His eyes were damp. "Why this can't work."

"Yes." That was it. She'd said everything there was to say. "I'm sorry, Brady. I promised God for a reason." She hesitated. "It's a reason that still matters."

There was one more thing she needed to do. Jenna unclasped the key necklace and clutched it in her hand. "This is yours. I've wanted to give it to you for a long time." She held it out to him.

"I can't . . ." He shook his head. "It's yours."

"I'm there, Brady. Like you said, I live in 9:03." This time she took hold of his hand and gently placed the necklace in his palm. "It's yours now. And as long as I live I'll pray you get there someday."

He looked at the key for a long moment, at the time stamp at the center. Then he slipped it into his pocket, his movements slow as if he didn't want to damage the chain. His eyes found hers again. "Thank you." Brady stood. There was nothing more to share, nothing else to discuss. Despite the hurt in his eyes, he held out his hand one last time. "Come on. I'll take you back."

As they walked past the reflecting pool Jenna caught the image of the two of them. And in that instant she saw what Brady saw. Two people desperate. Holding hands so they wouldn't fall to the ground. Heartbroken.

Changed forever by the bombing.

• • •

WHEN THEY REACHED Allison's house, Brady came around to her side of the truck and helped her out. It seemed his physical strength had remained today, no matter how much the conversation had destroyed him.

Both of them.

This was it, the goodbye Jenna had known would happen. The one she had dreaded more than any in all her life. Brady closed the passenger door and leaned against the truck.

When he took hold of both her hands, she didn't resist. Instead she came closer, inches from him. "I hate this."

For a few seconds, determination flashed in his eyes. Like he might beg her to change her mind or let go of her promise to God. But the look was gone almost as soon as it came. "So that's it? You leave tomorrow . . . and don't look back?"

All she wanted was to be in his arms. *Something hopeful. Think of something hopeful.* "You know how to reach me."

"Why?" His eyes were dry now, marked by futility. "Jenna, you've made up your mind. You need to keep your promise." He released her hands and slid his into the pockets of his jeans. "This is it." He paused. "Right?"

Jenna stepped forward. "I don't want it to be." She felt herself melting, falling into him. The space between them closed and she put her arms around his neck. "I love you, Brady."

That was all it took. He placed his hands on either sides of her face, his fingers up in her hair, and like that his lips were on hers. The kiss was slow and unforgettable. A dizzy mix of longing and desperation and finality.

She could've stayed there forever, but one kiss became another and another. And a minute later, Jenna knew it was time. If she didn't step away from Brady Bradshaw now, she never would.

Her breathing was jagged, her lips still hungry for his, but she did the thing she could never have done in her strength. She pulled away and took hold of his hands. They were trembling, tears brimming in their eyes. "Goodbye, Brady."

"I love you. I always will." His voice said he was past asking why, past trying to figure out a way to make her stay. "Goodbye."

Jenna let go of his hands and moved back a few feet. "I love you, too." She hesitated. "If you change your mind . . . you know where to find me."

His eyes told her he understood. Not if he changed his mind about her. But if he changed his mind about God. "I can't, Jenna." His voice was barely a whisper. "God took the only people I've ever loved." He blinked back tears. "I can't believe in a God like that."

She looked at Brady for a long moment, memorizing him, certain that for everything they shared, this really was goodbye. Not just for a while.

But forever.

By the time she turned and headed up the steps into

Allison's house, she was crying hard. She closed the front door behind her, leaned against it and slid down to the floor, her sobs coming from a place so deep and raw, Jenna wasn't sure they'd ever stop.

She heard Brady start up his truck, heard him drive away. As he left, Jenna realized they hadn't gotten a sapling for Ashley's niece. It was another loss, though it paled in comparison to losing Brady.

Jenna wasn't sure how much time passed. Ten minutes or fifteen. Thirty. But suddenly while she was sitting on the floor, while sadness racked her body and made her wonder how she'd ever move on, she had an idea.

A crazy idea.

Her phone was in her pocket, and she pulled it out. Through bleary, tear-soaked eyes she began to write a text message. She explained the situation and asked for help. Any help at all. Then she sent it to the one person who might be able to do something, the person who would always want Brady and Jenna to find a way.

Ashley Baxter Blake.

22

Ashley got the text during the seventh inning of Devin's summer league baseball game. As she pulled her phone from her purse, she figured the message must be from Amy, who was playing with Janessa at the playground adjacent to the ball diamond. But it wasn't.

It was from Jenna Davis.

Landon was sitting beside her, cheering for Devin's friend, who was up to bat. Landon didn't seem to notice as Ashley shaded the phone screen to read it. The baseball game faded as the words came to life.

> I'm sorry to bother you, Ashley. I would've called but I can't stop crying, and I had to talk to you. I said goodbye to Brady a few minutes ago. Forever. Like I told you, we're too different. He doesn't believe. Which means I have to let him go. I knew you'd understand.

Ashley's heart immediately engaged. She hadn't heard from Jenna in a few days and she'd wondered how things were going. Clearly not well.

She kept reading.

This is the situation. What I never told you. A few years ago I promised God I wouldn't fall in love with someone who didn't believe in God. If I couldn't share my faith with the person I fell in love with, then I wouldn't fall in love.

Well, with Brady it's too late. I love him more than I've ever loved anyone. But he won't believe. He can't. He still blames God for what happened on April 19, more than twenty years ago.

I understand that, really. But that means we're too different. I can't consider having a relationship with him. All of which is destroying me. I'm devastated. We both are.

Tears stung the corners of Ashley's eyes. *Oh, no.* Brady didn't understand what he was walking away from, how complete his healing would be if only he'd turn his heart over to God. *Dear Lord, this is terrible.* Ashley found her place and finished reading the text.

I don't know, I just thought I would tell you. Could you please pray for Brady? Pray that something happens to get his attention, to show him about God. Pray that he'll change his mind and choose to believe. The way his mom believed before she died.

Otherwise, this summer has been beautiful. I couldn't help but fall in love with him. But I can't let things continue. Not unless he changes.

I guess I'm asking you to pray for a miracle. I know this isn't your problem, but I appreciate all you did to get us together, and I just thought . . . I knew . . . that you would pray. I'll call you soon. Thanks again. Jenna.

Ashley sighed as she lowered her phone. *Dear Lord, please speak to Brady. Let him hear Your voice. Give him a miracle, Father, please.* Ashley lifted her eyes to the action on the field.

Devin was walking up to bat.

"You got this, Devin . . . nice and easy!" Landon's tone was positive. Devin had struck out twice already this afternoon. But Landon's encouragement was endless. Another reason Ashley loved him so much.

With the count two and one, he connected with a fastball. Devin hit it over the shortstop into left field, right in the gap.

Ashley and Landon were both on their feet as Devin tore off toward first base. He beat the throw by a mile, prompting the entire fan section to clap and cheer. Ashley high-fived Landon and then sat down. "Yes! He needed that." She looked up. "Thank You, God."

As Landon sat, too, Ashley remembered the conversation they'd had this morning over breakfast. God probably doesn't care about hits and strikeouts. But He's absolutely concerned with His children.

When they finally got home, Ashley and Landon poured glasses of iced tea and went out onto the front porch. The sun was setting, and the summer breeze was cooler than before. The humidity less intense.

They had just leaned back in the porch swing when Ashley gasped. How could she forget? "Jenna's text!"

"What?" Landon glanced at her, clearly concerned. "Jenna who?"

"Jenna." Ashley sat up straighter. "The young teacher from Ohio."

Landon seemed to process that for a moment. Then it gradually hit him. "The firefighter's girl. From the Oklahoma City memorial?"

"Yes." Ashley smiled and put her hand on Landon's knee. "I love how you keep track of my craziness."

"I'm good at it." He grinned. "Okay, so what's this text?"

"I'll be right back." She handed her iced tea to Landon and ran into the house. Once she found her phone, she returned and took her spot beside Landon again. "Listen to this. It's from Jenna. About Brady."

"The firefighter." Landon looked slightly unsure. He set their glasses down on the table next to the swing.

"Yes. The firefighter." Ashley couldn't wait to read the text. She started at the beginning. "Okay, here's what she said: '*I'm sorry to bother you, Ashley. I would've called but I can't stop crying, and I had to talk to you . . .*' "

Landon put one knee up on the swing like he wanted to be completely focused as she read. When she finished, Ashley set her phone on the porch railing. Then she turned to Landon. "Isn't that terrible?"

"Yes." Her husband was serious now. "It's very sad. After they had such a great summer." He looked at her for a few seconds, his brow raised a little. "You're not going to Oklahoma tonight, are you?"

The hint of a smile tugged at her mouth. She leaned close and kissed his lips. "No, Landon . . . I'm not going to Oklahoma."

He was quiet for a minute. "I have an idea."

"Uh-oh." She felt the sparkle in her eyes. "Don't tell me *you're* going to Oklahoma."

"No." He smiled. "What if you text him? Tell him you've been praying for him." Landon leaned forward. "Just see where it goes. Maybe God will open a door so you can talk to him about faith."

Ashley felt her heart soar. "Why didn't I think of that?"

"Because"—Landon kissed her again—"we're a team."

"Yes." She ran her fingertips over his brow. "We are that. Your heart to mine, Landon Blake. You are the brush I paint with in life."

"And you"—he searched her eyes, the two of them lost in the moment—"are the colors in my painting." He leaned back and grinned.

"Let's pray for him. For a miracle."

"Yes."

Landon led the prayer, and it was beautiful. That God would change Brady's heart and that he would see that the God he'd been avoiding was the very same God who had brought Brady and Jenna together.

When Landon was done, they stayed there on the porch swing, quiet in the gentle breeze. And Ashley did just what Landon had suggested. She sent Brady a simple text:

> This is Ashley Blake. God keeps bringing you to mind. This probably seems a little out of left field. But I thought I'd let you know anyway.

She reviewed it and then read it to Landon.

"Perfect." Landon smiled. "That should start the conversation."

Ashley hit send and waited. It wasn't until later that night when she was curled up in the living room recliner reading Devin's book report that Brady texted back.

> Hi Ashley. I know you mean well, and I appreciate that. But please keep God out of this. He took my mother and does nothing to stop the tragedies and heartbreak in this world. You want me to believe in a God like that?

Ashley sat up a little straighter and read his message again. She could almost hear the anger and hurt in his voice, almost see the pain in his eyes. His questions weren't easy.

Lord, what am I supposed to tell him? How can I get him to understand that You're real and You care? She looked out the window at the dark night.

My daughter . . . remind him that in this world you will have trouble. But I have overcome the world.

The words ran through her soul as if God were sitting beside her in the living room. Ashley felt chills on her arms. *Lord, is that You?* The message was clear, and it was something Brady needed to hear. The world had trouble. It always would. But God had overcome the world.

That's what she needed to tell Brady.

She started to text, and then changed her mind. A real conversation was the only thing that could help at this point. She was sure. But even so she was afraid. What if he got mad or thought she was being too pushy? What if she made things worse? *Okay, Father . . . give me the words. Please.* She took a deep breath and placed the call.

Brady answered on the second ring. "Ashley."

"Hi." The two of them had never actually talked. "I thought it would be easier if I called. Jenna has kept in touch all summer. I feel like I know you."

He sighed. "I can't . . . Ashley, I'm not interested. I'm sorry."

Ashley held her breath. *Please, God* . . . "I want to answer your question. That's all."

"My question?"

"Yes." She exhaled. At least he was still on the phone. "You asked why you should believe. How you could believe in a God who allows pain and suffering." Her heart was pounding. "May I answer?"

Silence filled the line for a long moment. "I really don't want an answer." He drew a sharp breath. "All right. Go ahead. Maybe I should hear this."

Yes! She walked out onto the back porch and stood at the railing. The stars danced overhead. "Your mom believed in Jesus, right?"

"Yes." His answer was quick, frustrated. Barely patient enough to listen. "Right up until a terrorist took her life."

"Okay." Ashley gripped the wooden rail. "So if she was a Christian, she believed in the Bible. And she believed in Jesus."

"She did." Brady paused. "She loved the Bible." His voice softened a little. "At least from what I remember."

Ashley stared at the sky, but suddenly all she could see were the words to the Scripture. "In the book of John it says in this world you will have trouble. It's a promise." She let that sink in. "But then it says to take heart . . . Because the Lord has overcome the world."

He didn't say anything for a few beats. He paused. "Take heart? So, we're supposed to chock it up to earth. These things happen?" His tone was gentler. But the hurt remained.

"It's *just* earth. I think that's the point." Ashley didn't want to talk longer than he was willing to listen. She tried not to be wordy. "See, all of us deserve."

"Ashley . . ." He sounded tired. "I know this."

"Okay." She leaned against the rail, her eyes still on the sky. "I guess all I'm saying is that this isn't the end. Every one of us will die." She was careful not to rush her words. Not to sound forceful. "Jesus offers us a life rope out of this place. Because as great as it is . . . it's not heaven."

Another pause. "Thank you, Ashley. Really." He was only putting up with her. She could tell. "I gotta go."

One more thing. That's all she wanted to tell him. "You can see your mother again. If you believe Jesus died for your sins, if you accept that gift, you will join her in heaven." She hesitated. "Just think about that. And know this, Brady. I'm praying for you. That God will show you somehow."

Silence.

Ashley looked at the phone, to be sure he was still on the call. "Brady?"

"You think . . ." His voice was more emotional. "You think she's in heaven? You believe that?"

"Absolutely." Ashley felt a ripple of hope. Finally, he was hearing her.

Brady was quiet again. When he spoke, his words were softer. "I need to go, but thanks." He hesitated. "Really."

She offered to talk to him again, if he needed anything. He seemed genuinely grateful, and then the call was over. Ashley stared at the phone. The whole conversation had lasted just under eight minutes.

Was it enough to make a difference?

Ashley wasn't sure. But there was one thing she could do, whether he called her again or not.

She could pray.

• • •

BRADY DIDN'T WORK that Sunday. He had planned to go to the river with a few buddies from the station. But ever since the call from Ashley, all he could do was think about what she'd said.

The only way to see his mom again was to believe. Believe in the very God who had taken her from him. His thoughts battled and fought for position in his aching heart until all he could do was deal with them.

And there was only one place he could do that.

He arrived at the memorial an hour after it opened. This time it was more crowded, not that it mattered. Brady didn't see the people around him, didn't hear their voices. Sunglasses on, he walked to the bench where he and Jenna had sat two days earlier. The place where she had told him why she couldn't stay. Why it wouldn't work between them.

Brady sat, and for the longest time, he only stared at the wall and the time stamp six feet high, engraved at the top.

9:03.

Jenna had found her way there, found a way to believe in God and move forward in her healing. She was a true survivor. No doubt. Ashley's words came back to him. If he believed, he would see his mother again. In heaven.

He was contemplating it all when a tall blond guy walked up and sat on the other side of the bench. "Serene, isn't it?"

Brady was confused. Had he looked like he wanted company? He nodded. "Definitely."

The guy held out his hand. "I'm Jag. Good to see you again."

"Brady." The sun was bright on their faces, so Brady kept his sunglasses on. The stranger wore none. Even so, the sun didn't seem to bother him. He wasn't even squinting. "Have . . . we met?"

"A long time ago." Jag smiled. "You were five. And one other time not too long ago."

"Okay." He had no memory of the man. But something about him was familiar. Brady could see that now. Was he part of the club? "Why are you here?"

Jag stared at the wall across from the reflecting pool. "Do you know the motto of the memorial?"

"The motto?" Brady sat up straighter. Who was this guy?

"Yes." Jag turned to him again. "Come to remember. Leave with resolve."

Brady hadn't heard that. "I thought I knew everything about this place."

"It's on their website." Jag hesitated, his eyes locked on Brady's, like the guy could see straight through his sunglasses. "You've spent a lot of time here. Remembering."

How did the guy know? Despite the summer sun, a shiver ran down Brady's spine. "How . . . ?"

"You lost your mother here. I know that." Jag put his hand on Brady's shoulder. "A lot of people lost much on these grounds." His look grew more intense, and at the same time, more peaceful. "Leave with resolve, Brady. Resolve to move on. Resolve to make this world a better place." He paused. "Resolve to believe. You know why?"

"Why?" Nothing about the conversation made sense. How did Jag know him? And how could he know about Brady's beliefs?

"Because . . . God loves you. More than you know." Jag stood.

"How do you . . . ?" Brady's voice trailed off. He had a dozen questions, but before he could ask a single one, Jag shook his hand again. "By the way, there are a few saplings at the main office."

"At the office?" Brady's head was spinning. The man knew about the saplings?

"You were looking for one, right?" Jag smiled.

"Yes. For a little girl. But there weren't any left until . . ."

Jag took a step back and pointed to the museum. "I found two. They're holding them."

"I . . . that's amazing." Nothing about this made sense. Brady felt tears in his eyes. "Thank you."

"I gotta go." Jag stepped away. "See you around, Brady. Leave with resolve." With that, the man turned and walked off toward the museum.

"See ya . . ." Brady's words became a whisper.

Brady stared at the time stamp on the wall. What in the world had just happened? How had the stranger known him when he was little? The guy couldn't have been more than ten years older. And what about the two saplings?

Brady turned to look at Jag again. The guy should've been twenty, thirty yards ahead on the sidewalk. But he wasn't.

The path was empty.

Another shiver ran through him. Where had the guy gone? Nothing about the last few minutes made sense. Brady blinked a few times. *Could the guy be an angel?* He let that thought sit for a few seconds. No. That wasn't possible.

For the next hour Brady stayed there, sitting on the bench, thinking about Jag and his words. Leave with resolve . . . Resolve to believe. Whoever the guy was, his message came at the exact right time.

Suddenly the words from Jenna and Ashley ran through his mind.

Words from the Bible.

In this world he would have trouble. That was true, right? That was the whole problem, the trouble in the world. The way evil seemed to win far too often and pain seemed ignored by God.

If there was a God.

But what if there was? What if He really was the way Ashley had described Him? Brady felt the warmth of the sun to the center of his being.

Or maybe that was the conviction spreading from his heart to his soul.

Could they be right? Jenna and Ashley? Was it possible that God loved the world so much that he sent Jesus? Not to protect people from the pain of earth, but to save them from it? Not as the reason for the bad things in the world.

But as the rescue.

Brady pictured his mother, the hazy memory he still carried with him. Yes, her body had been destroyed by the bomb. But because of her faith, Jesus had rescued her. Lifted her right out of the rubble and into His kingdom.

Life to life.

Suddenly, Brady understood what Jag had told him. This was his place to remember. More times than he could count, he had come here to honor his mother, to recall her talking to him. *I love you to the moon and back, Brady. To the moon and back.* Yes, he had come here to remember.

Now it was time to leave with resolve.

Like Jag said.

Brady took a deep breath and felt an urgency rise within him. He had to exit this place, had to get out of the memorial. With a final look at the time stamp he hurried to the office. There they were. Two saplings from the Survivor Tree. Just like Jag had said. He carried them to his truck and set off through the city. He knew exactly where he had to go, what he had to do.

Minutes later he was knocking on the door of Cheryl and Rodney Fisher.

Cheryl opened the door. Her eyes lit up. "Brady!

Why . . . what are you doing here? You look all healed up." She stepped back. "Come in. Rodney's in the other room."

Brady was breathing hard, his heart and head pounding. He remembered a detail from the last time he was here. How Rodney had prayed that something would happen. Something that could only be from God. Like Jag, whoever he was, suddenly appearing.

Like Jenna.

He steadied himself.

"Mrs. Fisher . . . I want to talk. About God."

"Hallelujah." She whispered the word. Her smile was as warm as the summer sun. "I knew you'd ask one day."

He stepped inside and like that his tears came. Quietly, without fanfare. They spilled from his eyes down the sides of his cheeks. "I . . . I have so many questions."

Cheryl took him in her arms. "You came to the right place, Brady." Then she looked straight at him. "Rodney and I . . . we have answers."

Brady nodded and found his composure. He felt a peace and acceptance he hadn't felt since Jenna left. And for the first time something told him the feeling wasn't from the Fishers.

But just maybe from God, Himself.

• • •

ANSWERS WEREN'T ENOUGH.

That week fighting fires and responding to accident calls, Brady thought about the things he'd heard recently.

First from Ashley, then from the Fishers. God was the rescue in hard times, not the reason for them. Jesus loved Brady enough to die for him. On and on it went. The people he loved had answered every question Brady asked, except the one that bothered him still.

Why?

Why did God take his mother when he was so little? Why did He do that to Jenna? And so, though Rodney and Cheryl had done their best to help Brady believe, he had walked away from their house that day unconvinced.

He couldn't get past the idea that God could've stopped the tragedy, prevented the bombing altogether. A quick zap from heaven and the terrorist never would've made it to the Murrah Building.

No fertilizer bomb. No explosion. No devastating destruction.

Brady and Jenna would still have the people they loved. Same with countless others changed by that April day. Confusion about his questions consumed Brady's every waking hour.

But they didn't work their way into his bedroom until one stormy night later that week. Brady couldn't fall asleep. His legs and head ached—something that had been happening less and less frequently. Every ten minutes he had to find a different position—his right side, his left. On his back with one arm over his head.

Whatever he tried he couldn't get comfortable.

He couldn't remember actually falling asleep, but in

a blurry instant Brady was in the burning warehouse again. The one where he nearly died. Blazing fire exploded all around him and he was pinned beneath the rubble. Suffocating. Dying.

Help me! he cried out, but no one could hear him. What was happening to him? Why was he reliving the ordeal all over again? The heat grew more intense and Brady could see the skin on his hands start to bubble.

Help me, someone!

And then suddenly he could see his mother calling to him. Pretty and kind with the most loving eyes. And she was yelling for him, crying out for him.

"Brady! Come home!" She held out her hand, but it didn't reach him in the fiery debris. "Please, Brady . . . I'm waiting for you! Come home!"

"Mom . . . I can't move!" Brady screamed the words. "Send someone! I'm dying."

He couldn't breathe, couldn't keep his eyes open much longer in the searing heat. And his mother's hand was right there, right in front of him, but he couldn't grab it. Like it was more apparition than reality. Still he could see her, hear her. Even above the roaring fire.

Come home, Brady! Please, come home!

One last time, Brady tried. With everything in him he shouted at her. "Send someone to help me!"

And the moment the words left his mouth a man appeared. Tall and strong, he tossed aside burning pieces of roof and red-hot metal beams like they were made of paper. One after another, the man moved scorching sections of building away from Brady. He could see the man now. Surreal blue eyes. Blond hair. Even in the midst of the terrible fire Brady knew who it was.

Jag.

The stranger at the memorial.

"It's time to come home, Brady." Jag took his hand and helped him to his feet, and at the same time the heat and fire and flaming debris around them disappeared. Brady's skin was normal and he could breathe again.

Jag's eyes pierced his own. "Your mother is waiting for you. Your Father, too."

With a shattering gasp, Brady opened his eyes and sat straight up, tangled in his bedsheets. His shorts and T-shirt were drenched with sweat, his lungs heaving. "What in the . . ."

He jumped out of bed, eyes wide, and looked around. No fire, no broken building parts pinning him to the ground. His breaths came in rapid succession. He was in his bedroom, whole and alive and exhausted.

But unlike any other dream Brady had ever experienced, this one had been real. He could remember every detail. Smell them. Feel them. And then—in a slow and steady rush—a strange reality dawned on him.

Jag—whoever he was—had rescued him from the warehouse fire.

There was no other way Brady would've escaped from the collapsed building that day. No one in the department knew how he'd made it out alive. And not only that but maybe Jag had rescued him from the Murrah Building. Wasn't that what he'd said the other day at the memorial? That he'd seen him when Brady was five?

A shiver ran down his arms. And now that same Jag had been part of his dream. The man's words echoed again. *It's time to come home, Brady . . . Time to come home.*

He could see his mother crying out to him, begging him to join her.

Brady's heart pounded against the wall of his chest. What did it mean? What was the message? Was Jag a person or was he . . . could he really be an angel? His mind flashed back to their conversation at the memorial.

Brady had no way of knowing for sure. But Jag's message was unmistakable. There was a reason Jag had freed him, a reason his mother had appeared to him in the dream.

And slowly, like all of his life had led to this moment, Brady dropped to his knees. His legs and arms shook and his heart raced within him. He grabbed the edge of his bed and pressed his forehead into the mattress.

All of it was real. The rescue at the warehouse, the dream, and the cry from Jag and his mother. It was time for Brady to come home. Time for him to stop fighting against the God who was clearly pursuing him.

"I'm sorry, Lord." Brady whispered the words into the fitted sheet. "I'm so sorry."

With everything in him he could feel himself changing.

The dream had changed everything, and with his entire being Brady suddenly believed in the truth that his mother was safe in heaven and that he would see her again. And in the reality that Jag had been sent to rescue him. He believed in the obvious fact that Jenna had come back into his life for a reason, and he believed in something else, something he had never expected to believe in again.

Brady Bradshaw believed in God.

23

Rain was forecast that August morning, so Ashley had moved her painting of the Survivor Tree into the kitchen. She was nearly finished. Amy knew, now, that the painting was for her.

Ashley could hardly wait to hang it in her niece's room.

She stood in front of her easel. It had been nearly a week since her call to Brady. If he'd found God, she knew nothing of it. A few days ago she'd received a random text from Brady asking for Ashley's address. She figured maybe he was going to send her a card or a letter. She had texted back that she was still praying for him, and he had thanked her. That was it.

Jenna hadn't reached out again, either.

The paint on the end of her brush was more brown than green. She dipped the bristles in the palette. Today she was highlighting the trunk of the great elm. Bringing it to life, she liked to say. This part of painting required her greatest skill, her most careful hand. She was focusing on a specific area when the doorbell rang.

She set down her brush and frowned. If someone had

come up the drive, she hadn't heard the car. It was too early for the kids or Landon to be home. And her father and Elaine were out of town for a few days. Maybe it was one of her sisters.

She padded across the wood floor to the front door and opened it. For a few seconds she didn't quite understand what she was looking at. Who she was looking at. But then her mind began to right itself.

The man standing on her porch was Brady Bradshaw. He had to be, right?

He was dressed much the way he'd been that day at the memorial. Dark jeans, sweatshirt. In his hands was something Ashley couldn't believe. She lifted her eyes to his. "Brady?"

"Yes." His expression was humble, his face kind. "It's me."

"Is that . . ." Ashley looked at his hands again. He was holding a sapling, a small baby tree with its roots covered in a paper bag.

"It is." Brady smiled. "It's from the Survivor Tree." He handed the bundle to Ashley. "You asked about getting one for your niece."

She took the tree and stared at it. This was the only thing Amy had wanted for the better part of a year. Ashley couldn't move, couldn't do anything but gaze at the little sapling. "I . . . I can't believe it." She stepped back and ushered Brady inside. "Please . . . come in."

"I need to go." Again his tone and expression were gentle. The frustration from the other night completely gone. "I have to make it to Ohio before school gets out."

Ashley searched his face. Had he really said that? Did he mean . . . ? "You're going to see Jenna?"

"Absolutely." Brady reached out and shook Ashley's free hand. "Thank you. For calling me." A single laugh and he raised his brow. "That couldn't have been easy."

"It wasn't." Ashley still didn't believe this was happening. "What are you saying, Brady? You believe?"

Brady's smile filled his face. "Let's just say God got my attention. I've been praying about seeing Jenna ever since I left home."

Joy came over Ashley all at once. She set the sapling on the floor and hugged Brady. Then she stepped back and squealed. "Are you serious? Brady . . . this is amazing."

He couldn't stop grinning. "I can't say I have it all figured out. But I believe." For the next few minutes he told her about an older couple, the Fishers, and how he had gone to their house the day after Ashley called. And then he told her about his dream.

Ashley could hardly wait to hear more of the story. "So these people . . . the Fishers . . . they're Christians?"

"Definitely." Brady raised his brow. "They've been waiting for me to ask them about God for years."

The feelings in Ashley's heart were more than she could comprehend. She listened while Brady told her about how the Fishers had opened the Bible and looked at a dozen different verses from John and Romans and James. "And then, my dream . . ."

He seemed overcome by a rush of emotion. He shook his head. "There's more to it. I don't know. After that, I could see. Clearly." The corners of his lips lifted again. "For the first time since I was that five-year-old little boy waking up in the hospital."

Ashley thought about her painting. If anyone would want to see it, Brady would. "Let me show you something. In the next room."

The two of them walked into the kitchen and Ashley pointed him to the painting. His eyes softened and he nodded slowly. "It's perfect. Beautiful." He looked at her. "You must've been really affected by the memorial."

"Because of my niece. The one I sent you the message about." Ashley stared at the image. It was almost finished. "Amy, my niece, she lives with us."

The situation seemed to make sense to Brady now. "She lives here?"

Ashley told him about Amy, how her family had been killed in a car accident, and how she was determined to live a life that made them proud. And that was the reason she wanted a sapling from the memorial.

Again Brady stared at the painting. "No wonder she loves the old tree."

"Exactly. Amy . . . she draws strength from her faith every day."

Each word seemed to land deeply on Brady. "What a wonderful truth." He pulled his phone from his pocket and looked at the time. "I need to get on the road."

Ashley led him back to the foyer and Brady motioned to the sapling. "Tell Amy to take good care of the tree." His smile faded a little. "And tell her I'm proud of her. For being a survivor."

"I'll tell her." Ashley was touched that he would go out of his way to come here.

For a few seconds, Brady hesitated. "Can I ask you for something?"

"Of course."

"Follow me." He stepped outside.

The air was warm, but clouds gathered in the distance. All of Bloomington embracing another summer day. She walked beside him to his truck, and saw it before he said anything. There in the bed of the truck.

Another sapling.

"You got one, too." Ashley looked at Brady as he opened his door. Was he taking the little tree to Ohio? A possibility dawned in her heart and worked its way to a hesitant smile. "You're taking it to Jenna?"

His eyes lit up with what looked like hope. "Just pray for us. For a second chance."

Ashley nodded. "I will. Absolutely."

Brady hugged her again and then he slid behind the wheel and closed the door. Ashley watched him go and a thought occurred to her. She wasn't watching a frustrated, hurt young man set off to whatever was next in his life.

She was watching a miracle.

• • •

JENNA DAVIS WAS in the last half hour of the first Friday in the school year when the principal stepped into the classroom and motioned for her. The woman's face didn't look alarmed. But there was an urgency in her expression all the same.

The new second graders sitting at their desks noticed the interruption. Jenna smiled at the children. "One minute, boys and girls. Please stay in your seats."

She walked to the door and moved into the hall with her principal. Ms. Brown spoke first. "You have a visitor. Waiting in the office." She raised her brow slightly. "Please come straight there ten minutes before the bell rings." The woman smiled. "I'll have the vice principal take your students to the buses."

A visitor? Who could possibly be here for her? "A man or woman?"

Ms. Brown paused. "A man." She smiled. "A very handsome one."

Who would be here? And why come to the school without contacting her first? Jenna had no idea. "Thank you. I'll be there." She returned to her class. And just like Ms. Brown had said, ten minutes before the bell rang, the vice principal arrived to take over.

Jenna thanked him and grabbed her things.

On her way to the office, she tried to imagine who could possibly be waiting for her. The dad of one of her new students, maybe? One of the little girls had told her yesterday that her daddy wasn't married and he wanted to take Jenna on a date. Jenna hadn't given any thought to the matter.

But now . . .

Curiosity fueled her pace, but it wasn't until she turned the corner and could see the glass wall of the main office that she stopped short. The man was there, standing near the counter. Jenna could only see his back, but his shoulders were familiar. His dark hair, too.

What?

Could it be . . . ?

She walked to the office door, her heart racing. As she stepped inside, he turned and saw her. Jenna's breath caught in her throat and she brought her fingers to her lips. It was him.

Brady Bradshaw. Standing three feet away.

"Jenna." He moved toward her. No man had ever looked better. But there was something different about him. Like the hurt was gone for good. He kept a slight distance between them, but his eyes didn't leave hers. "Can we talk? Outside?"

If the office staff was watching the moment play out, Jenna wasn't aware. All she could see was Brady, all she could hear was his voice, soothing the hurt she still carried in her heart.

She nodded. *Breathe, Jenna. You have to breathe.* Was she dreaming? "I . . . I can't believe you're here."

He smiled. "I'll explain everything." He followed her outside. Not until they reached the school's front walk did they both stop. "I can't believe you're really here, Jenna."

"Brady . . ." Tears sprang to her eyes. Again, something was different about him. She could sense it. "Tell me I'm not dreaming."

He took her in his arms and held her the way she was aching to be held. They stayed that way for a long moment and then Brady whispered, "I believe, Jenna."

"What?" She eased back and searched his face. "You believe?"

"In God." His eyes were damp. "It's a long story. God spoke to me in a dream." He smiled and she could see he was absolutely telling her the truth. "I'll tell you everything later, but God changed my heart. My mind. I've given my life to Him."

His life? Brady was a believer now? Jenna couldn't stop her tears. "You're serious?" She reached for his hands. Her knees were shaking, her hands trembling. The feeling of his fingers between hers was too real for this to be a dream. "Is that . . . why you're here? To tell me?"

The smile started in his eyes. "It's part of it." He released one of her hands and motioned toward the grassy yard in front of the school. "I have something to ask you."

Only then, as Jenna turned, did she see what he was looking at. She gasped and stared at the scene.

Half the school was gathered on the lawn, watching them. The only bare spot was a small circle of grass. And at the center . . . a small potted sapling. "Brady?" Her voice was part cry, part whisper. *How could this be hap-*

pening? When had he made a plan with her school? Jenna could barely breathe. *Was he going to . . .*

She couldn't finish the thought.

It was all too good to be true.

"Jenna . . . come on." This time he led her toward the crowd. With a hundred teachers and students watching, Brady stopped at the center of the open patch of grass and picked up the little tree. He held it out to her. "It's a sapling."

She took the gift as tears fell down her cheeks. "From the Survivor Tree."

"Yes." He nodded. "I thought it would look good in our backyard."

She was laughing and crying at the same time. *Their* backyard? This was really happening. *Dear God, I can't believe it . . .* Her heart was bursting inside her.

Brady was still looking at her, taking his time. "I talked to the fire department in Columbus. They're ready to hire me . . . and I'm ready to move here. Depending . . ." He took the sapling from her and set it on the ground. Then he took a ring from his jeans pocket and dropped to one knee.

A buzz ran through the crowd standing nearby, but Jenna couldn't hear a single word, couldn't focus on anything but Brady.

He held the ring up to her. "Jenna, I'll never love anyone but you. To the moon and back." Tears fell onto his face, but they didn't dim his smile. "Will you marry me?"

Her hands flew to her mouth and she nodded. Then she took the ring as he stood. "Yes, Brady." She had kept her promise to God, and now she would pledge Brady her life, her heart. "A million times yes."

The teachers and students burst into applause; several of them had their cell phones out, capturing the moment. Brady slipped the ring on her finger. Then he took tender hold of her face and kissed her. "I have a long way to go. A lot to learn and understand." He kissed her again. "Together, Jenna," he whispered. "We'll grow closer to God. Every day of our lives."

"We will." Her tears and laughter mixed. "I love you."

"I love you, too." Their lips met again, and around them the crowd cheered.

Jenna would remember this moment forever. She was certain. Everything she had prayed about was happening in a single instant. Brady was here and he was hers. But so much more than that, he believed now. She couldn't wait to hear what had happened, how the old couple had helped him.

She looked at the ring and then back at Brady.

They were both survivors now. And the sapling would grow up in their backyard, somewhere here in Columbus. They didn't need the memorial any longer. They were whole and alive and the future was theirs.

Brady kissed her once more. "I can't wait to be your husband. God has great things ahead for us, Jenna. I know it."

Chills ran through her as she nodded. "He does." And

suddenly she felt like a princess again. Princess Jenna. Not just because she was going to marry Brady Bradshaw after all these years.

But because she was going to spend eternity with him.

• • •

AMY'S HEART WAS full. The family had gathered that Saturday to celebrate her birthday. And for another reason. Amy walked into the backyard where her cousins and aunts and uncles, and Papa and Grandma Elaine were already gathered. Papa and Uncle Landon had the shovel ready.

Today they were going to plant her little survivor tree.

Amy had chosen the spot, not far from her grandma Elizabeth's rose garden. Aunt Ashley had agreed it was the best place. The tree would give shade to anyone who wanted to smell the roses.

That sounded like a nice idea to Amy. Plus it was close to the house. So Amy could always do her homework out there or sit against the trunk when the tree got bigger. Just to think about God and life.

And the family she had waiting for her in heaven.

"Okay . . ." Uncle Landon walked up and handed her the sapling. "Are you ready?"

Amy nodded and grinned at her uncle. "I can't wait."

Cole came up and put his arm around her as she carried the little tree to the hole her Uncle Landon had dug. "You're amazing, Amy. If I haven't said that enough."

"Thanks, Cole." She smiled at him. He was always kind, always looking out for her. Today was no different.

As they reached the spot, Cole dropped back. "This is all you, Amy."

She nodded. Then with all her family gathered around, she stepped up to the hole and set the baby elm inside. Uncle Landon had already uncovered the roots, so it was ready to be planted.

Amy knelt down in the dirt and positioned the tree so it was straight. She looked over her shoulder at her papa and Uncle Landon. "Is that good?"

"Perfect!" they both answered at the same time. Aunt Ashley and the others gave her a thumbs-up and nodded. "Perfect," they all agreed.

And so it was. Amy took handfuls of the dirt piled near the hole and pressed them around the roots so the tree wouldn't fall over. When it was steady, she stood and took the shovel from her Uncle Landon.

This part was a surprise. She scooped one shovelful of dirt and sprinkled it on the roots. Then she looked at her Aunt Ashley. "Your turn."

"Me?" Her aunt looked surprised. "Honey, this is your tree. You can do it."

Amy had been waiting for this day for months. She looked around at her family. "What happened to my mommy and daddy, what happened to my sisters when they went home to heaven that day . . . it happened to all of us." She didn't want to cry, but tears came anyway. She blinked a few times. "We're all survivors."

Everyone had tears now, even Cole.

Her throat was tight. For a few seconds she couldn't talk, but then she did a little cough and her words came. "Please . . . I'd like everyone to pass the shovel and put some dirt in the hole. So we all plant this tree together." Her tears made it hard to see, but she smiled anyway. "Okay?"

Everyone nodded and moved in closer. Aunt Ashley went first and then Uncle Landon, her papa and Grandma Elaine, Amy's aunts and uncles and all her cousins. Cole was last, and when he was done he handed the shovel back to her. "You finish, Amy."

She smiled and put the last few shovelfuls around the tree. Then she and Cole got on the ground and patted the dirt in, nice and tight. When they stepped back, Amy could see the elm clearly. Not just how it looked today, a baby tree in brand-new dirt. But how it would look a year from now. Twenty years from now.

Their very own survivor tree.

Her papa looked around. "Let's pray."

Amy wiped her eyes. "Yes." Praying was just what they needed to do. She held out her hands. Cole took hold of one, and Aunt Ashley the other. Then everyone else added in and they made a circle around the sapling.

"Father, it's like Amy said." Papa's voice was tender. "We are all survivors because of You. We have lost much, but through Your strength we have also loved much. Please, Lord, let this baby elm tree be a reminder to us that You are for us, not against us. You are the Healer of our broken hearts. And one day You will bring us home with those who've gone before us. Thank You for Amy. In Jesus' name, amen."

Amy's family started talking all at once, about how pretty the tree was and how well they'd planted it. Everyone came up and hugged Amy, and they hugged each other. Their voices and smiles and faces filled Amy's soul and her tears stopped.

What they'd done today would stay in Amy's heart forever. Her idea had worked. That all of them would take turns planting the tree. The Baxters were always stronger this way. Together. They were Amy's family, her favorite people on earth. Survivors, all of them.

And now they had the little tree to prove it.

ACKNOWLEDGMENTS

No book comes together without a great deal of teamwork, passion and determination. That was definitely true for *To the Moon and Back*!

First, a special thanks to my amazing publisher, Judith Curr, and the team at Howard Books. Judith, at the Simon & Schuster offices, you're known as the Rainmaker. How blessed I am to be working with you and your passionate team. You clearly desire to raise the bar at every turn. Thank you for that and for everything!

A similar thanks to Carolyn Reidy and my family at Simon & Schuster. I think often of our times together in New York and the way your collective creative brilliance always becomes a game changer. Thank you for lending your influence in so many ways. It's an honor to work with you!

This story is so very special because of the incredible talents of my editor, Becky Nesbitt. Becky, you have known me since my kids were little. Since the Baxters began. How many authors actually look forward to the editing process? With you, it is a dream. And always you find ways to make my book better. Over and over and over again. Thank you for that! I am the most blessed author for the privilege of working with you.

Also thanks to my design team—Kyle and Kelsey Kupecky—whose unmatched talent in the industry is recognized from Los Angeles to New York. Very simply, you are the best in the business! My website, social media, video trailers and newsletter along with so many other aspects of my touring and writing are what they are because of you. Thank you for working your own dreams around mine. I love you and I thank God for you every single day.

A huge thanks to my sisters, Tricia and Susan, along with my mom, who give their whole hearts to helping me love my readers. Tricia as my executive assistant for the past decade, and Susan, for many years, as the head of my Facebook Online Book Club and Team KK. And Mom, thank you for being Queen of the Readers. Anyone who has ever sent me an email and received a response from you is blessed indeed. All three of you are so special to me. I love you and I thank God for each of you!

Thanks also to Tyler for joining with me to write screenplays and books that—for now—readers don't even know about. You are a gifted writer, Ty. I can't wait to see your work on the shelves and on the big screen. Maybe one day soon! Love you so much!

Also, thank you to my office assistant, Aurora Galvin. You create space for me to write! This storytelling wouldn't be possible without you.

I'm grateful also to my Team KK members, who use social media to tell the world about my upcoming releases and who hang out on my Facebook page, answering reader questions. I appreciate each of you so much. May God bless you for your service to the work of Life-Changing Fiction™.

There is a final stage in writing a book. The galley pages come to me, and I send them to a team of five of my closest, most special reader friends. My niece Shannon Fairley, Hope Painter, Donna Keene, Renette Steele and Zac Weikal. You are wonderful! It always amazes me the things you catch at the final hour. Thank you for loving my work, and thanks for your availability to read my stories first and fast.

Also, my books only happen with the help of my family, especially my amazing husband, Donald. Honey, thank you for your spiritual wisdom and leadership in our home, and thanks for talking through books like this one from the outline to the editing. The countless ways you help when I'm on deadline make all the difference. I love you!

And over all this is a man who has believed in my career for two decades: my amazing agent, Rick Christian of Alive Literary Agency. From the beginning, Rick, you've told me to dream big, set my sights high. Movies, TV series, worldwide reach. You imagined it all, you prayed for it to be. You believed. While I write, you work behind the scenes on film projects and my work with Liberty University, the Baxter family TV series and details regarding every book I've ever written. You are brilliant and driven, compassionate and dedicated. I used to dream of having you as my agent. Now I'm the only author who does. God is amazing. Thank you, Rick, and thank you for praying for me and my family. That most of all.

Finally, my greatest thanks to God Almighty, who is First and Last and all things in between. I write for You, through You and because of You. Thank you with my whole being.

Dear Reader Friend,

On a cloudy day several years ago, I stepped foot on the Oklahoma City National Memorial. I walked the grounds and touched the Survivor Tree and stood for fifteen silent minutes near the chairs representing those killed. Long before I left that day I was sure of two things.

First, the memorial is one of the most beautiful, reflective places I've visited. And second, I knew I'd write about it one day.

You may be too young to remember much about April 19, 1995. But either way the terrible tragedy of that day happened. Lives were lost, families were ripped apart, and Oklahoma City was forever changed. The United States was impacted for all time.

I hope as you read Brady and Jenna's love story that you found yourself connecting to the tragedies and hard times in your own life. The truth is this: God wants to make good out of your darkest days. And as time passes, He wants you to find love and hope, redemption and healing.

Beauty from Ashes.

As with my other books in this new Baxter family collection, this story and the ones to come will allow us the chance to live with the Baxters. We will see what matters to them, and how their work and family affect the people and culture around them.

The next Baxter book, *When We Were Young,* is another of those! I know you'll love it! These are among the most favorite books I've ever written. I'm grateful you're sharing in the journey!

Being back with the Baxter family has been the greatest gift. Always when people ask, "How are the Baxters?" I have an answer. I honestly do. I see them at work and play, holding close conversations, and looking for new horizons. Participating in adventures.

You've probably heard by now that the Baxter family is coming to TV. The series is expected to become one of the most beloved of all time. I know you'll be watching. You can find out more details about that and how to connect with me on social media or through email at my website—KarenKingsbury.com.

But in the meantime, I'll see you in the fall with my next book.

Because the Baxters aren't just my family. They're yours.

And with them at the middle of our lives, we are all connected.

Until next time . . . thanks for being part of the family.

Love you all!

THE BAXTER FAMILY: YESTERDAY AND TODAY

For some of you, this is your first time with the Baxter family. Yes, you could go back and read twenty-some books on these most-loved characters. The list of Baxter titles—in order—is at the beginning of this book. But you don't have to read those to read this one. In fact, there will be other Baxter books coming in the next few years. These books are a collection, and can be read in any order.

If you wish, you can begin right here.

Whether you've known the Baxters for years or are just meeting them now, here's a quick summary of the family, their kids, and their ages. Also, because these characters are fictional, I've taken some liberty with their ages. Let's just assume this is how old everyone is today.

Now, let me introduce you to—or remind you of—the Baxter family.

• • •

THE BAXTERS BEGAN in Bloomington, Indiana, and most of the family still lives there today.

The Baxter house is on ten acres outside of town, with a winding creek that runs through the backyard. It has a wraparound porch and pretty view and the memories of a lifetime. The house was built by John and Elizabeth Baxter. They raised their children here. Today it is owned by one of their daughters—Ashley—and her husband, Landon Blake. It is still the place where the extended Baxter family gathers for special celebrations.

John Baxter: John is the patriarch of the Baxter family. Formerly an emergency room doctor and professor of medicine at Indiana University, he's now retired. John's first wife, Elizabeth, died long ago from a recurrence of cancer. Years later, John remarried Elaine, and the two live in Bloomington.

Dayne Matthews, 43: Dayne is the oldest son of John and Elizabeth. Dayne was born out of wedlock and given up for adoption at birth. His adoptive parents died in a small plane crash when he was 18. Years later, Dayne became a very visible and popular movie star. At age 30, he hired an attorney to find his birth parents—John and Elizabeth Baxter. He had a moment with Elizabeth in the hospital before she died, and years later he connected with the rest of his biological family. Dayne is married to Katy, 41. The couple has three children: Sophie, 8; Egan, 6; and Blaise, 4. They are very much part of the Baxter family, and they split time between Los Angeles and Bloomington.

Brooke Baxter West, 41: Brooke is a pediatrician in Bloomington, married to Peter West, 41, also a doctor.

The couple has two daughters: Maddie, 20, and Hayley, 17. The family experienced a tragedy when Hayley suffered a drowning accident at age 4. She recovered miraculously, but still has disabilities caused by the incident.

Kari Baxter Taylor, 39: Kari is a designer, married to Ryan Taylor, 41, football coach at Clear Creek High School. The couple has three children: Jessie, 17; RJ, 11; and Annie, 8. Kari had a crush on Ryan when the two were in middle school. They dated through college, and then broke up over a misunderstanding. Kari married a man she met in college, Tim Jacobs, but some years into their marriage he had an affair. The infidelity resulted in his murder at the hands of a stalker. The tragedy devastated Kari, who was pregnant at the time with their first child, Jessie. Ryan came back into her life around the same time, and years later he and Kari married. They live in Bloomington.

Ashley Baxter Blake, 37: Ashley is the former black sheep of the Baxter family, married to Landon Blake, 37, who works for the Bloomington Fire Department. The couple has four children: Cole, 17; Amy, 12; Devin, 10; and Janessa, 6. As a young single mom, Ashley was jaded against God and her family, when she reconnected with her firefighter friend Landon, who had secretly always loved her. Eventually Ashley and Landon married and Landon adopted Cole. Together, the couple had two children—Devin and Janessa. Between those children, they lost a baby girl, Sarah Marie, at birth to anencephaly. Amy, Ashley's niece, came to live with them a few years ago after Amy's parents, Erin Baxter Hogan and Sam Hogan, and Amy's three sisters, were killed in a horrific car accident. Amy was the only survivor. Ashley and Landon and their family live in Bloomington, in the old Baxter house, where Ashley and her siblings were raised. Ashley still paints and is successful in selling her work in local boutiques.

Luke Baxter, 35: Luke is a lawyer, married to Reagan Baxter, 35, a blogger. The couple has three children: Tommy, 15; Malin, 10; and Johnny, 6. Luke met Reagan in college. They experienced a major separation early on, after having Tommy out of wedlock. Eventually the two married, though they could not have more children. Malin and Johnny are both adopted.

• • •

IN ADDITION TO the Baxters, this book has revisited the Flanigan family. The Flanigans have been friends with the Baxters for many years. So much so that I previously wrote five books about their oldest daughter—Bailey Flanigan. For the purpose of this book and those that might follow, here are the names and ages of the Flanigans:

Jim and Jenny Flanigan, both 46. Jim is a football coach for the Indianapolis Colts, and Jenny is a freelance writer who works from home. Bailey, 24, is married to Brandon Paul, 27, and they have one child, a daughter, Hannah Jennifer, almost 1. Bailey and Brandon were once actors in Hollywood—Brandon, very well known. Today they run the Christian Kids Theater in downtown

Bloomington. Bailey's brothers are Connor, 21—a student at Liberty University; Shawn and Justin—both age 18 and seniors at Clear Creek High; BJ (James), 17, a junior in high school; and Ricky, 15, a freshman.

In addition, Flanigan family friend Cody Coleman has resurfaced in recent books. Cody lived with the Flanigans when he was in high school and had a long-standing crush on the family daughter, Bailey. But all that changed when Brandon Paul entered the picture. Even before the relationship between Brandon and Bailey got serious, Cody began to have feelings for Bailey's former college roommate, Andi Ellison. Over the following years, Andi and Cody shared two failed engagements. Now, though, the two are married and may appear in future story lines.

ONE CHANCE FOUNDATION

The Kingsbury family is passionate about seeing orphans all over the world brought home to their forever families. As a result, Karen created a charitable group called the One Chance Foundation.

This foundation was inspired by the memory of her father, Ted C. Kingsbury. Ted always said, "Life is not a dress rehearsal. We have one chance to love, one chance to truly live!"

Karen often tells her reader friends, "You have one chance to write the story of your life!"™ Now, with Karen's One Chance Foundation, readers can join her in the belief that all of us have one chance to make a difference in the lives of orphans.

In the Bible, James 1:27 says people with pure and faultless religion look after orphans. The One Chance Foundation was created with that truth in mind.

If you are interested in giving to Karen's One Chance Foundation and having your dedication printed in one of Karen's upcoming novels, visit www.KarenKingsbury.com. Below are dedications from some of Karen's reader friends who have contributed to the One Chance Foundation:

- To my mom, Vivian! I Love you To The Moon and Back! I thank God for YOU! Shelly
- In memory of my brother, John Fosmer. Love you "To the Moon and Back," Eleanor
- Endre, you and me under the full moon. What a gift! Love, Catherine
- In loving memory of my mom, Annabell! Love your daughter, Adelia Rippetoe
- To Shannon—love of my life—my best friend & my "lil' monkey face." Love, AC
- Tammy, you are my best friend and I would be lost without you! Love, Lisa
- Caryn and Jared, God bless your marriage! We love you to the moon and back! Love, Mom & Dad
- Love to my granddaughter Emma Nelson of Bloomington, IN. Your Grammy Dena Patrick
- I love you, Moma! Thanks for being the Jenny to my Bailey. Love, Little Lulu
- Hudson & Nolan, we love you to the moon and back! You are our greatest joy. Love forever, Mama & Daddy
- To Gloria, the most godly woman I know and the best mom! I love you! Jessie
- To my daughter & friend, Melissa Milkie. I wanted to see your name in an inspirational book, as you

so graciously dedicated your books to me. You, Michael & Mark are the best happenings of my life. —Love, Mom

- To my big sister & first best friend, Elizabeth! I love you so much & I am so proud of you! Love, Lydia
- To my family—Rick & Cori (grandchildren, RT & Ali, AJ & Josh), Ron & Kori. 8 Blessings from God! Luv you, G'ma Margery
- In loving memory of our mom, Hazel Owens, who read all of your books, Love & miss you always —Barb and Jean
- Dottie, 12.24.60–7.3.11 Always in my thoughts; Forever in my heart! Love, Mimi
- God is doing great things through you, Evan Miller! Proverbs 3:5–6 #Pray4Ev
- To Dennis—the love of my life. You are missed. Love, Mary Mikel
- Aunt Faye—my 2nd Mom—you taught me the love of books. Love, Sharon
- To my family: B, R, P, J, T, A, A, A, C, N, R, M, L & M, all in God's loving care! B+R 50yrs!
- In Loving Memory of the Most Amazing Mom, Patti Berg! Blood did not define family . . .
- In loving memory of sister Martha Elizabeth Offer, 1986–2012. Miss you! Love, Sarah

- To Kurt—Celebrating 35+ yrs of loving you to the moon and back! Forever, Sheila
- Mom—Words can't express how truly thankful we are for you. Love, Kristen & Kade
- In Loving Memory of My Husband, Jay —Janice Helmkamp
- To my babylove, thank you for helping me chase sunbeams to the sun. Love, Staci
- In Memory of "My Chuck"..."Remember When" —Sharon Crist
- Jonnye Dickson, thanks, Mom, for encouraging my reading. Love, Annette
- Tara and Mary—Dedicated to our friend Eva Mayer. Love you to the moon and back!
- Karen Taylor—Miss you, Mum & Dad, always here for you, Sandie. Love you all forever
- MaryBeth Cannon, I carried you in my womb for 9 months, in my arms for 2 months, and I will carry you in my heart forever. LOVE, Mom
- Aunt Pam, your encouragement and support mean more to me than you will ever know!! Love, Jonica
- Precious Kennedy Grace, Be Humble & Kind. Live Boldly. Papa & Lala Love You BIG!
- Mom/Tammy: Just like you always say, "Love you to the moon & back!" Daidra & Family

- To my sisters Becky & Missy for loving our family To the Moon and Back! Rose McCauley
- Diane K. Weimer: With love and thanksgiving for my son Theron Edward Weimer, Jr.
- Grandma MaryAnn Marley, We love u 2 the moon & back! Nicole, Renee, Sophia, Annette
- In memory of Robert Perez, my husband and best friend—always and forever!
- Jocelyn Tow . . . no one will ever know how much we love you, not even you! Love, Mom and Daddy
- I Love You, Katy Goll! You're Amazing! Love, Your Husband, Raymond
- Jodi Jordan, my daughter: I love you to the moon & back!! —Your mother, Joyce
- To our Law Enforcement Officers. Thank you for your service! May God bless you! —Mary Johnson
- Vernon, I would do it all over again. It's hard to believe we have celebrated 52 years already. Love & prayers, Sharon
- Natalie Garber—"And Beyond." Happy Graduation. Reach for the stars. Love, Memaw
- In memory of Donna. You're always in our hearts. Love, Your Family and Friends
- To my Grams in Heaven, I will always love you to the Moon & Back! Love, Shelly

- Helen A. Smith, Forever my Best Friend. I LOVE YOU MORE! Love, Littlefoot
- Dr. Wilcox, loving and sharing Jesus for 42 years! Best 1st grade teacher ever!
- To Barb Rysavy, an example of love & grace! Thanks for the gift of life! Love, Sue & Karen
- In honor of my best friend and beautiful mom, Cindy. I love you more! —Becca Turner
- To Maw: Thank you for always being our angel here on earth. You've loved us through it all & we love you always. You show Jesus Eyes to everyone. Love, Hope & Kingston
- Mom, we miss you but know you are watching over us from Heaven. Love always, Lydia Seabron
- Fred, we miss you and love you so much!! Love, Jerri Ann, Dawn, Kevin, Katie, William
- Mom, my true Strength, Grace, and Faith. Love, Dad (Matthew Landavazo)
- Allie & Hannah, you're a gift from God. I love you to the moon & back! Love, Mom (Lauren Morris)
- To Justin, Kellie, Faith, and Carl! I love you "to the moon and back"!!! 731 Aunti Joni
- To Arleen, my mom and best friend! I love you forever!!! Joni xoxoxo . . .

- To Jennifer Powell & Janet Tilford: My Power 100 Heroes!! Thank you for the hours of love & support you give each week as you "walk the talk" in helping all of us become healthier. God bless you! —Janice Kukkola-Miller

- To our precious daughter Angela Dilling from Romania, an angel messenger sent from God. With love, Mom and Dad, Ellen & Pete Miller

- To Tina Dunson & Joyce Bush, Your lives are an inspiration to all! With love, SB

- Tori Brianne, You are precious beyond words; we love you, TTMAB! —Dad, Mom, Landon & Cade

READING GROUP GUIDE

TO THE MOON AND BACK

KAREN KINGSBURY

1. How would you define "survivor"? Tell about how you or someone you know is a survivor.

2. Before reading *To the Moon and Back*, what did you know about the Oklahoma City bombing? What do you remember? What did you learn?

3. Did you know about the famous Survivor Tree? How does that old elm and its symbolism speak to you and your life today?

4. Why was it important for Amy to have a sapling from the Survivor Tree? In what ways did Landon and Ashley honor their niece's wishes and her goal to survive loss?

5. How have you commemorated someone you loved and lost? Why is this important?

6. In what ways does Brady Bradshaw deal with his very great loss? How have you or someone you know dealt with tragic loss?

7. Explain the significance of 9:03 on the wall at the Oklahoma City National Memorial. What does it mean to you personally, in your own story?

8. Jenna and Brady separately took time every year to remember their losses and the events of the Oklahoma City bombing. Why is it important to remember the people you've lost . . . or the most difficult days in your life?

9. Brady was convinced God had abandoned his mother and him. Explain why this makes sense and the impact of believing this way.

10. Jenna was determined to hold on to God, the way her parents had. Explain why this makes sense and the impact of believing this way.

11. Why is it important to have people in your life who understand your greatest joys and your deepest losses? How can talking to God about those moments help you?

12. Ashley Baxter Blake reached out to a stranger because she felt God leading her to do so. Have you ever felt led to talk to a stranger or help someone in need? Talk about that time.

13. Ashley and Landon struggle in this story, but they find a way to work things out. What were some of

the ways this couple grew stronger through a trial?

14. What did you learn about conflict resolution walking alongside Ashley and Landon in this season? How important is it to have honesty and trust, and to expect the best from each other?

15. Jenna made a promise to God that she would only fall in love with someone who shared her faith. Why was this important to her? How important is faith to you?

16. Explain the role of Jag in Brady's life. Have you or someone you know ever experienced an angel encounter? Talk about that.

17. Brady's life was changed by a dream. How important are the dreams we have while we sleep? Talk about your most interesting dream. Do you think God can speak to us in a dream? Why or why not? Give an example.

18. *God is not the reason for the bad things that happen, He is the rescue.* What does this sentence mean to you? How have you seen proof of this in your life?

19. Jenna stuck to her convictions. In a world where anything goes, why is it important to have standards

and stick by them? Give an example from your life or the life of someone you know.

20. Why would you give this book to someone trying to survive a difficult season in life? How might it speak to them?

Pass this book on.
A book is only life-changing if it's being read.
—Karen Kingsbury

Catch up with
The
BAXTER FAMILY
#1 NEW YORK TIMES BESTSELLING AUTHOR
KAREN KINGSBURY
The BAXTER FAMILY
IN THIS MOMENT
A NEW YORK TIMES BESTSELLER
KAREN KINGSBURY
The BAXTER FAMILY
LOVE STORY
KAREN KINGSBURY
A BAXTER FAMILY Christmas
PICK UP YOUR COPIES TODAY.
PROUDLY PUBLISHED BY HOWARD BOOKS
AN IMPRINT OF SIMON & SCHUSTER, INC.
A CBS COMPANY
60283

READ THE BESTSELLING
ANGELS WALKING SERIES
ANGELS WALKING SERIES • 1 •
angels walking
KAREN KINGSBURY
#1 NEW YORK TIMES BESTSELLING AUTHOR
ANGELS WALKING SERIES • 2
KAREN KINGSBURY
#1 NEW YORK TIMES BESTSELLING AUTHOR
chasing sunsets
A NOVEL
Brush of Wings
KAREN KINGSBURY
No. 1 NEW YORK TIMES BESTSELLING AUTHOR
PICK UP YOUR COPIES TODAY.
PROUDLY PUBLISHED BY HOWARD BOOKS
AN IMPRINT OF SIMON & SCHUSTER, INC.
A CBS COMPANY
60284